INVEST IN DEATH

Also by the same author:

Murder Stalks A Mansion

Gilded Death

Keep My Secret

INVEST IN DEATH

A Newport Mystery

ANNE-MARIE SUTTON

Invest In Death

A Newport Mystery

© 2018 by Anne-Marie Sutton. All rights reserved.

Published in the United States of America

by Newport Mysteries September 2018

Cover Illustration by Claudia Wolf

Newport Mysteries

P.O. Box 5055

Milford CT 06460

www.newportmystery.com

ISBN-10: 1719048886
ISBN-13: 978-1719048880

For Tony and Jack

"I'm glad I have you, said Mother."

PROLOGUE

Ocean Drive appears on many street maps of Newport, Rhode Island as *Ocean Avenue*. Its eight miles of winding road skirt the rocky southern coast of Aquidneck Island, the island which is home to the towns of Portsmouth to the north, Middletown in the middle and, most famously to the south, Newport.

The Drive, as you will hear the locals call it, is a stunning road. On one side is the mighty Atlantic Ocean. Imposing houses have long been built with a view of this historic water. Some of these "summer cottages"- for the wealthy residents have always referred to their summer homes in Newport as *cottages* - date to the nineteenth century. Today's visitors can see these stately stone and shingle residences, none of which bears the remotest resemblance to Mr. Webster's dictionary definition of a *cottage*.

The newer houses on The Drive came into existence in the second half of the twentieth century and more recently the twenty-first. These equally luxurious homes were built by later Newport inhabitants. Not the ones who made their fortunes in the Gilded Age industries of coal, minerals and railroads, but by those who found success in modern enterprises centered on technology and finance.

It is in one such modern Newport *cottage* that our story begins.

CHAPTER I

Jason Cava came out of the French windows onto the terrace. He went over to the table where breakfast had been laid by the housekeeper and poured himself coffee. The wide rambling house was named *Di Sole*, meaning *sunny* in Italian. Its grey shingles were trimmed in white, but with so many oversized windows it appeared to be made entirely of glass.

"Althea, darling, you look dreadful," he said to the woman shading her eyes from the morning sun. "I don't think you're sleeping well," he added helpfully.

"I don't see how you can know that," Althea said crossly. "You sleep on the other side of the house." The truth was that Althea Tanner hadn't been sleeping at all, but she thought that it was mean of Jason to comment on her appearance.

The younger man sat down in a deck chair facing the blue sunlit ocean shimmering with white cap waves. The warm sun felt good on his face. He loved this view and the way it made him feel happy to be alive.

"Stay home today," Jason said as he sipped the coffee. He was a short, compact young man with dark eyes, Roman features and a fashionably bald head. "Sit by the pool and recharge the old batteries. I'll be in the office to handle things."

"Recharged batteries isn't what I need, and you know it."

Jason recognized the fear in her tone, and his heart beat quickened. "What *are* you going to do, Althea?"

"That damned Teddy Ainsley!" Althea spat out the words. "Everything's been fine for the last eight years. Perfect really. Everybody is thrilled to have their money with Tanner Associates. And now *he* has to be so selfish." She brushed a cascade of thick coppery red hair back from her left cheek.

Jason watched the tips of Althea's long fingers glide through her shoulder length hair. Her slender hands were one of the best of her

2

many good features. Funny how physically attractive he thought she was, and how strange that her sexuality didn't tempt him. He did admire beautiful objects and Althea Tanner, with her high cheek bones and creamy white skin, was a thing of beauty. The pale yellow peignoir coated her slim sensuous body like lemon cake frosting.

"It's not selfish of a man to want access to his own money," Jason said. "You know, I think I envy him, wanting to make his life's dreams come true."

"And your life's dreams haven't been coming true these last eight years?" Althea challenged him.

"What I do is hardly the stuff dreams are made of."

"What Teddy wants to do is absurd. It's a ridiculous waste of thirty million dollars!"

"Perhaps," Jason said. Suddenly life in this gilded cage made him restless.

"What's that saying?" Althea frowned, her blue eyes narrowing. "Yes," she said. "I know. *A fool and his money are soon parted.* Yes. That will be Mr. Teddy Ainsley. You wait and see."

Suddenly a smile was on her red lips. "We need more money."

This time her voice was defiant. "And I know where to get it."

The grand salon was one of the most underused rooms in the Inn at Kenwood Court. Built in a period when more - and even more - was always best, the salon was a fine example of nineteenth century Gilded Age style. Designed for lavish parties and balls, the yellow and gold room had tall rectangular mirrors trimmed in elaborate gilt on each of its walls. Two enormous chandeliers, laden with the bodies of several chubby cherubs, hung from the painted ceiling. The room's furniture was placed around the perimeter and the pieces, including several benches, were of hard upholstery and an uninviting ornate design.

"Perfect!" pronounced Teddy Ainsley as he surveyed the room.

"Do you think so?" responded the inn's owner, Caroline Kent, doubtfully. She looked around the room again, wondering if she had missed a portrait of a long dead Kent ancestor which could be attributed to Whistler or perhaps a lost Childe Hassam landscape. Seeing none, she turned back to the man standing beside her. "I've never thought so, Teddy."

"But, Caroline, this is a perfect music room. How are the

acoustics?"

"I don't know. I've never heard music played in this room."

"Never!" Teddy looked astonished. His slight build was at odds with his six foot frame. With pale yellow hair and faded hazel eyes, his face at first glance appeared forgettable. But there was a resolute intensity about him which couldn't be ignored.

"I've only been living in the house since Louise and I turned it into the inn. Reed and I never stayed here when we were married." Caroline paused and looked wistful. Teddy kindly gave her some time to reflect on her marriage to the late Reed Kent and his untimely death in a motor accident.

"You could ask Louise," Caroline said finally.

"Yes, that's a good idea," Teddy said, sounding relieved to be back on the topic of music. "But I don't think sound will be a problem. I love this room. I always have. Val and I were often here as children. It's just so right for the concerts I'm planning."

"Yes, well, we'll have to talk more about what all this entails. First I have to look at the fall schedule for bookings--"

"Bookings," Teddy interrupted, bringing his hands together in a clasp. "Yes. Of course. We should talk about rooms as well." When Caroline looked surprised, he continued. "Mother will take the artists with us at Bellehurst, but there will be others coming up from New York for the productions who will need to be accommodated. I hoped you would have rooms for them here."

"Teddy, let me be clear. I haven't said yes to this proposal. There are several things I have to consider before I agree to have you stage your concerts here at Kenwood. It could cause great disruption to the guests."

"But surely the concerts will be great publicity for the inn. You can't possibly turn me down, Caroline." Teddy's soft pleading eyes met hers. "You have to do it. This means so much to me."

CHAPTER II

The Inn at Kenwood Court was a relative newcomer to the Newport hotel scene. Caroline had inherited the house, known as Kenwood, from her husband Reed Kent. At first she had been unsure of what to do with the property. The grand old house had a mortgage, was in need of repair, and its original purpose as the Kents' *summer cottage* in Newport had long ceased to be economically practical. For the past two decades the family had rented the estate to various well-to-do newcomers whose goal was to enter Newport society.

The Kent family fortune which had its roots in the nineteenth century no longer existed. It had been lost in the twentieth century with the financial speculations of which her husband Reed's father was so very fond. When Frederick Kent had died twenty years earlier, his only child and his widow Louise had been left in genteel poverty. Louise, who loved old black and white movies, often thought that she and Reed were like impoverished British aristocrats in a 1930s film whose need for money forces them to rent out their Manor House to the owner of a biscuit factory who is anxious for his family to mingle with the upper classes.

Caroline had never been interested in the stories of long lost Kent fortunes. She had married Reed because she loved him passionately, not because of his family's history. Upon becoming owner of Kenwood, the sensible plan would have been to sell and realize whatever money was left once the mortgage had been paid.

But grief and sorrow teamed to provide an alternative plan. Caroline's career as a stage actress in New York City had never brought great fame, but acting had always nourished her inner soul. After Reed was gone, that balm vanished. Mourning put her adrift.

Then one night Caroline dreamed of being at Kenwood where her husband had spent the happy summers of his youth. The next weekend she drove up to Newport to visit the house set majestically above the Cliff Walk, the famous stretch of public pathways overlooking the Atlantic Ocean. She fell in love with the house's elegant design - two compact wings on either side of the main wing. Tall Palladian windows with their topping curves trimmed in white dominated the gray stone facade. When Caroline smelled the sea air and felt the push of the ocean breeze on her face, she felt life once more.

And so the Inn at Kenwood Court was born. Caroline moved to Kenwood and became its resident innkeeper, letting the enthusiastic tourists who came to Newport be the instrument of paying off the house's mortgage. She and Louise would have a permanent roof over their heads - for her mother-in-law was as eager to return to her former home as Caroline was to make it her own.

Louise Kent never regretted her decision to return to her family's old summer home. She was a tiny, energetic woman with lively grey eyes and an optimistic outlook. The prospect of doing the menial jobs necessary to the running of the inn didn't discourage her. Life in her Manhattan apartment had been ordinary. This new existence was a life full of new work, new people and new challenges. That one of the inn's first guests had been murdered was, in retrospect, the most thrilling of all the things that had happened since she and Caroline had come back to Newport.

Caroline had solved that first murder case and then two more puzzling murders in the city. If Louise would admit it - and she never would to a living soul - she had begun imagining herself as Dr. Watson to Caroline's Sherlock Holmes.

This morning, however, was a day with less adventure and more of the ordinary. Several guests were currently staying at the inn where breakfasts were advertised as lavish affairs. Cleaning up the dining room was one of Louise's morning tasks. Today was no exception as she carried chafing dishes, coffee pots and plates back to the kitchen.

"Missus, that's too much for you," Mattie Simpson cried, wrestling the big silver tray from Louise's hands. "You can't carry all this yourself."

"Mattie," Louise said. "Stop fussing. We go through this every morning. I carry in the breakfast things. You cook the breakfast, remember? That's your job. I don't fuss over you while you are at the stove."

Mattie, grim-faced, ignored her employer. They had been together for more than forty years, through the good times and the bad. The cook was a thin, angular woman whose stern features masked the affection she felt toward Louise. Mattie had remained in her household during the years of Louise's widowhood, cooking and cleaning for her and lifting her spirits. That Louise was also performing domestic duties at the Inn At Kenwood Court was, in her loyal retainer's mind, completely unacceptable.

Louise sighed as Mattie continued to unload the tray, her strong hands moving quickly to load the dishwasher and put the pans to soaking.

"Where is Caroline?" Louise asked.

"Don't think she's done with that man who came to see her," Mattie answered.

"Oh, Teddy Ainsley. Of course. I did forget he was coming this morning. I think I'll go and find them."

Mattie's response was little more than a grunt as she worked on the pots. Louise saw her chance and escaped.

"I don't know if I can take it all in, Louise," Caroline said.

Louise had found her daughter-in-law in the salon, but the room was empty of her recent visitor.

"What did Teddy want?" Louise asked.

"Well," Caroline said slowly, "he told me that he wants to put on a music festival this fall. Several programs of classical music. Live performers, a small orchestra, an opera perhaps."

"Teddy has always been a music lover. As a child he was constantly taking lessons, going to music camp. I'm not sure that he didn't study it in college. Not that I ever knew him to perform or do anything practical with it. But tell me why Teddy came to talk to you about this festival."

"Very simple, Louise. He wants to have it here. At Kenwood." Louise's mouth gaped, and she closed it without speaking. "He's thought it all out and decided that Kenwood is the place for it. Our salon is unusually large, you know. Larger than any room his mother has at Bellehurst. And I got the impression that she wouldn't have approved of its being there anyway. Better someone else's home for all the upheaval it will cause. In our case, the inn."

"Yes," Louise said, finding her speech at last. "He would think of Kenwood. Teddy and Val were here a lot while they and Reed were growing up."

"I'm not sure what to do, Louise. Teddy's offering a lot of money, which you know that we could definitely use. The festival would be in October. We're still busy then after the summer rush, but not always full. He would take all the rooms, plus pay extra for the facilities the musicians will use."

"And how many people does he expect to be in the audience?"

"He thinks a great many will come. We'll have to see what the fire marshal says about that, but I think we could hold at least seventy or so for each program."

"Heavens, that's a lot."

"We'd have to hire some people to help us set up. Of course I would pass the costs onto Teddy."

"I'm still amazed by all this. I can't see Teddy planning all of it, and then following it through. It's not the Teddy I knew when he was a child."

"He told me that Val will help him."

"I'm not surprised. She's always been the big sister even though they are twins. I expect she was born first."

"Teddy's like a child who wants a puppy for Christmas," Caroline said, shaking her head. "It's going to be hard to say no to him."

"But I do think we need to consider this carefully before we make a decision," Louise said. "I am part of the decision making, aren't I, Caroline?"

"Of course," Caroline said, giving the older woman a hug. "You know I don't make a move around here without you."

CHAPTER III

Lt. Hank Nightingale beat his hands impatiently on the steering wheel of his car as he waited to make the left turn onto Memorial Boulevard. He should have driven the back way down Old Beach Road, but he had been distracted on Bellevue Avenue and missed the turn. What a policeman he was. Changing a disc in the car's audio player when he should have had his eyes on the road.

The police detective was listening to *The Great Gatsby*, a book he had read earlier in his life. Hank was caught up in the story, even though he knew now that Jay Gatsby's persona was invented and that the book's hero was in reality a crook. But such a likable law breaker. Hank made a mental note to ask Caroline if she had read the book. He was pretty sure she had. But raising the topic would certainly lead to a lively discussion the next time they met.

Hank made his turn and hastened toward the beach. He glanced at the dashboard clock. 12:04. He was late for his second class. The whole purpose of taking the Tai Chi class was to help him relax, and rushing to Easton's Beach on his lunch break was only adding to the stiffness he felt across his shoulders and up the back of his neck.

Parking his car, he saw the class had already started. He took off his shoes and socks and ran across the sand toward the group of men and women, taking his place at the end of the line. Temple Exercises had begun, and Hank stretched his right arm in an arc over his head toward his left shoulder. Alex Seeger, the instructor, gave him a disappointed look, then a wink. Hank nodded sheepishly, then reversed his move and brought his left arm slowly up over his body.

The class lasted forty minutes. The dozen or so participants, mostly male, all seemed to be in the class for the same reason as Hank. Someone had told them, or they had read somewhere, that Tai Chi relaxed you. Some stressed the body movements, others the mind's concentration. A few said that they liked to practice the breathing, insisting it helped them to fall asleep during a restless night.

To relieve his chronic neck pain, Hank's doctor had suggested that he do yoga or Tai Chi. A small article in the *Newport Daily News* about a Tai Chi class beginning on First Beach at noon on Tuesdays caught his eye and he signed up, his choice made.

The forty minutes passed quickly, and it was time to end with the Temple Exercises. The ocean air was bracing, and Hank felt loose and relaxed. He breathed in and exhaled, blowing the air out of his mouth. Sea gulls jumped back from the incoming tide and scurried across the sand at the water's edge. The beach was wide and inviting. He debated whether to take a walk before returning to the office. His computer, the demon which he was sure was responsible for the constant cricks in his neck, awaited and Hank would think of any excuse not to return to its glaring screen.

The handsome dark-haired man next to him was zipping up a black fleece jacket. He withdrew a gold wrist watch from his pocket and slid it onto his arm. Hank tried to get a glimpse of the brand. The jacket was certainly expensive, and curiosity was one of Hank's official qualities. He smiled and extended his hand.

"Hi, I'm Hank. Hank Nightingale. We haven't met." The other man smiled back and shook Hank's hand vigorously.

"Leo. I'm Leo Vargoff. You from Newport?" Leo looked to be in his late forties. He was tall with a full head of curly brown hair and intelligent dark eyes.

"Yeah," Hank said. "Yourself?"

"I'm over in Jamestown. I wanted a dock for my boat."

"Sailboat by any chance?"

"Nah. Power boat. You a sailor?" Hank nodded. "Got a boat?" Hank shook his head. "Well, come out on mine sometime."

"Thanks," Hank said, not being a fan of power boats, but supposing he would be happy to be out on any boat. "That would be great."

"O.K., we'll do that," Leo said. He pulled out his phone from his jacket, his fingers moving rapidly over the screen. Hank wondered if Leo was checking his calendar for a boating date. But instead he frowned and exclaimed "Damn." With a brief goodby, Leo turned and walked briskly in the direction of the parking lot.

"See you met our Leo."

Hank recognized the gravely voice of Alex Seeger behind him

and turned around. Alex was wearing white Bermuda shorts and a faded cherry red T-shirt. His sparse grey hair was cut close to his head and showed a scalp as well as a face that was pink from the sun. He had told the class on the first day that he studied Tai Chi at a camp in the western United States run by a Grand Master, returning every year to hone his skills. He enjoyed introducing the discipline to others and was teaching this class as a volunteer.

"Hey, sorry about being late," Hank said. "Got tied up at work."

"That's OK. Cop business, huh?" Alex laughed. "I still can't believe you're a cop. You just don't look like a cop."

Hank raised his right foot to display a well-defined arch. "No flat feet."

"Yeah, right." Alex laughed again, this time not so jovially. "I just feel like I've got to watch myself around you. Be on my best behavior." He winked again.

Hank had checked out Alex Seeger after he signed up for the class. Googled him so he knew something of his background. There were business interests in Providence. Trucking, food distribution, real estate. The detective had found no criminal record, but Providence was a city where money could change hands in casual ways. Hank was enjoying the class, but his policeman's antenna never stopped working.

CHAPTER IV

Tanner Associates was housed in a small Gothic cottage on the commercial end of Bellevue Avenue. The white shingled house had been renovated to Althea's exact specifications in 2006 when she founded the company. While the building's exterior reflected its historical roots, the interior was modern, all black and white with plenty of chrome and light.

Althea Tanner's introduction to the world of high finance had come when she was fifteen years old, and her mother had asked her for help in understanding the investment choices in her 401(k) pension plan. Althea did some basic research for her and found that she enjoyed analyzing the various mutual funds offered and choosing the right ones for her mother's needs. The teenager began to follow the financial markets, eagerly awaiting her mother's next statement to see how her investments were growing. At her high school the young girl started an investment club and became its president.

In college Althea had a double major in economics and accounting. After graduating from Salve Regina University in Newport, she landed her first job with the Newport bank where John Ainsley, the patriarch of one of the oldest families in Newport, kept several accounts.

John Ainsley had always enjoyed making his own financial decisions. He read widely, talked with other wealthy individuals to see which way they thought that the wind was blowing (sometimes resulting in contrarian decisions on his part), and liked to be ahead of popular shifts in the stock market. Ainsley relished finding a winner for his portfolio and enjoyed the high which came from seeing his stocks rise steadily under his personal management. He disliked financial planners and had long felt he had no peer in choosing investments. Then he started talking about the stock market to Althea Tanner after the bank had assigned her to his account as a personal banker.

When John Ainsley first met Althea he was in his late sixties. He was muscular and fit, a strong swimmer, a strong sailor, a strong polo player. All in all a strong, virile man. The young woman with the long blond hair - for Althea was a blond in those days - and slim well-rounded figure had already caught his roving eye when she was first hired at his bank.

If John Ainsley had an ulterior motive when he agreed to a first meeting with his new personal banker, it was never revealed. For Althea blew him away with her knowledge of the stock market and her confidence in what she knew. The older man quickly forgot all about any non-business thoughts he might have harbored. She was all about making money, and John was stopped in his tracks. Attractive women were not in short supply in Newport, but stock pickers were.

When Althea correctly predicted the tech sell-off in the spring of 2002 and Ainsely sold his stocks before the downturn, the young woman's future was assured. Ainsley offered her a full time job with him and a generous salary and commission on the investments she was to help him make.

For the next four years, Althea was busy helping the Ainsley fortune to grow. It was a comfortable existence. John had so much faith in her that she never felt pressured to perform. She was free to study the markets and make her investing decisions, balancing risk with her instincts.

Then everything abruptly changed. In early 2006, John Ainsley had a heart attack while playing squash and died within minutes. Althea was shocked, devastated by the loss of the man who had become the center of her life. She assumed that John's death meant the end of her association with the Ainsleys. But she was surprised to learn that his widow Margaret took for granted that Althea would continue to manage the family's money. Within a month of her mentor's death, Althea Tanner made the leap and became *Tanner Associates* with a big name client to start her own firm.

Maya Vereen, Althea's administrative assistant, was taking lunch orders. Jason went with the Reuben sandwich the nearby deli always had for special on Tuesday. He ignored Althea's disapproving face at his choice as he always did. He could make the same grimace at her kale and quinoa salad. What the hell was that all about? You may as well eat the newspaper. One day the deli had put avocado on her salad and Althea had screamed. Screamed, mind you. All for a few extra calories of avocado fat or whatever was wrong with enjoying the taste of something that actually had taste.

After Maya had left, Jason leaned back in his desk chair and looked at Althea. "Do you want to talk now? Before Maya gets back."

The office was open plan, which he hated, but which Althea thought was so contemporary. There was little privacy except for a small conference room they sometimes used for clients.

"Sure," Althea said. "What do you want to talk about?"

"What you said this morning at breakfast. I believe you made a reference to getting more money. As in *you knew where to get more money.*"

"I did say that."

"So what's your plan? We can't pay out thirty million dollars to Teddy Ainsley. We just don't have it on hand. I think we could manage about twelve million, and that's after keeping back the money we need to pay out the second quarter's dividends in July."

"First of all," Althea said, leaning on her elbows and bracing her chin as she bent forward toward Jason, "we are not giving Teddy Ainsley thirty million dollars anytime soon. His agreement with us is the same as all the rest. He's got to give us proper notice before withdrawing funds from our management. Three months, I believe."

"Teddy is not going to give us three months. He's going to squawk to the other investors, and they are going to get the wind up. He wants to buy that damned estate over near Fort Adams for his music center, and he wants to make an offer for the property now. He told you it needs extensive renovations to make it into what he envisions. He's not going to wait. He's like a dog with a bone."

"As I was saying," Althea continued as if Jason had not spoken, "we have some time." When Jason snorted, she once again ignored him. "The plan is ridiculously simple. We'll get new investors. We have a $10 million threshold for new clients, so we don't need too many. Two would do for starters."

Now Jason sighed heavily and sunk his head into his hands. "New investors. Of course. Why didn't I think of that?" He put his head up and his fingers on his computer's keyboard. "I'll just go online to--"

"Stop it," Althea commanded. "Stop and listen for a change.

You know, you are getting very difficult to deal with these days. You can walk anytime."

"No, I can't," Jason said in a steely voice. "That I cannot do."

"All right. Now if you will just work with me, I have this figured out." She watched him, waiting for him to give her his full attention. When she was satisfied that she had it, she went on. "You know that our clients tell their friends about us, and some of them have asked to be referred. Most I wouldn't touch. I like to keep things select in here. But there are two I've decided that I'd like to consider."

"I'm listening."

"They're referrals. Both from Alex Seeger. One is his wife's brother, the other is a friend of his."

"Names?"

"The brother-in-law is Richard Somebody. Richard... Richard." Althea prided herself on remembering names, and Jason gave her time to jog her memory. "Richard Tompkins. He's a surgeon. No, my mistake. He's an anaesthesiologist."

"Those guys make a lot of money."

"Yeah. They do." She smiled. "And the other one's a developer. Builds apartments, strip malls, office buildings. Mostly over in Providence."

"What's his name?"

"Vargoff. That one I remember because it made me think of a Russian spy. His name is Leo Vargoff."

CHAPTER V

In the years after she was a teenager sailing in Narragansett Bay with Reed Kent and her twin brother Teddy, Valerie Ainsley had gone on to become a world class sailor. Busy racing on sailboats all over the world, she returned to Newport only occasionally. She had never married, preferring the life of a wandering nomad, comfortable in the easy camaraderie of men and women at sea. Lean and muscular, she had a perpetual tan, her short blond hair bleached from the sun.

But two years ago, during a rare trip home, Val's life changed when she spent a night drinking with Andrew Rourke, an old friend who was a fixture in the local sailing community. Rourke had recently been diagnosed with cancer, and he told Valerie that he needed someone to take care of his charter business while he was undergoing treatment. Without hesitation, Val told him not to worry, she would take care of things in his absence.

In the morning Valerie regretted her hasty promise to Andrew, but there was no going back. She was a woman of her word, and she changed her schedule to stay in Newport that winter to mind the charter company. Val quickly realized that the level of Rourke's business skills was directly opposite to his renowned skills as a sailor. Most of her time was spent getting the books in order and using her own resources to pay for repairs to his deteriorating fleet of boats.

As winter became spring, Andrew's prognosis for a recovery grew dim. Val tried to keep his spirits up with news about the resurgence of his small fleet of boats and plans for the coming sailing season. Rourke always smiled when Val, full of cheerful updates, visited his small apartment. But she wasn't fooled; he knew he had little time left.

That May Andrew died, but not before signing the papers to give ownership of Rourke's Charters to Val. The business was not something she wanted, but Val was gracious when Andrew insisted that she should have his company after his death. She thanked him for his faith in her, although she knew that once Andrew was gone, she would be getting on with her former life.

But after Andrew's death Val made no move to put the charter boats up for sale. She continued to maintain them, taking care of each one with special pride. She went to the small ramshackle office on lower Thames Street daily and checked on the bookings. Somehow she never seemed to be able to tell people that Rourke's Charters was closing up shop.

It was her brother Teddy who pointed out that she was procrastinating and he knew the reason why.

"You're enjoying it, Val," Teddy said one day when he came by the office to take her to lunch. "Why don't you admit that you've found something you love more than roaming all over the world looking for the next thrill?"

Val was nonplused and began to argue with her twin. But Teddy only smiled.

"Are you going to change the name to Ainsley's Charters?" he asked.

"No," Val said without hesitation. "I like the sound of Rourke's Charters."

Rourke's Charters prospered under Val's hand. Teddy was right when he described his sibling as thrill-seeking. He knew that she wasn't content to sit still, but now her energy was used for a new test of her abilities.

Val's goal became to offer the best sailing charters in New England. World class. So she began buying bigger boats with state of the art amenities. Over the years Newport had hosted America's Cup races and challenge races. These contests had featured 12-meter yachts, and when several of these had come up for sale, Val bought them. While the boats continued to enter races with expert crews under her management, she also used them for charters. When the 12-meter boats weren't racing or out on charter, she took out groups of tourists on one of the old America's Cup boats, teaching them elementary sailing skills and encouraging them to handle the tasks of crew.

Now, at the age of 41, it still surprised Val to realize how much she enjoyed her current life and just how little she missed the excitement of ocean racing and journeying all over the globe.

To increase income, Rourke's Charters had begun offering sunset cruises. Groups who wished to charter one of the larger boats for an evening's entertainment could enjoy a combination of good food, drink and sightseeing. Val captained the boat along with a small crew. Depending on how much the guests had to drink, she would allow them to take over the wheel, trim the sails and sometimes bring the boat about.

These cruises had become increasingly popular with the rise in the economy. Already this spring Val had multiple bookings into the summer months. An article in the local paper had highlighted the cruises, and they were featured in several of the guidebooks put out for tourists in Newport.

This morning Val was in the charter's new office on Bowen's Wharf in the center of downtown Newport. When the door opened, she looked up from her laptop.

"Althea, hello," Val said. "It's been a while, hasn't it?" She rose from her desk and walked toward the newcomer, extending her hand.

Althea took Val's hand and pressed it gently. "It's been too long, Valerie. So nice of you to see me on such short notice."

"Come in. Sit down."

While Althea settled herself in a chair, Val poured two cups of coffee. "Cream? Sugar? I forget how you take your coffee."

"Black is fine."

When the two women were seated, coffee in front of each, Val took out a pad and pen. "How can I help you, Althea?"

"As I said on the telephone, I want to book one of your cruises. How is your schedule looking for the next several weeks?"

Val turned to her computer and brought up her scheduling file. "Week day or week end?"

"It's a business event so I'm thinking a week night. A Thursday? People are ready to relax near the end of the week."

"O.K." Val studied her screen. "I do have next Thursday, and then the following Thursday. Either one suit you?"

Althea thought for a minute. "I suppose I should take the second one. I have to let everyone I'm inviting know about it. I do want a good response to this."

"And this is business, you said."

"Absolutely. I want to treat some of my long time clients to a nice party. And also introduce some prospective clients to what Tanner Associates offers. I'll invite your mother, of course, and Teddy. You will already be onboard." She paused. "The Ainsleys are my oldest clients, you know."

"Mother would never step on a boat." Val gave Althea a *didn't you know that* look. "She won't come."

"I suppose I should have realized that. I never remember her going sailing with your father."

"That's right."

"So we are set for two weeks from tomorrow?"

"The 27th. I think that I'll put you on *Kandu*. That's our newest 12-meter. We usually leave at six from the dock here."

"Good. What about the catering?"

"I'll email you the menu, and you can look at it. Let me know by the end of the week what you want us to serve."

"And the bar?"

"Wine, beer. The usual soft drinks. We can offer simple mixed drinks like gin or vodka and tonic. And I always have scotch and brandy onboard."

"Who serves?"

"I have someone. That's all taken care of. These trips work very well. We do them all the time."

"This one has to be very special. Tanner Associates does everything first class. And I'm sure that with your usual pursuit for perfection in everything you undertake, Val, this will be a fantastic party."

"That's nice of you to say."

Althea looked around the office. The walls of faded barn board gave the space a clean look, and the nautical trimmings were few and tasteful. Several black and white photographs of sailing races dominated the wall behind Val's desk. There was a case with a glass front which held a few of the many trophies which Val had won in her racing career.

"You've got a good business going here, Val. I congratulate you. You've made this quite a successful operation."

"I remember when I started to buy the 12-meter boats and had to withdraw the money from the Ainsley investments to do it. How you said it was an idiotic idea."

"I was wrong to be negative," Althea said smiling. "I thought you were all about the sport of sailing, not the business of sailing."

"And you were wrong, as you said. As you are now with my brother."

Althea bristled as she answered. "Teddy's very different than you are, Val. He's no manager. And what he wants to take on with this wild idea of his--"

"The music center is not a wild idea," Val said.

"Spending thirty million dollars is a wild idea, Valerie, and deep down you know it."

"Teddy has big plans, and his ideas are going to cost a lot of money just like mine did."

"Yours didn't cost a big chunk of your family's fortune."

Val stared hard at Althea. "But you seem to forget - again - that it's our money. Ainsley money." Althea frowned. "Teddy wants to buy Laurel Hill and turn it into a world class center for classical music. There will be concerts and teaching programs, musicians in residence. He's been planning this for a long time. Mother and I support him one hundred per cent."

"I see."

"You just said that our family were your oldest clients, Althea. You wouldn't be where you are today without my father. And you damned well better never forget that."

CHAPTER VI

Val's words were still ringing in Althea's head as she walked across the cobbled surface of Bowen's Wharf. *She* owed the Ainsleys. Well, the Ainsleys owed her. After John Ainsley died, that family would have been up the proverbial creek without a paddle without her. She had always made sure that they continued to live in the style to which he had accustomed them. They got their quarterly checks, and they were generous ones. If only Teddy had not decided to cash out a big portion of the holdings, there would be no problems.

There were several large sailboats tied up at the end of the wharf, and Althea stopped to examine them. She didn't see any boat called *Kandu*. Kandu. She liked that name. *Can do*. I can do, she thought. I can get myself out of this if I don't panic. She took out her cell phone and pressed some numbers.

Her call was answered on the second ring, but there was no sound from the other end.

"Cameron? Are you there?" she asked into the phone.

There was a pause before the other voice came on the line.

"What is it?" a man's voice asked in a neutral tone.

"I'm sorry to call you. I know we don't usually, but I needed to hear your voice."

"Why?"

"I just need a little boost, and I thought of you."

"I don't like you to call. You know that. It's not a good idea."

"I know," Althea said regretfully. "I know what we decided. But I miss you. That's all."

Before the voice could respond, Althea pressed the red button to end the call. Slowly she put the phone back into the jacket pocket of her suit. Cameron was right. She shouldn't have called him. She was taking a terrible risk.

His colleagues at the Newport Police Station were getting used

21

to the sight of Lt. Hank Nightingale practicing his Tai Chi movements in his office. One minute the lieutenant would be seated at his desk, staring at his computer screen. The next minute he could be seen standing next to his desk with his feet wide apart, knees bent and moving his hands in a wide circular motion in front of his body.

Sgt. Keisha McAndrews had provided the explanation.

"That's called *grinding the corn*. It's a popular Tai Chi exercise. Haven't you ever seen those videos of people doing it in parks in San Francisco?"

Her comments sent several officers rushing to their computers to see the film for themselves.

Keisha herself was a regular at the gym. Tall and athletic, the young black woman maintained her strength through vigorous daily running and a regular weight training program. She was familiar with yoga as she had friends who were devotees. But her only exposure to Tai Chi had been the films of people in Golden Gate Park which she had seen online. Their fluid movements and the gentle rhythms of their motions had captivated her, and she looked forward to seeing the benefits that Hank would obtain from his new regimen.

Sgt. Ben Davies, her fellow detective on Hank's team, took another approach to health.

Ben, who was middle-aged with the beginnings of a paunch, disdained exercise, embracing it only when it was coming up to the time of his annual physical. Then he was all for taking walks at lunch, watching his diet and proclaiming that he was never going to eat another fried onion ring.

It had been three months since Ben's last physical, and he was currently sitting at his desk outside Hank's office, crunching the remains of a yellow and brown bag of peanut M&M's.

"Sure you don't want any of these, Keisha?" he asked.

"I'm good." She was busy entering data into her laptop.

Ben finished the bag and looked at his watch. "Three o'clock, Keisha. Lieutenant wanted our final report on the burglaries before he went home for the weekend."

"I'm doing it now," she said. She hit a few keys of the computer and waved her right hand with a flourish. "It's going right in there."

Ben shook his head. "You are amazing. I don't know how you do those reports so fast. It takes me days."

"It's all in the touch," she said, waving both her hands now.

"That and learning how to type in high school. My father said I could always make a living if I could type."

"How is that?" Ben asked.

"Oh, he grew up in the days of typewriters and remembered all the secretaries at his office."

"Ah, secretaries," Ben said rapturously. "Whose dumb idea was it to get rid of secretaries?"

"I guess you can blame Bill Gates. Or Steve Jobs. We all have computers now, and we are expected to know how to use them." She tried to look stern, but couldn't hold the expression for long. "I'm sure it's not your fault you didn't learn to type in school."

Ben held up his hands with their short stubby fingers. "These babies were never meant to use a keyboard."

"Your hands are too wide for one of these laptops. I could see about ordering you one of the ergonomic keyboards from supply. You hook it up to your laptop. A couple people over in traffic have them."

"Please don't. Whatever an ergonomic keyboard is, I don't want it." Ben sat back in his chair and closed his eyes. "I want a secretary."

Hank Nightingale, who chose this moment to come out of his office, a file in his hand, stared at Ben in confusion. "You want a what?" he asked.

While Keisha laughed, Ben sat up in his chair and crumpled up the empty M&M's bag on his desk and closed his hand over it. "Hello, Lieutenant. What can we do for you?"

"Thanks for the report, Keisha."

"You're welcome, sir."

"Now that we've closed the books on these burglary cases, I hope we can relax for a few days."

The team had just arrested a suspect in several burglaries around Washington Square, and the accused was currently in custody. The evidence looked solid, and Hank was feeling confident of a conviction once the slow course of justice made its way to trial.

"Who's got big plans for the weekend?" Ben asked. "Kids and me'll be raking out the lawn and putting down fertilizer. Weather is supposed to be sunny."

"Sounds like fun, Ben," Keisha said. "I'll think of you while I'm at the beach. What about you, Lieutenant?"

"Well, I'm never sure. Caroline's job at the inn is sometimes worse than mine for planning ahead. There's always some emergency. But I'm hoping we'll be able to do something tomorrow. As Ben said, the weather forecast is great."

Hank looked out a nearby window at the blue sky. There was a breeze blowing through the branches of the two trees visible from their second floor office. "Be some good days for sailing. Maybe I'll hook up something for Sunday." Hank took every opportunity to crew on *Fancy Boy*, the boat owned by one of his buddies, which was often entered in local races.

"One of these days you'll have your own boat, Lieutenant," Keisha said. She had seen that wistful look appear on Hank's face more than once when sailing and boats came into the conversation.

"Yeah, maybe when I retire. I'll take my pension and buy a boat."

Teddy Ainsley's proposal to hold his music festival at the inn continued to weigh on Caroline's mind. On one hand, the idea intrigued her. She loved Kenwood, and she was excited about the prospect of showing it off as a formal venue for concerts. The grand salon didn't get much use these days. There were no big parties such as the ones which had taken place in the old days. When was the last time a ball had been held at Kenwood by the Kents? She guessed in the days of Frederick Kent's youth or even his father's era. It would be nice to bring the room alive again.

But there was the other side of the proposal. For all Teddy's enthusiasm, he had no background in entertainment and promotion. What if nobody came? What if the whole thing was a fiasco and Kenwood's name was irretrievably linked to the failed enterprise? She had spent the last three years building up the inn's reputation, and she couldn't take a chance of tarnishing it.

Louise considered the idea impractical. But her mother-in-law hadn't seen the look on Teddy Ainsley's face as he had explained his plan to Caroline. She understood that it was his dream, just as hers had been in coming to Kenwood. Back then she didn't know the first thing about running an inn. She'd never had to balance figures on a spreadsheet. In fact she'd never even unplugged a clogged drain.

Friday afternoons were busy times at the inn with the arrival of the weekend guests. Once she had settled everyone in and acquainted them with the house, Caroline made sure that the bar in the library was well-stocked and that everyone's questions about restaurants and what to do were answered. Afterwards she liked to retire to her office for a break. Louise usually joined her, and they had tea and some of the cakes or cookies that Mattie had baked for the guests.

This Friday, however, Louise was busy working in the garden so Caroline decided to use her free time to go to Val Ainsley's office on Bowen's Wharf. If Val could reassure her that she planned to be involved in Teddy's music festival, Caroline would consider the proposition.

CHAPTER VII

Val was studying a chart when Caroline arrived at Rourke's Charters.

"Caroline, hello," Val said, getting up from her desk. "What a nice surprise. How is Louise?"

"Fine. Terrific, really. You know how living in Newport again agrees with her. Right now she's working in the gardens. She is determined to get the grounds back to the way they were. We can't afford much help, so she's doing most of it herself."

"Well, then I shall call on her soon to see what she has been doing. Can I bring Mother? She loves her garden and will enjoy talking shop."

"Of course. We're both generally around. The inn keeps us busy."

"Like this place."

"Yes," Caroline agreed. "I'm sure it does. And that's what I was hoping to talk to you about."

"Do you want to charter a boat?"

"That's not why I came, but now you've given me an idea. I have a good friend who loves to sail but doesn't have a boat of his own. Now I think I know what to get him for his next birthday. A charter."

"That can be arranged. Is he local?"

"Yes. What's the minimum time for a charter?"

"Usually it's a week, but I can make an exception if you want something shorter. A day or two. There's always a boat at the dock I can let you have."

"Thank you. I'll have to decide on a plan and let you know."

"O.K.. So tell me why you did stop by."

"It's about Teddy."

Val smiled. "I should have guessed. He's been to see you."

"Yes, and I admit I'm a bit overwhelmed with his plan for these concerts. I'd like to help, but I'm just not sure. I got the impression you're encouraging him and that you'll be helping him."

"I told him I would do anything. And I will."

"But how much time will you have to do the nuts and bolts of putting these programs on? He admitted that he's never taken on anything like this before."

"Mother and I were very encouraging when he came to us with the plan to buy an estate in town and renovate it for a music center. He's been fairly aimless these last few years, and we were pleased to see him with a purpose. This idea of doing a concert series in the fall in a rented facility came up afterwards."

"Buying a music center? He didn't tell me anything about that."

"Do you know the house called Laurel Hill over by Fort Adams?" Caroline shook her head. "It's a big place that's come up for sale, and he wants to put in an offer for it. The house needs a lot of work. Which translates to needs a lot of money. The grounds are extensive, about three acres. There are over twenty rooms, and some of them are quite large. A ballroom and a music room."

"He's going to renovate it?"

"Teddy got an architect to look at it, and she's working on some preliminary plans and estimates. The house was built in 1860. There have been some renovations, but far too long ago. Everything needs updating, the plumbing, the wiring. There are some other buildings on the grounds, a carriage house for one. They will all have to be repurposed."

"And Teddy is going to oversee all of this?"

"He says so. Founding this music center is his heart's desire. He's been in love with music since he was child."

"I'm amazed," Caroline said, "and I wish him luck. But it makes me wonder even more if he has the time to do these fall programs at Kenwood."

"You want an honest answer? Probably not."

"What should I do, Val? Should I tell him I can't have the concerts at Kenwood?"

"Let me talk to him. Perhaps he could stage one or two concerts to give people a preview of what they can expect when he opens Laurel Hill. Could you handle that? One or two programs."

"Probably. Something on a small scale. He did say the salon would be perfect."

"We used to play games in there as children. It wasn't being used for much else at the time."

"He didn't tell me about playing games when he came to see me."

"Probably didn't want you to tell Louise. We used to play soccer in there. Barefoot, of course, but I don't think that did the parquet flooring any good." Val smiled. "Teddy and I both have a lot of fond memories of Kenwood. I'm sure that's why he thought of the house for his music."

When the bell on the door of the charter office jingled, both women turned to look.

"I was in the neighborhood," a smartly dressed woman said as she came in, closing the door behind her. "And I thought I'd come by to talk to you about the menu you sent me. There are a few things I was hoping we could change." The woman seemed to notice Caroline for the first time and looked at her curiously.

"Caroline, this is Althea Tanner," Val said. "Althea, Caroline Kent. I'm thinking you two don't know one another."

Caroline smiled and extended her hand. She found herself staring at Althea's face. The woman was beautiful. Althea held Caroline's hand for a few seconds before letting it go. Hardly a conventional hand shake, Caroline thought.

"Are you here to charter a boat?" Althea asked. "This is the best place in Newport."

"No. I'm not."

"Caroline owns The Inn At Kenwood Court, Althea. You must have heard of it. It's over by The Breakers."

"Yes, of course. I've read about your place. You get the cream of the visitors I'm told."

"We do try to position our inn as a high end accommodation."

"*Life as lived in Newport's Gilded Age.* Didn't I see that written somewhere?"

"Yes," Caroline said. "We've used that phrase to promote the inn."

"I sometimes need a place for overnight guests. Your place sounds perfect for us. I'm sorry I haven't thought of it before now."

Caroline took a business card from her handbag and offered it to Althea. "I'd be happy to show you around the inn."

"Thank you," Althea said as she studied the card. "You know,

I'm just thinking." She glanced at Val who had been listening to the conversation with a minimum of interest. "I'm planning a sailing cruise with Val on the 27th. I'm having a few of the firm's clients, and also some prospective ones. Why don't you join us? Are you free that night? It's a Thursday."

Caroline looked uncertain. "Are you thinking I am a prospective client? I'm afraid that I don't know what your firm does."

"We offer financial advice." Althea paused and looked at Val. "We also look for the cream."

Caroline laughed. "Well, that's not me. I can assure you that it will be a long time until I need the services of a financial advisor."

"Don't worry about that, Caroline. I'm asking you because I think my guests would enjoy meeting you. And you can do some networking. We females have to stick together."

"Yes we should."

"We'll be using one of Val's America's Cup boats for the evening. And please bring... your husband?"

"I don't have a husband," Caroline said.

"You must have someone in your life," Althea said playfully.

"There is someone who would enjoy coming out on one of the sailboats."

"Then ask him," Althea said. "It is a *him*, isn't it? Although you never know these days."

"Yes, he's a *he*," Caroline said. She knew how much Hank would enjoy the invitation to sail on one of the 12-meter boats. They had often seen them tied up at the dock, and she remembered how much Hank's eyes lingered lovingly on them.

Althea took out one of her cards and handed it to Caroline. "Give me a call and let me know if you can come to my party. I'd love to have you both."

CHAPTER VIII

"That's interesting you should bring up reading *The Great Gatsby*, Hank."

It was late evening, and the couple were sitting on one of the wicker settees in the inn's gazebo, located at the rear of the property next to the Cliff Walk. It was a clear night with a full moon. Cool breezes off the ocean blew through the open windows of the structure. The only sounds seemed to be the breaking of the waves on the cliffs below.

"Why is that, Caroline?" Hank asked.

"I had once wanted to play Daisy Buchanan."

"In the movie? The one with Robert Redford and Mia Farrow?" Hank had seen the movie because several scenes had been filmed in Newport. It had been a huge event around town, and everyone was eager to see the finished product when the film had been released.

"No," Caroline said. "Not the film. I wanted to do her in a stage play."

"And you never did?"

"No," she said, the tone of her voice suggesting regret. "There never was a play. I had a friend who was a playwright. I tried to interest him in the idea of adapting the book into a drama, but it didn't appeal to him. So the chance never came."

Hank put his arm around Caroline and pulled her close to him in a comforting gesture. She easily let herself be consoled.

"It was a long time ago," she said. "I've gotten over it."

"If you're still talking about it, then you haven't." Hank kissed the top of her head and let his mouth linger in the folds of her soft brown hair.

Hank considered that his relationship with Caroline was in a good stage. Her husband Reed, the man Hank never knew but who was so much a part of his life, had been dead for over three years now. Becoming a fixture in Caroline's world had made for a slow and often rocky journey. When they first met it had been too early in Caroline's widowhood for her to be thinking about romance. Hank understood that, but he had been impatient on more than one occasion while he tried to convince her that there was no disloyalty in feeling love for a second man.

He loved her, had said it often. She loved him, but said it rarely. Hank wondered if Reed would ever be gone from between them.

"Tell me why you wanted to play Daisy."

"Daisy and Gatsby are such famous characters in literature. In the book she is always reacting to other characters - her husband Tom, Nick Carraway, Jay Gatsby. I don't think that Fitzgerald wanted more out of Daisy than to use her to emphasize Gatsby's striving for respectability. Daisy could have been brought more alive on the stage than she comes across in the book. I wanted the audience to see her as her own person. With her own hopes and dreams. And ultimately her own tragic inability to realize any of them."

"Wow. I'm impressed."

Caroline gave Hank a good natured poke. "Actors give a lot of thought to what is inside a role. Now you tell me what's brought up this sudden interested in the novel."

Hank explained how he had been listening to the audio book and his own take on Jay Gatsby.

"The reader doesn't know until the end of the book that the character we thought we knew is a fake."

"Exactly," Caroline said. "You see what I mean about interpreting Daisy. If you played Gatsby you could give small clues to his real personality from the beginning of the play. Gatsby can't be as confident as he appears early in the story. He's insecure. A good actor could bring that out."

"Do you miss it?" Hank asked.

"What? Miss what?" Her bright green eyes narrowed.

"Acting. The stage. You left all that behind in New York when you came up here."

"It was the right thing to do," Caroline said quickly.

Too quickly, Hank thought as he hugged her close again and buried his nose back in her hair. She was a strong woman, always appearing so capable, and he must remember how she needed support like any other human being.

"Oh, here's something I need to ask you," Caroline said, her abrupt change of topic interrupting his thoughts. "How would you like to go sailing?"

The question was completely unexpected. Usually Hank was the one asking Caroline if she could take some time to go out with him when he was able to borrow *Fancy Boy* from Dave Fletcher for the afternoon.

"Sailing? Sure. What did you have in mind?"

Caroline told him about Althea Tanner's invitation.

"That's interesting," Hank said carefully. "A sailing *party*?"

"Yes, but I talked to Val afterwards and told her about all your experience, so she knows you know what you're doing. She'll let you take the wheel, trim the sails, whatever you want to do."

"Yeah?" Hank said skeptically. He wasn't sure what the atmosphere would be on this party cruise.

"Hank, don't tell me you are going to pass up a chance to go out on one of the America's Cup boats."

"No, I probably shouldn't. When is it? Thursday night the 27th." Caroline nodded. "Sure I'll come along." He pulled her close again. "I'm your date, right?"

"I was asked to bring one," Caroline said. "And, yes, I picked you."

A few miles around the coastline from where Hank and Caroline were enjoying each other's company, Jason Cava was pacing his bedroom, trying to calm his mounting anxiety.

When he had first started working for Tanner Associates, Althea had recently purchased *Di Sole*. The house had been built for a hedge fund trader who used it for two summers before he decided he'd rather be in The Hamptons. It was Althea who had given the property a name, a remnant of a recent trip to Italy where she had found everything she encountered *magnifico*.

Jason rather liked the name, and he was impressed with the house. It was Althea's suggestion that he use the east wing for his own living quarters.

"Why rent somewhere when you can live here for free," she pointed out. It was an offer he couldn't refuse. *Di Sole* was a spectacular place to call his home, and as the years went by Jason had come to love living there.

The house was too big for one person's needs. Even with the

two of them, they often padded around in solitude, their paths within the house running in different directions. Althea's original suggestion was that they could get work done away from the office. In truth, this collaboration rarely if ever happened. Althea had her own way of doing things, and Jason soon realized he was a tool to get her what she wanted. He didn't mind. The financial compensation became more than he had ever imagined it would be. How could he complain?

And now that was the problem. Too much money. Jason had too much money. He wanted to take it and leave. Leave before it was too late.

But he was only fooling himself when he made these plans. How could he leave? What Tanner Associates had become was as much a part of him as it was of the others.

CHAPTER IX

2008 had begun as a crisis year for Althea Tanner. Along with the rest of the country she had watched nervously as the sub-prime mortgage crisis, government bailouts and falling stock prices dominated the headlines.

When Tanner Associates had begun accepting clients in late 2006, the Dow Jones Industrial Average was rising steadily. The stock market would reach its record high of 14,164.32 in October 2007. After being battered by the financial events of 2008, that same Dow number would be 8,776.39 points at the end of that same year. Because the stock market had lost almost half its value, investors saw their portfolios hemorrhage billions of dollars. Retirement savings lost value. Pension funds faltered.

For Althea Tanner, who had used the reputation she had earned as John Ainsley's personal stock advisor to attract other clients to her new firm, the timing couldn't have been worse. While the Dow was climbing during 2007, her firm was making eye catching profits for its new investors. Word of mouth around Newport was that you were very lucky if you could get your money into Tanner Associates. With a minimum investment of $10 million, Althea made sure that she got only the most desirable clients.

On New Year's Day 2008 Althea had no reason to believe that the coming year wouldn't surpass the previous.

Then the business news stories started to make her apprehensive. In March, the Federal Reserve intervened to help the global investment bank Bear Stearns with an emergency loan to meet its debt obligations, a rescue which ultimately failed. Four months later the government again stepped in by taking over Freddie Mac and Fanny Mae, the government-sponsored mortgage enterprises, so they could each meet their financial obligations.

Throughout this period the stock market bobbed up and down. While investors were cautious, it seemed that few people were ready to believe that the country was on the verge of an economic collapse. But as Althea studied the Tanner investment statements for 2008's first and second quarters, she couldn't shake the feeling that the downturn was real and, more worrying, had yet to reach its bottom.

The problem was that Althea couldn't go to her new investors and alert them to this news. Any sign that your money wasn't going to grow at a record rate when Tanner advised you, even if the cause was behind her control, would send her new clients running for the exits. She had earned their trust by way of her reputation. She had to maintain it with her results. And Althea could clearly see that investment rates of return in 2008 were plummeting. How could she keep her clients and save her business?

As Althea had feared, the stock market continued to show weakness during the summer of 2008. Tanner's third quarter profits were going to be non-existent. In September the Lehman Brothers investment company declared bankruptcy and the Dow dropped over 500 points. Althea, like many in the country, waited anxiously that fall as Congress debated whether to approve the Treasury Department's proposal for a government bailout which would supply cash directly to banks hit by the sub-prime mortgage crisis. When the bill did not pass Congress, the stock market plunged again.

In response, Althea Tanner did something she had never done before: she ran away.

The Bristol Club has always been one of Bermuda's most luxurious resorts. Located on a private peninsula, its turquoise blue water and pristine sandy beaches provide a serene oasis for the two dozen pink cottages which are spread across its twenty secluded acres.

Althea and John Ainsley had stayed at the club shortly after he had hired her to advise him. John had proposed a *working vacation*, and Althea had been pleased to go. The couple went for a week, but each had occupied a separate cottage. Althea had been surprised by John's arrangements; she had been fully prepared, even eager, to accept him as a lover. But John coolly maintained his distance during their stay. Ainsley was too smart a businessman to jeopardize his new resource by letting the potential of future sexual conflict threaten his financial well being.

The vacation had achieved John's purpose. He and Althea had

the leisurely time to make their plans for future Ainsley family investments. At the week's end, the couple, despite their lack of physical closeness, had established a strong working relationship.

Althea looked back on the time shared with John Ainsley at The Bristol Club as a turning point in her life. And now as her world was about to crash down around her, she decided to return to Bermuda to take stock of her own options.

During the first few days at The Bristol Club, Althea rarely left her cottage. The atmosphere was as relaxing as she had remembered it. She was sleeping better, eating the healthy meals delivered by golf cart three times a day, and even reading the best selling novel she had brought with her. Each late afternoon she took a walk on the club beach advertised as *quiet*. She talked to none of the other guests.

On the fourth day she decided to take her book with her to the quiet beach. Her fair skin did not allow her to expose it to the sun, and she wore a large-brimmed hat, sunglasses, and a billowing white linen caftan. Settled in a shaded chair, she opened her book.

"What are you reading?" a deep masculine voice asked from above her head.

Startled, Althea looked up to find herself staring at one of the most ruggedly handsome faces that she had ever seen. The newcomer had prematurely grey hair and ice blue eyes bracketed by deeply etched laugh lines. He was tan, wearing navy swim trunks and a grey T-shirt that showed off his well-toned body. Althea's first instinct to let her intruder know she didn't want to be interrupted quickly reversed itself.

"Stephen King," she replied. "Are you a fan?"

The newcomer laughed. "I'm more of a Grisham guy myself. Have you read his new one, *The Appeal?*"

Althea shook her head. "This is probably the first novel I've read all year." When her companion looked surprised, she added, "It's been a grisly year for me."

"Tell me about it," he said with a winning grin as he lowered himself onto the sand next to her.

Althea was not ready to share her plight with a stranger, even one as attractive as Cameron Epsberg. Without giving him much detail, she told him that she was worried over her underperforming business. The present economic situation was blamed, and Cameron seemed to understand how easily that could happen in the current business climate.

After half an hour on the beach, Cameron extended a *come to my cottage for a drink* invitation. One drink led to another and soon Althea was in his bed.

For the next several days, the couple relaxed in each other's company and took advantage of the pleasant September weather. It was during their last day together on the beach that Cameron asked again about her work.

"Why did you say this has been a 'grisly' time for you, Althea? Grisly is an unusual word to use."

"It's nothing," she said lightly. "Let's not let that trouble ruin a lovely vacation." She reached across the sand and grazed the blond hairs on his arm with her fingers.

"I don't think it is nothing. I've seen a look in your eyes when you think no one is watching."

"You don't need to know. Let's just be two people who meet on the beach and pretend that nothing else is happening in the whole world."

Cameron frowned and looked thoughtful. Althea studied him warily. The two stared at one another for almost a minute, as if each was wondering how much to share with a person who had been a total stranger only a week ago.

"You can trust me, you know," he said. "And, besides. I like you. I want to help you if I can."

"And I like you, too," she said, her voice hinting at sadness. "I didn't expect to find you on this trip."

"So you better had tell me about *grisly*." He reached out for her hand. "I'm a good listener."

So she decided to tell him.

When she finished, she saw that Cameron was smiling.

"Is that all it is?" he asked. "You should have told me right away."

"Why?" Althea was puzzled.

"Because I *can* help you. That is if you don't mind bending a few rules."

CHAPTER X

The plan was so simple to execute that Althea later wondered if she was dreaming it all.

Cameron Epsberg was a mergers and acquisitions lawyer with a high-powered firm in New York City. He had access to confidential information known to only a few insiders. During his career he had carefully used some of his knowledge to make a small number of judiciously placed stock purchases. Infrequently trading and spreading the trades over several accounts, he had so far seemed to evade any notice of his profits by the regulatory authorities.

As it happened - and so providential for Althea's current predicament - the announcement of a merger between two drug companies, which Cameron's law firm was working on, was going to be made public in two weeks. Cameron had been careful not to profit from this deal. There would be too much scrutiny when well known pharmaceutical companies were involved. But Althea was far removed from the law firm and its clients. That she would act on a tip she could have overheard anywhere, or that she deduced what was going to happen from the financial press rumor mill, could be reasonable explanations for her stock purchases prior to the merger announcement.

All Althea had to do to make Tanner's third quarter 2008 results meet her clients' high expectations was to sell large blocks of the stock in their portfolios and move the money into the soon to be rising drug company shares. Once the shares had gained big profits, she could sell them and use the money to write the usual quarterly dividend checks for her investors.

Back in Newport, Althea liquidated enough of her clients' accounts to make the trades. The stock she bought rose as Cameron promised. The blocks were quickly sold and the next quarter's generous checks went out to all the clients. She was still the premier investment advisor in Newport whose clients had bragging rights all over town that they were beating the markets while their less fortunate friends suffered substantial losses in their own portfolios.

Althea's gratitude to Cameron Epsberg was enormous. Once she had safely produced the desired third quarter results, she met him in Boston for the weekend.

That he was happy to resume the relationship they had started in Bermuda pleased her. But she could not get the need for another rabbit - which would have to be pulled from the magician's hat to make Tanner's fourth quarter results - out of her mind.

"Hey, take it easy," the lawyer had told her. "I only do one of these every year or so. What the feds don't like is a pattern."

"But it was so easy to make money, Cameron."

"If it was so easy, Althea, then everyone would be doing it. There's a reason that they're not."

She knew he was right but the gambler's instinct, always there in a stock trader, was urging her on.

"If I could get somebody to make the trades," she began. "Somebody who trades a lot of stock, big blocks because to them a half a million shares is nothing, what would you say to that?"

Cameron nodded reluctantly. "I'm listening."

"This is how it would work. You give me the information on the merger or acquisition, I pass it on to this person who makes the trades in his accounts. I know for a fact he has several."

"Several as in how many?"

Althea put up her hand as a stop sign. "Don't ask." The truth was that she'd been having an affair with the unnamed person, and she wasn't ready to share that information with Cameron.

"The stock market is going to be difficult to read for a long time, believe me. I know. Predicting where it will go will be absolutely impossible. Doing this plan is a sure way to make the money I need to pay out to my investors. And it seems to me that there could be a lot left over for us in the bargain. The three of us."

"I don't know," Cameron said, still hesitant. "I don't know this third person."

"You can be sure he's well equipped to do this. Would even enjoy it. We'll do a three way even split."

"This is someone you trust?"

"Yes. Unequivocally."

"Where does he live?"

"Newport as it happens."

"You know that if I agree to this, we have to break off anything we have started and are thinking of continuing." Althea hadn't, but she quickly nodded her assent. John Ainsley had taught her how to make that decision. "There can be no connection between us. No contact whatsoever. Not even a Christmas card."

"I understand."

"I've been thinking for a long time that I should make more money." He smiled for the first time since they had begun this conversation. " I believe that I deserve it."

"You do, darling," Althea said. "And so do I."

"All right. You contact... your friend. I don't want to know his name."

"That's fine with me."

"And about the split. I'm going to send you someone who will work in your office. He'll be your employee and earn a salary. You'll need him to make sure your computer records and the clients' statements appear legitimate and above board. His name is Jason Cava and he'll contact you within the week. He'll get ten percent for his contribution. The rest of us thirty percent each."

"How do you know this Jason?"

"He's a friend. That's all you need to know. He'll take care of protecting the records."

"But how will I get the stock information from you?"

"Jason will take care of that, too."

CHAPTER XI

"I still think this party tonight is a mistake, Althea," Jason Cava said. "And I wish Teddy Ainsley wasn't going to be there. Suppose he starts talking to you about wanting his money out of the firm in front of the other guests?"

Althea was sitting at her desk, reading a commodities report. Tanner had never steered their investors into commodities. Prices could be very volatile, but Althea had begun to wonder if this instability was something she might use for cover in the future if the need ever arose.

"Mmn?" she said, absorbed in her reading.

Jason repeated his question. Althea turned away from the report and sighed.

"Don't be such an old spinster aunt about this. Everything is going to be fine. Teddy knows how to act at a cocktail party. He's not going to cause a scene."

"I don't like it. I can't be as sure as you seem to be that nothing will go wrong."

"Of course I'm sure. And look at the weather today. Picture perfect for a sail in the bay. I'm really looking forward to tonight. It's going to be a perfect evening."

Well, she certainly hoped so. Her fingers were crossed. In truth, Althea was more worried about Val's letting something slip than anything her brother might say. It was important that both Dr. Tompkins and Leo Vargoff be brought into the fold. A quick injection of their capital would give her some breathing room while she dealt with Teddy Ainsley's demand for his money.

Scott Forsythe was waiting for Althea at the bar at the Clarke Cooke House on Bannister's Wharf. She greeted him with a generous kiss on each cheek. He responded by stroking the small of her back, taking his time letting her go from his hold. Scott was, like all the men in Althea's past and present life, good-looking. His steady black eyes and dark, slicked back hair gave him an air of authority and control. The cut and style of his clothes indicated they were expensive and had been chosen with particular care.

The restaurant's large windows faced the water and provided a post card view of the harbor. The tall masts of the yachts tied up at Bannister's Wharf rocked gently in the breeze. Althea sipped the vodka martini which Scott had ready for her and took some time to enjoy the scenery. The historic wharf was the sailing heart of Newport, the place where Ted Turner had once brought home the America's Cup. A hundred and fifty years earlier, Oliver Hazard Perry had also returned here after his decisive naval victory on Lake Erie during the War of 1812.

"Penny for your thoughts," Scott asked.

"I would need more than a penny," Althea laughed.

The vodka had already relaxed her. She was dressed in a flowered sun dress with a pink cashmere shawl draped across her shoulders. Around her neck was a multi-strand necklace of green jade beads and white pearls, perfectly set off by her thick red hair.

"Is there anything I should know about this evening?" Scott asked. He had a tumbler of dark brown single malt on the bar in front of him. "I assume it's the usual suspects."

"Yes. And the two new investors I told you about. Richard Tompkins and Leo Vargoff. I want them impressed enough tonight so they decide to write checks."

"You're still sure that we need them. Cameron Epsberg hasn't been able to turn up something that would help us?"

"Jason says not."

"You know that I hate the idea of bringing more people into this."

"I don't see another way. I'm sure that you haven't forgotten we've also got a lot of money tied up in that media stock you shorted last month."

Cameron Epsberg had provided a tip that the Federal Communications Commission wasn't going to allow one entertainment giant to take over another major digital player in the industry. The decision would come as a surprise to most of the financial world. But someone inside the FCC had given Cameron advance warning of the ruling the commission would make.

"We can't profit," Althea continued, "until the FCC announces that the deal isn't going through, and the price of the shares goes down." The drop in share price would have the effect of making Scott's 'shorted' stock investment increase handsomely in value. "We don't know when that's going to happen."

"So we do need more capital because of Teddy."

"Yes, and these two new investors can give it to us. I had thought we were more than covered to pay out the dividends for the quarter ending next month before I was completely blind sided by Teddy's request."

Althea drank a large measure of her drink. "I suppose you could say that we've been a little greedy lately, darling. I mean, an island in the Caribbean," she said, meeting his eyes. "That put a bit of a strain on our resources."

"I'm thinking of sailing my boat down there this winter. You know I've wanted that island for a long time."

"You know we accommodated you with the funds out of future profits."

"We did the same for Cameron when he bought that villa in Tuscany two years ago."

"That we did. What were we thinking?"

"That this would never end," Scott said. "We're lucky you haven't gotten around to a second home."

"I don't need one," Althea said tartly. She drained her glass. "Come on. Let's get this show on the road."

Scott paid the check and they left the bar. The evening dinner crowd had arrived on Bannister's Wharf and jostled them as they left the restaurant. Scott took Althea's arm and guided her through the push of people across the bricks and cobblestones to reach the adjacent Bowen's Wharf where the boat was waiting for them at the dock.

"Don't worry," Scott said, his voice easy. "We'll cover things. We've got ourselves this far, and we're going to continue to make this golden goose keep laying eggs."

"That's a picturesque way of putting things," she said with a laugh.

Scott squeezed her arm. "It's true, isn't it?"

"Yes," Althea agreed, lifting up her head and holding out her chin determinedly. "Then let's go and greet the geese."

CHAPTER XII

Caroline stood at the dock next to where *Kandu* was tied up. It was a large red-hulled vessel with a lean graceful look. She was wearing what she hoped was the proper party attire: a sleeveless mint green dress and matching cardigan.

All the guests were on board except for her and Hank. She was there, ready to board. But there was no Hank. Her cell phone, held tightly in her hand, stubbornly refused to ring.

She alternated looking across the wharf and back to the boat where she saw Val's crew, a young man and woman, making the boat ready to leave. Finally, with her anxiety mounting, she pressed Hank's number. After five rings he answered "*Yeah*" in a harried voice.

"Hank, where are you? I'm at the boat. We're getting ready to leave."

"I know, I know. Look, you'll have to go without me. Sorry." Caroline could hear the noises of traffic behind him.

"Where are you? What's happening?"

"We had a call, an emergency. I can't talk now, but I'm tied up here." He stopped speaking to her to talk to someone who was with him. Caroline couldn't understand what he was saying. "I'm sorry," he said, back on the phone with her. "I'm really sorry. But maybe some other time. O.K.?"

"Yes," she answered, wondering when might be the next time they would be offered the chance of sailing on an America's Cup yacht. "It's fine, Hank. Things happen."

"Bye," he said. "Thanks." And the phone went dead.

The sun glowing in the early evening sky was becoming a brilliant orange color as Val started the engine. Two crew members cast off the boat's lines onto the dock as she began to back *Kandu* out into the harbor. The noise from the busy the restaurants along the water's edge grew fainter as Val moved away from the wharf and threaded her way slowly through the boats moored in the crowded harbor.

With slow precision the crew raised first the main sail and then the head sail. Caroline felt a thrill in her chest as she saw the sails going up. The two huge triangular canvases, making a heavy ruffling sound as they were unfurled to blow free in the wind, gave the boat a majestic bearing. She wished that Hank were here to see this with her.

Most of *Kandu's* guests were taking advantage of the opportunity to see the imposing view of the stone fortress of Fort Adams guarding the entrance to the harbor. A few of the passengers were standing. Others had found a seat on the deck. Althea slipped easily among them, making sure that everyone had a drink in his or her hand. A uniformed steward offered canapés from a tray.

The night air was cool, and there was a light wind. The engine was soon turned off, and in the sudden quiet of the open water, the boat began to glide effortlessly forward under sail power.

Caroline had felt like an outsider when she first stepped onto the boat. Except for Val and Teddy, she knew none of the elegantly dressed guests onboard. But Althea had quickly pressed a glass of white wine into her hand and introduced her to several people.

Val remained at the wheel as the boat sailed in the direction of the Newport Bridge, passing Goat Island on the starboard side and then the smaller Rose Island on the port side. Two of the male guests, whom Caroline had yet to meet, stood next to Val. One was tall and good looking with dark curly hair. He wore a large gold watch on his left wrist. His unsmiling companion was several years older. Shorter and heavier, he had a large head with a thin dusting of grey hair.

Val gestured toward the wheel and the older man nodded. She eased back in the cockpit to let him take her place. Caroline watched his hands as he gripped the wheel forcefully, the expression on his face rigid.

"Ready to come about, Jill," Val called to one of her crew.

"Ready," came the answer.

Standing beside him, Val guided the new helmsman through a port tack. Conversation stopped as the swinging boom began to move. The two crew members carefully protected the guests to keep them away from the path of the boom's progress.

The maneuver was completed, the vessel now positioned to sail in the direction of Castle Hill. The noise of cocktail party chatter resumed.

Only the woman next to Caroline continued to keep her gaze on the man at the wheel. She was middle-aged, trim and well-exercised, with an up sweep of blond hair and lots of sparkling diamonds. She wore a short white dress trimmed with clusters of red stars. After a minute or so, her attention turned to Caroline.

"Hello," she said pleasantly. "I haven't seen you at one of Althea's do's. Are you a new client of the firm?"

"No. I'm afraid that I'm a bit of a party crasher. I recently met Althea, and she invited me to come along tonight. Caroline Kent."

"How nice to meet you, Caroline. I'm Leslie Seeger." Leslie touched Caroline's hand in greeting. "That's my husband Alex at the wheel."

"He looks like he knows what he's doing."

"Oh, Alex can do anything he puts his mind to."

"Good for him."

"I expect you'll soon be one of us." When Caroline's face must have shown confusion, Leslie added, "That is, you'll be with Tanner Associates." Caroline didn't contradict the statement. "And you'll be damned lucky - if you'll excuse my language - to sign with her. That woman is a miracle worker."

"So I've heard," Caroline murmured. She finished her drink. "If you'll excuse me, I think I'll get a refill."

Caroline didn't need more wine as much as she wanted to move to the less populated area of the boat. As she made her way forward, she picked up strains from several conversations.

"The Fed is going to have to raise interest rates in the fall."

"There's going to be turbulence in the market, I'm telling you."

"Europe's not growing. I told Althea to keep me out of Europe."

An older couple was listening to Althea's assistant Jason Cava, whom Caroline had met when she first came onboard.

"I'm afraid that the market was reacting to what is expected to be a disappointing retail sales report tomorrow," Caroline heard Cava explain. "Also there was a global bond sell-off yesterday. So that's why the market was down *today*, Mrs. Dalworthy. But these daily fluctuations aren't serious."

Mrs. Dalworthy, a tall woman of about seventy who was dressed in a beige linen suit, managed a smile. The white-haired man next to her, wearing a bottle green blazer, crisp white shirt and yellow paisley tie, nodded solemnly.

"Of course," Jason continued, "some big companies came in with poor earnings today. It doesn't help their shares when the revenue falls short of the analysts' forecasts."

"Those damned analysts," the white-haired man said with irritation. "A bunch of new MBA's who don't know anything about business."

"You might be right, Mr. Dalworthy," Jason said with a practiced chuckle, "but their comments have their effect. There's not much we stock investors can do about that."

Caroline didn't know a lot about investing, but she found it surprising that nothing she was hearing was very informative. It sounded like so much boilerplate. She looked around for Teddy Ainsley. This might be a good opportunity to find out if Val had talked to him about limiting the number of concerts he wanted to have at Kenwood.

Caroline heard Teddy's voice before she could see him. As she reached the forward hatch, she knew that the angry voice coming from the cabin below was unmistakably his.

CHAPTER XIII

"—never would have tried to get away with this trick while my father was alive."

Caroline's ears strained to hear what was being said below.

"I want my money. And I want it now. I *need* it." Teddy's voice was plaintive. "Don't you understand?"

The response was barely audible. A few disjointed words. *Patient... I... time.*

"I don't *have* time. I told you that."

Caroline looked around the deck and her eyes locked with those of another of the guests. He was a man about her own age attired in a blue and white striped seersucker suit, navy T-shirt and matching espadrilles. His straight blond hair was pulled into a pony tail. He gestured toward the hatch.

"Who's that speaking?" he asked in a distinctly British accent.

Caroline shrugged as she if she didn't know.

"You can't stand in my way," Teddy's voice said, angry once more.

Again the reply was difficult to understand.

"I won't let you get away with this, Althea. I want the money, I mean it. I'll make you pay."

"Sounds like someone is quite upset with Althea Tanner," the young man said. "But I'm not sure that I recognize the man's voice. Do you think they're talking about some investments?"

"I'm not sure. Perhaps we shouldn't listen," Caroline said as she moved away from the hatch. Her new acquaintance followed her.

"They probably went below because they thought no one could hear them," he said.

Caroline introduced herself.

"Jonathan Granger," Jonathan responded. "I'm onboard with my wife."

"I don't think I've met her yet."

48

Jonathan pointed across the deck. "She's over there with Scott Forsythe. Talking money, I'm sure. Melody loves to talk about money." Granger smiled, showing even white teeth. "And lucky for me she does."

Caroline studied Melody Granger. She was fifty at least, with long black hair and a round friendly face. She was dressed in a billowy yellow pant suit with a chunky black onyx necklace around her neck.

"Melody thinks yellow suits her. What do you think?" Caroline was taken aback, unsure of what was the polite thing to say. "Don't be afraid to say what you think. I do." Caroline stared at him. "All in yellow, she makes me think of a big sunflower."

"Well, it is summery," Caroline said, recovering herself. "I can't wear yellow myself. And I love the color."

Jonathan regarded her, appraising her figure. "Fall colors would absolutely look best on you. Summer's not your season. I wouldn't wear that light shade of green if I were you." Caroline winced.

"You sound like you know a lot about fashion, Mr. Granger."

"Jon, please. And I used to be a model. Before I met Melody, that is. Now I'm what they call a toy boy."

"Really!" Caroline couldn't help blurting out.

Jonathan Granger grinned. "I don't think I'm the first one of those you've met in Newport."

"Well," she said with a smile, "I think you are the first one who's admitted it."

"Come on," he said, grasping her elbow. "Let's get some more of that wine. I'm parched."

They found the steward who provided them with two glasses of perfectly chilled Pouilly Fuissé.

"I expect we'll turn around at Castle Hill," Jonathan said, looking at his watch. "We've been out for more than an hour."

The male member of the crew was piloting *Kandu*. Val was deep in conversation with Teddy, who looked anxious. From the grim look on her face, his sister must be learning about the argument he had just had with Althea. Val's face grew darker as Teddy said something to her. Finally she whispered in his ear, and he nodded his head miserably.

"So what do you do, Caroline?" Jonathan asked, breaking into her thoughts. "You look like a woman who does things."

Caroline was about to reply when Alex Seeger came running up the steps from the cabin below. His face was a furious shade of red. As he reached the deck he stopped in front of Caroline.

"Do something," Alex shouted at her in a cracked voice. Caroline involuntarily moved back, bumping against Jonathan Granger's chest. He put his hands protectively on her shoulders. "Somebody's got to do something."

Val, looking vaguely annoyed, pushed her way toward Alex Seeger. When he saw her he cried out, "Call the police. Call the harbor police."

An eerie quiet had descended on the boat. Everyone seemed in a freeze frame, waiting for anything that would explain what was happening.

Alex Seeger looked over his shoulder. "She's down there. I saw her."

Caroline found her voice. "Who is it?" she asked. "Who did you see?"

"Althea," he answered, sounding bewildered.

"What about Althea, Mr. Seeger?"

"Somebody's killed her. My God. Somebody's killed her."

CHAPTER XIV

There were audible gasps from the guests after Alex Seeger made his startling announcement that Althea was dead. Scott Forsythe rushed down the stairs before anyone could stop him. Quickly following him was a slight, balding man. From somewhere among the guests, Caroline heard a woman's voice say, "My husband's a doctor." Mindful of other murder scenes that she had witnessed, Caroline quickly moved to the stairway to block any further attempts to go below. Was it possible that Alex was mistaken, and that Althea was injured but alive?

Any hope that this was true was dispelled when Caroline saw the somber look on Scott's face as he came back up the stairs. He was followed by the doctor who shook his head.

"I've notified the police," he said, his cell phone clutched in his hand. "They'll be there to meet the boat when it comes in." He looked at Val. "I suggest you get us back there as quick as you can."

Val Ainsely took command of *Kandu* and began issuing brisk orders. The engine was turned on, and soon she was piloting the boat with all haste directly back to the dock. The young members of the crew, their faces solemn, began the business of lowering the sails and preparing the boat for docking. The awkward silence among the guests was broken intermittently by a few whispered words. The steward had stopped serving drinks, although Caroline suspected that had he not, he would have had several takers.

Caroline hadn't known Althea Tanner when she was alive, but she had liked meeting her in Val's office and had been pleased to accept her invitation to the boating party. Now, as her investigative instincts kicked in, she began to consider what could have caused this woman to be the target of a killer.

She watched as many faces as she could, wishing she'd had the time to meet everyone and put names to faces. She knew that her observations now, before the shock of the crime had finished sinking in, would be invaluable to Hank whom she fully expected to be given the task of investigating this murder.

Scott Forsythe was standing by himself near the cockpit, rubbing his hands nervously as he stared ahead. Caroline saw that Jason Cava seemed about to approach him, but then stopped. Jason looked ghastly, as if he couldn't make sense of what had happened. His fists were clenched and he looked shaken. Had there been a personal relationship between him and Althea? Caroline had sensed a camaraderie between the two in their body language which might be deeper than the usual employer-employee association.

Jonathan Granger was holding his wife's hand, stroking it gently and murmuring reassurance to her as she cried softly into his shoulder. Leslie Seeger had also joined her spouse to offer comfort after his grim discovery of the body. Alex's look of determination while at the wheel of the boat had now been replaced by a look of confusion. The doctor spoke to him, but Alex did not respond. A woman touched Leslie's arm, and Caroline saw the resemblance between the two. Sisters, perhaps.

The older couple, whom Jason had addressed as the Dalworthys, sat silently side by side, their faces with the almost identical look of worry.

Teddy Ainsley was near to where Caroline was standing. Val's twin looked strangely calm, as if he alone of all the people on the boat was not affected by the murder.

The three remaining guests were still unknown to her. A middle-aged man with a trim beard and thinning fair hair who looked vaguely artistic. A well dressed auburn-haired woman smoking a cigarette. And the tall, handsome man who had stood in the cockpit with Alex Seeger, looking now as if he would like to be anywhere else but on this boat of death.

There was only one question in Caroline's mind. Which one of these people was a killer?

CHAPTER XV

Hank Nightingale stood at the dock, impatiently scanning the harbor for sight of *Kandu*. Uniformed police officers were busy keeping curious onlookers, whose numbers seemed to be growing as word spread of the presence of so much law enforcement in Bannister's Wharf, from entering the area.

High above in the fading twilight sky, large grey and white streaks of clouds gave the appearance of an everyday tranquility to Bannister's Wharf. On the cobblestones below, however, the bright red and blue flashing lights of the official cars and vans indicated a much different atmosphere.

"Where the hell are they?" Hank muttered to Ben Davies. "How long does a boat like that take to get back here?"

"You would know, Lieutenant. You being a sailor yourself."

"Ten minutes from Castle Hill with the engine on. Tops. I've been standing here for five at least."

"Look. Isn't that them now?" Ben said as a large red-hulled boat came into their view.

"Finally," Hank said. He crossed onto the dock where the boat's lines were waiting. "Come on, Ben. Help me throw the crew these lines. I don't want any civilians down here."

Ben, who had never done this before in his life, followed Hank's lead and picked up the heavy coil of rope. As the woman at the helm brought the boat toward them, first Hank and then Ben threw the lines to the crew. A young man and woman moved quickly to secure the boat as the engine went silent.

As soon as the boat was tied up, Hank looked for Caroline. He finally spotted her standing by the stairway as if guarding the opening. Then he realized that was exactly what she was doing. Why did she always seem to be there when murder was committed? He took a deep breath as he jumped onto the boat and addressed the captain.

"Ms. Ainsley?" She nodded. "I'm Lt. Hank Nightingale of the Newport Police Department. I understand you've had a serious incident onboard."

The body of Althea Tanner lay sprawled on the floor of the cabin next to the open door to the head. The top of a dark green-handled knife was protruding from the left side of her chest. Right about where her heart is, Hank thought. Too bad. Anything further away would have meant she'd probably still be breathing. Of course, he didn't know the time of death, how long she had been lying there. He checked his watch: it was 7:58. The call from the boat had come in at 7:33.

Hank's eyes surveyed the interior. A service bar had been set up in the galley, with about a dozen bottles of white wine chilling in a large silver wine tub on the counter. Some plastic wrapping from food was in the small sink, and there were two soiled serving trays nearby. A cardboard box with trash stood on the floor. Another was piled high with empty wine bottles.

The rest of the cabin's interior looked equally disorderly, but Hank didn't think there had been a struggle between victim and killer. Hank recognized *Kandu* for what it was built to be: a racing boat. There were sweatshirts and jackets piled on cushions. Extra sails of all types were stowed in the forward V-berth under the open hatch. The boat's captain had made little effort to tidy up the space for visitors who would only need to come below to use the modest head.

Keisha came up beside him.

"Who is she, Lieutenant?"

"Althea Tanner. She lives in Newport, I understand."

"How beautiful she is," Keisha whispered.

"Yeah," Hank said, although he hadn't registered that fact on first seeing her. His eyes had gone to the chest wound surrounded by a wide circle of red blood. Now he examined her more closely.

Althea Tanner was wearing both her shoes, gold-toned sandals with a low heel, her slim white legs extending from the folds of her dress. The white fabric was decorated with large flowers. Their bright green leaves and peach colored blossoms looked out of place at a death scene. Some kind of fringed shawl, the material soft and smooth, lay fallen on the floor next to the body.

"Is Dr. Peters here yet?" Hank asked. Daniel Peters was the

medical examiner.

"Just driving in now. He was over in Jamestown having dinner."

"Some of us got dinner tonight?" At five o'clock the detective had been called to the Goat Island causeway where a man in an SUV had committed road rage, chasing a BMW sedan as it was returning to the Hyatt Regency Hotel which was located on a small island in the harbor. When apprehended by uniformed officers, the angry driver had claimed to be the son of a U.S. Senator from Pennsylvania. Hank had been ordered to the scene to manage what had the potential to become a difficult situation for the department.

The detective was able to defuse things after he determined that the perpetrator was no relation to any member of Congress, just a drunk from New Hampshire who had been hitting on another man's girlfriend. Still smarting from losing his chance to be out sailing with Caroline, Hank had taken particular joy in arresting the smug imposter and taking him to the station.

What Hank had not expected was this second emergency call, a summons which brought him to the very boat on which he should not only have been a passenger but a potential witness to murder.

Caroline's eyes met Hank's as she disembarked from *Kandu* along with the rest of the sailing party. He wanted to grab her as she neared him, be assured that she was safe, untouched by the violence onboard. But that would have been unprofessional, and he knew it, she knew it. Instead she nodded to him as she walked along the shifting gangway and up to the firm footing of the wharf.

To Hank's surprise, among the sailing party, he recognized Alex Seeger and Leo Vargoff. Each stared at him. Alex's face looked uncertain, while Leo's had a puzzled frown. But Hank made no move to acknowledge that he knew either. This was not the first time that the detective had encountered a familiar face during an investigation. The population of Newport was not that large that he didn't meet people whom he knew for reasons other than that they had prior dealings with the police.

"Ladies and gentlemen," Hank instructed. "Thank you all for leaving the boat. It is a crime scene now. However, I am sure you will understand that you each will have to be interviewed about what's happened here tonight. Ms. Ainsley's charter office is across the pedestrian plaza on Bowen's Wharf. My officers will escort you there and take some information from you. And I will be along shortly to talk to you as well."

Val had suggested Rourke's Charters as a place for interviews even before Hank had raised the issue of where he could safely store the group out of sight of curiosity seekers. The boat needed to be clear for the scene of the crime investigators to do their work. After Hank checked with Keisha that Dr. Peters had arrived and had begun his examination of the body, the lieutenant and Ben Davies also made their way across the cobblestones to Bowen's Wharf.

When Caroline had first informed him of the invitation to join the 12-meter cruise intended as an entertainment for some clients of a company called Tanner Associates, Hank had not paid much attention to the details. The name Althea Tanner meant nothing to him. His world was not one which crossed paths with the financial professionals who served the wealthy population of Newport. Now he supposed he would have to learn about that aspect of life in his city.

Where to begin?

As he and Ben entered the charter office they were greeted by the anxious faces of the dozen or so people crowded into the space. Val came forward.

"Lieutenant, I have a small private office upstairs. You can use that." He nodded, impressed with her take charge manner.

"Thank you." He turned to one of the uniformed officers. "Do you have the list for me?"

He was handed a sheet of paper which he began to study. The two officers had taken names and other contact information, including a short description of who everyone was - guest, crew or Tanner employee. There was only one name listed as working for Tanner Associates. Hank looked up.

Mr. Cava?" he said, surveying the group. A slim young man with dark eyes and a shaved head stepped forward. Hank was surprised to see that he was wearing soft black slacks and a black silk shirt. "Jason Cava?" The man nodded. "Come with me, Mr. Cava. We'll go upstairs."

CHAPTER XVI

"I still can't believe Althea's dead," Jason said before Hank could ask his first question. "Althea," he said in a low voice. "She was always so alive." He buried his face in his hands. The two men were sitting across from each other at the desk. Ben was seated on a chair next to them.

"You were close, Mr. Cava? Friends as well as business associates."

"We live together." Hank's eyebrows rose. "But it's not what you think," Jason said quickly. "We're not..." He shook his head. "Not... that."

Hank glanced at the contact list he had brought with him. He should have registered that Jason's address was the same as the dead woman's.

"What are you then?" Hank asked.

Jason took his time to answer. "I came to Newport nine years ago to work for Althea."

"Where are you from?"

"New York City. I was looking for a change. When I found out about this job in Newport, I thought wow, live in Newport, that's for me."

"And you were happy working for Ms. Tanner?" Ben asked. "Nine years is a long time these days to stay in one job."

"She treated me very well. Offered me a place to live rent-free in her house."

"Why was that, Mr. Cava? You just said that you weren't..." Here Ben smiled. "Together?"

"She said she had bought the place before she realized how big it was, too big for one person. I didn't argue. Maybe she didn't like being alone at night. It's pretty quiet out there, I can tell you."

"Tell me about your work," Hank cut in.

Jason started forward in his chair. "*My* work?"

"The work that's done by Tanner. I'm afraid I know next to nothing about investing money, financial advisors."

"Well," Jason said, relaxing his shoulders. "Let me try to explain." He described how Althea had gotten her start working for John Ainsley. And then how she had expanded into her own firm after Ainsley died, making her reputation as the premier investment advisor in Newport.

"And Val Ainsley and Teddy Ainsley are who exactly?"

"John Ainsley's children. The family has remained as our client. Along with his widow."

"I will need a list of all your clients."

"Why?" Jason asked, his dark eyes suddenly wary. "Surely the only possible people to suspect of this awful crime were on that boat tonight. What's the purpose of your knowing more names? Our business is extremely confidential, Lt. Nightingale. We have a select group of clients who intrust us to invest their money."

"Background," Hank answered evenly. "Tell me who else works at Tanner Associates besides yourself?"

"We have an office manager, Maya Vereen."

"That's it? All that money and only three people handling it."

Jason sniffed audibly. "You'd be surprised, Lieutenant. Everything is all computerized. You don't need too many people for that. Althea was a genius. She's really all we needed."

"So what is your job description?" Ben asked.

"I manage the files for all the client accounts, see that the numbers are there, everybody knows what their money is doing."

"I see," Hank said. But he knew that he really didn't.

"And, let's talk about tonight. When did you last see Ms. Tanner alive?"

"I had no real reason to talk to Althea once we were onboard with all the guests. We had set up between us that she would talk to the new prospects, and I would talk to all the clients in turn."

"You did talk to everyone?"

"No. Don't forget we were only half way through the trip."

"And where were you when Mr. Seeger came up from below?"

"Mr. and Mrs. Dalworthy had gotten me again." He sighed dramatically. "They fuss a lot, and I always have to reassure them that things were fine in the markets, no crash looming on the horizon, that kind of thing."

"And you were not near to where Althea was while you were speaking with this couple."

"No, no. I lost track of her when she was talking to Teddy Ainsley."

"But he was one of your current clients. I thought you said that Ms. Tanner was handling the newcomers onboard."

"That's right. But Teddy grabbed her away from Mrs. Tompkins."

"The doctor's wife?"

"Yes. She is Leslie Seeger's sister, and Althea was chatting with her."

"And what exactly did Mr. Ainsley do to get her away from Mrs. Tompkins?"

"I don't know what he said to her, but Althea got up."

"Did you see what happened next?"

"No, they seem to have disappeared."

"Disappeared?"

"The boat's not that big," Ben said. "Surely you saw where they went."

"Afraid not. Hamilton Dalworthy can be relentless. Some fellow at his club had just bought shares in a coffee plantation in Viet Nam. I had to discourage him from doing the same."

"We'll need information on next of kin," Hank said. "Does Ms. Tanner have family here in Newport?" Jason shook his head.

"Althea grew up in Connecticut in a small town somewhere around New Haven," he said. "She never visited down there that I'm aware of."

"Is their last name Tanner also?"

"I guess so. I do know that her mother is in a residence for Alzheimer patients, and Althea pays for that. I'm pretty sure the father is dead. Frankly I never gave them much attention."

"You weren't interested," Hank said.

"Not really, no."

"And yet you worked for her for eight years, lived in the same house."

"I don't mean to speak ill of the dead, Lieutenant. But I can assure you that Althea knew less than that about me."

"Yes," Hank said thoughtfully, "that is often the case nowadays. So I suppose you can't tell me about any romantic attachments Ms.

Tanner had."

"No."

"That's too bad," Ben said. "An attractive woman like that is bound to have had someone."

"She didn't confide that sort of thing in me," Jason said primly.

CHAPTER XVII

Caroline watched as Hank and Ben climbed the steps with Jason Cava. She was sorry that she couldn't be interviewed first to tell Hank everything she knew. Instead Caroline concentrated on what she had seen on the boat at the time of the murder. She had been standing with Jon Granger, first at the mid-section of the boat, and then they had moved toward the cockpit. If she was looking for suspects, the charming Brit had to be crossed from the list. They had been together from the time they had heard Teddy arguing with Althea until Alex had appeared with the news that she had been murdered.

Jon's wife Melody had been chatting with Scott Forsythe around this time period. She decided to eliminate Mr. and Mrs. Dalworthy as suspects because of their age. It was a leap of faith, she knew, but she couldn't get her head around either of the aristocratic pair plunging a knife into Althea Tanner. If she was wrong, well she would be taught a valuable lesson.

And Caroline considered Teddy Ainsley. He, the gentle lover of music and culture, also seemed to be an unlikely murderer. Yet his usual soft spoken demeanor had not stopped him from angrily confronting Althea over the subject of his money. '*I need it.*' He had said those words so pleadingly.

And there was a threat. As much as she didn't want to have to swear to it, she had heard Teddy threaten Althea.

"Caroline. Can we talk?" She didn't need to look up to see whose voice was speaking in that plummy British accent.

"Yes, Jon?"

"What are you going to tell the police detectives?" Jonathan asked.

"The truth, I hope," Caroline said. "Answer their questions."

"But perhaps they won't ask about the dust up Althea had with that bloke. We might have been the only people who heard it. Shouldn't we tell the police?"

Caroline had every intention to explain what had occurred below deck when it was her turn to speak to Hank. She knew that she couldn't withhold that information. But she was planning to frame the story with the firm declaration that the Teddy she knew couldn't possibly be a killer.

After Jason Cava left them, Hank asked for Alex Seeger to be shown up. In the few minutes before he arrived, the detective shared his frustrations with Ben.

"Not very helpful, was he?"

"No, sir. There's more to Mr. Cava than meets the eye. For one thing, I don't buy that bit about how they weren't sleeping together. A young guy like that. Of course he'd be all over her."

"Perhaps she didn't want him 'all over her.' She may have a lover we know nothing about yet. First thing tomorrow I want you to get over to the Tanner office and talk with this office manager. A woman will know a lot more about another woman."

"Yes, sir."

The door opened, and the man who walked slowly into the room bore little resemblance to the genial Tai Chi instructor Hank had come to know. Hank wondered how well Seeger knew Althea Tanner. Perhaps it was an affair with a married man which had nurtured her libido.

"Sit down, Mr. Seeger... Alex."

Alex slid onto the chair and stared vacantly at Hank.

"I know you must be in shock, but we must get the facts about the case on record."

"I'll try to help, Hank, but ..." Here Alex swallowed hard. "You know, I always thought I was such a tough guy." He swallowed again. "But I think this has proven I'm not."

"Violent death is shocking."

"Yeah," Alex said quietly.

"I'll try to be brief so you can go home. Let's start with the party itself. Why were you invited?"

"Leslie, that's my wife, and I have had our money invested with Althea Tanner for five years now."

"And you're pleased with the results?"

"Good lord, yes," he answered with some force. "We've made a lot more profit than we were doing with our previous advisors. That woman is, was..." Here, reminded again of her death, he shuddered. "... was the best."

"She was the firm, would you say, Mr. Seeger?" Ben asked.

"She knew how to play the markets and win."

"Did she often have these parties for clients?" Hank asked.

"She had one at her house last Christmas. And there was another time when she arranged a reception at one of the mansions. Very fancy that one was."

"The boat was a new event. Not a very big venue."

"She didn't have all the clients to this one, and she had invited some new people not on her client list."

"Did you know them?" Ben asked.

"Matter of fact I was the one who told her about two of them." He looked at Hank. "You know one. Leo from the Tai Chi class. And the other is married to my wife's sister, Becky. Richard's the doctor who looked at... the body."

"And called us," Hank said, looking for the doctor's name on his list. "Dr. Tompkins was planning to become a client?"

"He hoped so. Althea was fussy about who she let in. Her threshold for taking on clients is that you must be committed to investing ten million dollars minimum."

Ben whistled, and Hank, too, knew he must have looked surprised.

"Ten million," the detective repeated. "That's a lot of money."

"Yeah," Alex said.

"What did you do once you came onboard? Six I believe was the time the boat was to sail."

Alex explained how he and Leslie had arrived early on Bannister's Wharf so she could browse in the shops. While he was waiting for her, he had gone to use one of the public bathrooms tucked into a corner of the adjoining Bowen's Wharf.

"It's embarrassing, but I have this problem. You know, male stuff. I need to go often."

"Sorry, but let's get back to when you were first onboard," Hank said.

"Well, at first Leo and I stayed by the cockpit. I've done some sailing, and I wanted to see how Ms. Ainsley handled that big a boat." He told of his taking the wheel and Val's letting him turn the boat around.

"Did Leo take a turn at the wheel?"

"No, he didn't want to."

"What happened next?"

"I talked to a few people. Drank some wine. It was good French stuff. I had some of the food. All first class."

"Did you talk to Althea?"

"No. As a matter of fact, I didn't. I could see that she was interested in introducing Leo and Richard to the other clients. Those Dalworthys are high society people. The Ainsleys cut cheddar in Newport as well."

"Did you know everybody onboard?"

"I've met them at the other parties. Melody Granger and that juvenile English gigolo she married." He shook his head in disapproval. "And Selena Dawson. Her husband left her a packet. Tristan Marchand. His father was a big art dealer in New York named Alexander Marchand."

"And you eventually needed the head?" Hank asked.

"Twice actually. Once when I left the cockpit, and then again after I had the wine."

"When you went below the second time, who did you see?"

"You mean Althea?" Seeger looked puzzled.

"Who was standing near the stairway when you went below?"

"Oh, I see. Hmm." He paused. "Teddy was talking to his sister."

"Was anyone coming up the stairs?"

"No." He paused again, his face drawn. "You know, Hank, when I came to that boat tonight I wasn't thinking of anything else except having a good time sailing. And then, when I went down into the cabin and she was on the floor, I couldn't believe what I was seeing. I just stood there and stared at her. I couldn't move at first."

"What made you so sure she wasn't still breathing?" Hank asked.

"The knife, the blood. She had to be dead."

"And then?"

"I ran up the stairs. I screamed at that pretty young woman who was talking to Granger. I told her to call the police. I don't know why, I didn't know her. She was the first person I saw, I guess."

So Caroline was in the vicinity of the stairs at the time of the crime. Hank hoped she'd had her eyes open and not been so absorbed in conversation with the *gigolo* that she was unaware of a murder taking place.

CHAPTER XVIII

He was on auto-pilot as he drove the familiar route back to *Di Sole*. It was almost as if the car, a high-powered Audi TT roadster, knew its own way home. Jason Cava's brain was reeling. What should he do? What could he do?

Once the police had finished questioning him, he had no choice but to leave the charter office. Jason had been watching Scott Forsythe for a sign, any sign, but he saw nothing. There was no telling when the detectives would call for Scott to come up the stairs. It could be hours before he was free to go. Would he telephone Jason? Was that even wise?

Jason drove carefully into his garage bay. Once the car was parked, he sat motionless in the driver's seat for a few minutes. His mind felt like it was encased in a spider's web. Nothing was clear to him. He asked himself again what he needed to do, and he couldn't answer his own question.

Inside the house he went to the kitchen. Eva, the housekeeper had two rooms beyond the pantry, and he listened for the sound of her TV. He looked at his watch. It was only quarter after ten, but she went to bed early. She would be up with the sun tomorrow, and he sighed as he realized that he would have to be the one to break the news to her of Althea's death. Murder.

How would she take it? Eva Miller was a woman of indeterminate middle-age, hard working and energetic. She enjoyed taking care of the house. Baking was her specialty, and Jason had come to have an embarrassing addiction to the rich, sugary pastries she produced. The fruits of her labors were lost on Althea who was always watching her diet. Extra pounds never seemed to appear on his slender frame. He suspected that it was nervous anxiety about Tanner's business plan which kept him from being overweight.

Now he had more than obesity to worry about. The clients would want to know about the future of the firm. Know that their money was all invested as Althea had directed - surely the clients would feel secure in that for the near future. Perhaps, and here Jason felt his heart pumping, Cameron could find another stock picker to be introduced to the clients, someone who was a worthy successor to Althea. Of course this new person would be a figurehead, but was there a chance they could pass someone off?

Jason went into the library in search of alcohol. He poured himself a large snifter of cognac. After several large gulps of the brandy he went over to the desk and unlocked a drawer, taking out one of the prepaid phones he stored there. He used each one only once before getting rid of it.

A voice from another burner phone answered "Yes" on the second ring.

"We need to meet," Jason said. "Things aren't good."

Because they were the oldest of the guests, Hank had selected Hamilton and Alicia Dalworthy as his third interview.

"I won't keep you too long," the detective began. Like Caroline, he also had some difficulty seeing either of these people as knife-wielding murderers. He'd had some time to think about the method of Althea's murder, and he'd come to believe that the crime had the earmarks of an unpremeditated act done in anger or in passion. In his sailing experience, there were always knives onboard a boat, and one had presented itself as a handy murder weapon for the killer to use.

The Dalworthys had little to contribute beyond what Hank already knew.

"What's going to happen to Tanner now that Althea's gone?" Hamilton asked. "That's what I want to know. She's taken care of us for over ten years now. John Ainsley thought the world of her abilities. Who's going to take her place?"

"Do you have a contract with Tanner Associates, Mr. Dalworthy? What are the details?"

"Contract," the man across from him sputtered. "My good man. Everything was done on a handshake. The confidence John Ainsley had in her was more than enough for me."

"So you don't know what happens to your money in the event of the death of the firm's principal?"

"Why should anything *happen*, as you say, to our investments?"

Dalworthy looked incredulous, and Hank let the topic go. He

was looking for a killer, not the status of stock portfolios.

"What I need to know from both of you," Hank said, "is what you remember about the time period right before you heard that Althea Tanner was dead. Were you both together?"

"Yes," Hamilton said decisively. "We remained together during the entire trip." He patted his wife's hand.

"And were you at all aware of where Althea was, let me see." He consulted some notes. "The boat was just reaching Castle Hill when the body was discovered. That was a little before 7:30. Prior to that, when had you last seen her?"

"To tell you the truth," Hamilton said, "I didn't notice her at all after we had started talking to the doctor and his wife. I'm afraid we cannot help you there, Lieutenant."

Hank decided to see the *gigolo* next.

"How can I be of service to you, Inspector?" Jonathan Granger asked with his debonair British accent.

"I'd like you to tell me about your relationship with Althea Tanner."

"My relationship?" Granger asked amiably. "I don't have one."

"But you were invited to her party? A party for her clients."

"Oh," Jonathan laughed. "That's Melody, not me. My wife handles the money in our family."

"Did you speak with Ms. Tanner at all tonight?"

"Not really. Hello and all that."

"Who did you speak to?"

"There was a lovely woman onboard. Hadn't seen her before at one of these things. She and I rather hit it off."

"Her name?" Hank made a point of looking at his list. Beyond Granger's head he could see Ben suppress a smile.

"Caroline. Caroline Kent."

"Lovely woman," Hank repeated.

"Absolutely."

"And were you talking to this Ms. Kent when the murder was discovered?"

Granger hesitated. Hank stared at him, curious as to what was coming next. Perhaps, like Alex Seeger, Granger had mistaken Caroline for a wealthy investor and decided that he might like to exchange his current wife for a new, prettier benefactress.

But when Granger finally answered his question, Jonathan excitedly repeated everything that he and Caroline had heard through the hatch of the conversation taking place in the cabin below.

"And you are sure that the second person you heard was Althea Tanner?"

"Her voice was difficult to hear, Inspector. But the bloke she was talking to called her 'Althea.'"

"And you didn't recognize the voice of this man?" Ben asked.

"No. And neither did Caroline. But he gave one clue to his identity."

"Really?" Hank asked. "And what was that?"

"He said that whatever he was upset about wouldn't have happened 'while his father was alive.' You can understand what that means."

Yes, there was definitely one man Hank knew of in the sailing party whose father was no longer alive: Teddy Ainsley.

CHAPTER XIX

Whether to talk to Caroline next to corroborate Granger's information or to speak immediately to Teddy Ainsley was Hank's next decision. According to Granger, he had seen Teddy speaking with his sister Val near the stairway, but he hadn't noticed when Teddy had come up from below. Nor had he seen anyone else on the stairs, not even Alex Seeger making his descent to the head. It seemed that talking to Caroline had taken all the gigolo's attention. Hank wondered if she had been a bit more observant, and there was only one way to find out.

"We'll do Mrs. Kent next," he told Ben after Granger had left. "Call for her to come up." He turned away from his sergeant before Ben's face had a chance to show his reaction.

As Caroline passed Jon, he gave her a knowing look which told her that he'd informed Hank and Ben what they had overheard between Althea and Teddy. Now it was up to her to put her own interpretation on the meaning of their argument.

In the interview room Hank was reading some material on the desk. She waited for him to look up. He made a few notes and then clipped the papers together.

"How are you?" Hank asked, looking at her carefully. "I mean it. Don't say 'fine,' when you can't be."

"I'm hardly fine, Hank. I've just been in the company of a murderer. Do you realize that every other death I've helped you investigate happened in an open-ended environment? Tonight one of the people on that boat murdered Althea Tanner." She shivered. "And as far as those people downstairs are concerned, I could very well be the one who did it."

"But you didn't do it."

"And I don't know who did."

"I'm disappointed. Here I'm thinking that you would have the whole thing wrapped up for me. Didn't I say that, Ben?"

"Don't joke. You know that you should have been on that boat tonight. Have you thought about that?"

"Yes, but I wasn't, so I'm hoping you can tell me something about tonight that is going to help me."

"Jon told you about the argument we overheard, didn't he?"

"He said it was between Althea Tanner and a man. Sounds like it might be Teddy Ainsley. Was it?"

"Yes," Caroline said unhappily.

"But Granger didn't know that for sure. He told me so."

"I told him that I didn't recognize the man's voice."

"But you did. Why didn't you tell him who it was?"

"Teddy and Val have known the Kents all their lives. I've gotten to know him."

"And?"

"He's not a murderer, Hank. Believe me."

"But you didn't know that Althea was going to be murdered when you were listening through the hatch to their argument?"

"That's true. But I didn't know Jon; I'd just met him. I thought I would protect Teddy from gossip."

"O.K., tell me your version of the argument."

Caroline repeated the conversation carefully.

"So Ainsley wanted money, and Althea wasn't giving it to him? I don't understand. Didn't you think he was talking about his own money invested with Tanner?"

She told Hank what she knew about Teddy's desire to buy an estate in Newport to develop into a classical music center.

"Why wouldn't he be able to get his own money?"

"My understanding of how these firms work is that you need to give a required notice before you can withdraw your funds. I've heard of three months, as much as six. The company couldn't be dealing with abrupt demands for withdrawals. They'd need a steadier cash flow."

"You know a lot about this," Hank said.

"I did have to deal with Reed's advisor after his death. Of course millions of dollars weren't at stake then, as you know."

"What did you think when Teddy threatened Althea? He'd make her pay, I believe he said."

"I didn't think he meant anything serious by it. '*I'll make you pay.*'

It was just his frustration. She may have had legitimate business reasons, as I said."

"This murder was done in anger. Frustration might be an equally good propellant."

"Teddy frustrated did not kill anyone. He wouldn't."

"Did you see him after he came back up on deck?"

"Yes, I did. He was talking with Val. He was upset. It wasn't the face of a killer, Hank. The face of someone... frustrated," she added stubbornly.

"Could you hear what they were saying?"

"No," Caroline said quickly. For she was remembering the look on Val's face. That was more like anger.

"Did you see Alex Seeger go down the stairs?"

"I didn't. I did see him when he came back up. He shouted at me that he had found the body. It was horrible."

"I'm sure it was. But, Caroline, I need you to think. Who could have gone down those stairs after you heard Althea and Teddy arguing? That must have been a narrow window in time."

"Jon and I stayed at the mid-section of the boat for several more minutes before we moved forward. Then I could see Teddy and Val as I said." She shook her head. "But I wasn't watching the stairs."

"That's too bad."

"There's one more thing I thought of," she said eagerly.

"What's that?"

"That hatch where Jon and I heard the argument coming from. It was partially open to let air in the cabin, I imagine. But if you opened it a little wider, couldn't somebody climb in and go down below that way?"

"From the deck, you mean?"

"Yes. A nimble person to be sure."

"It's possible," Hank said.

"So it isn't just someone who was near the stairway who had the opportunity to attack Althea? It could be any one of several other people on that boat tonight."

CHAPTER XX

"What did you think of Mrs. Kent's theory that the murderer climbed down through that hatch?" Ben asked Hank after Caroline had gone back downstairs.

"You don't think someone on that boat would have noticed another passenger prying open the hatch? That would be bound to draw attention at a party." Hank shook his head. "No, I think our killer walked down the stairs. People were talking, having drinks. Who would remember who went down to the head?"

"What about that waiter? He must have been up and down several times to get more wine. From the looks of all the bottles in the trash, a lot was drunk."

"I was going to talk to Teddy Ainsley next, but you're right, Ben. Let's see what--" And here he consulted his passenger list. "--what Nick Dargis has to tell us."

As they waited for Dargis to appear, Hank considered what Caroline had told him about Teddy's need for money. Despite what she had said, Hank knew that money could create a powerful motive for crime. How many millions of dollars did Ainsley need to withdraw? Estates in Newport didn't come cheap. Just that morning in the *Newport Daily News*, among the recent property sales published had been one house over by Rosecliff which had sold for over $15 million.

Nick Dargis, wearing the white uniform of a steward, entered the room and looked around. He was medium in height with thinning brown hair greying at the temples. He had the lean look of a chain smoker who also enjoyed his drink.

"Sit down, Mr. Dargis. I'm Lt. Nightingale, and this is Sgt. Davies. We're hoping you can help us."

"Anything to assist the police, sir," Dargis answered respectfully.

"Good," Hank said. "Tell us, had you worked for Ms. Ainsley before this trip?"

72

"Yeah. Several times. She usually calls me when she has a party cruise."

"And did you know any of the passengers onboard tonight?"

"Mr. Ainsley. I've met him before. That's all."

"So you didn't know Althea Tanner?" Hank asked. Nick Dargis looked confused. "The woman who was murdered."

"No."

"What do you remember her doing this evening? Talking to the guests, moving about the boat, that kind of thing?

Dargis thought. "Well, she did want everyone to have a drink when they first came onboard. Kept telling me what to serve people, what they told her they wanted."

"I'm sure you were often below in the cabin to get more wine and food." Dargis nodded. "Did you see Ms. Tanner down below during the party?"

"Sure, when she was talking to Miss Ainsley's brother."

"What were they talking about?" Hank asked, feeling his chest quicken. "When was this conversation?"

"We'd been out for a while. I needed to get a fresh tray of food from the galley. When I went down the stairs, they were there. Like I said, talking."

"How did they seem?" Dargis looked unsure. "Was it a happy conversation, were they laughing?"

"Oh, no, not laughing. Mr. Ainsley's face was red. I saw he was real upset."

"And was Ms. Tanner equally upset?" Ben asked.

"No, I wouldn't say so. She looked serious, but like, well you know, like she was trying to calm him down."

"What did you hear him saying?"

"'You wouldn't do this while my father was alive'... no it was something more like *get away with this* while his father was alive."

"What happened next?" Ben pushed.

"Miss Tanner saw me and waved me back up the stairs."

"Did you go?"

"Yeah. I took the opportunity to go around again with the wine."

"Did you see Mr. Ainsley come up the stairs?" Ben asked.

"Yes."

"Tell me about that," Hank said.

"When he came up, he went right over to his sister. She wasn't in the cockpit. Matt was at the wheel."

"Could you hear anything they said to each other?"

"She said 'what's the matter, Teddy?' And he said, 'Althea wouldn't give me our money'."

"Are you sure he said 'our' money?" Hank asked.

"Yes, and Miss Ainsley said that she had to."

"Anything else?"

"I noticed Mr. Ainsley didn't look so red-faced any more. Now he looked more like the color of a ghost."

CHAPTER XXI

Despite a night which offered little sleep, Caroline was up at her usual 6 a.m. to start the following day. When she had come in last night, Louise was already sound asleep. The two women shared a suite of rooms on the second floor in the east wing of Kenwood, a bedroom for each and a sitting room in between. The suite had originally been designed as the private space of Mrs. Henry Kent, Frederick Kent's grandmother, who required a bedroom, a large dressing room which housed her extensive wardrobe and a room to entertain her friends at afternoon tea. The secrets they shared in that boudoir made for a chronicle of the social history of Newport during the first half of the twentieth century.

Caroline showered and dressed. She put on a pair of cream colored pants, reminded of Jonathan Granger as she topped them with a three-quarter forest green jersey tunic. He would approve of its definite fall color.

When she went into Louise's bedroom, her mother-in-law was sitting up in bed and drinking tea.

"The lady of leisure," Caroline said smiling. "I should get such service."

"Mattie would be pleased to bring up tea for you as well, Caroline, but you don't ask for it."

"I prefer coffee in the morning and Mattie, always a stickler for tradition, believes in morning tea trays." Caroline bent over and kissed Louise on the cheek. "It's fine. I can get coffee in the kitchen when I go down."

"Well, I must say that I'm grateful for the tradition," Louise said, sipping her tea and looking affectionately up at her daughter-in-law. "Maybe when you get to be my age, you'll appreciate the opportunity to have a leisurely start to the day."

"I can't wait," Caroline said. "A 'leisurely' morning. What will they think of next?"

"How was your sailing party last night, dear? Did Hank have a good time? I hope Val let him take the wheel. I'm sure she recognized his skills."

Caroline sat down on the bed and reached for Louise's hands. They were small with prominent blue veins, but their shape was graceful and the delicate pink nails perfect. The old diamonds in her platinum wedding and engagement rings were the color of grey ice, and Caroline loved their timeless elegance. Now her eyes fixed on them as she tried to regain her composure.

"Caroline? What's wrong?"

"Oh, Louise. What is it about me that I attract murder?" She was still holding tight to the older woman's hand.

"Murder?" Louise looked at her daughter-in-law with surprise.

"Yes, someone died on the boat last night. And Hank wasn't there. At the last minute he got called out and couldn't get to the dock in time."

"So it was just you to handle things," Louise said. She turned her hands and grasped Caroline's in hers. "Oh, my dear. Tell me. Who was it?" Suddenly she recoiled. "Not Val, or Teddy?"

"No," Caroline assured her. "It was the woman who invited me on the cruise. The investment manager."

"Althea Tanner," Louise said with astonishment. "But you said that she was inviting her clients to this party. And didn't you tell me she had a reputation for making people great sums of money?"

"That's her reputation. Yes."

"So why would a client kill her?"

"I'm not sure," Caroline said slowly.

Louise looked at her daughter-in-law. "What are you not telling me?"

"Oh, Louise, I'm sure it's nothing to worry about."

"What?"

"It's Teddy Ainsley. A short while before Althea was killed, they had an argument... over money."

"Teddy? You think Teddy might have killed this woman?" She shook her head. "That's impossible."

"I know he didn't, but it looks bad for him. There were only a dozen or so people on the boat, and one of them stabbed her." Caroline sighed. "And I'm a witness to the argument." She told Louise how she and Jon had been standing by the hatch and overheard the quarrel. "I had to tell Hank. I mean, Jon Granger already had."

"Of course you had to speak up, but how serious was this argument?"

"Teddy was upset. Frustrated. I think he wanted to sell some of the Ainsley investments to buy Laurel Hill, the estate he has plans to turn into a music center."

"And?"

"Well, Althea was telling him that he couldn't sell right away, that he had to be patient while she did... I don't know... whatever she would normally do to release the funds."

"And Teddy wasn't happy with that."

"No," Caroline said, her face downcast. "No, he wasn't." She hesitated but soon decided that Louise deserved to know everything.

"Louise, Teddy said that he would make Althea pay if she didn't give him the money immediately. *Pay.* That's the word he used."

"That was extremely stupid of him, don't you think?"

"Yes, I do. But we know that Teddy can say some idiotic things before he thinks, things that he doesn't mean."

"Of course, but now I see why you are worried. Because Hank doesn't know that about Teddy Ainsley, does he? And given your evidence, I see how he is bound to suspect him of the murder."

"There must be another person with a motive."

She didn't want to share her memory of Val's angry face as she listened to Teddy. Who would have noticed if the captain of the boat went below?

"Then perhaps you should do a little sleuthing of your own," Louise said.

CHAPTER XXII

Hank, too, had not enjoyed much sleep before getting out of bed to go to work that morning. As he stood under the warm shower, he considered his case. There were too many holes in the narratives of the witnesses. Once he got into the station, he would get Keisha working on a timeline for last evening on the boat. Once the team saw what they knew, they would know what they didn't know and needed to find out.

At the station, he told Keisha what he wanted done, and the huge white board in Hank's office soon began to fill with her neat printing of names, times, corroborations and questions. It was impressive how organized the young sergeant was and how little difficulty she had making sense of his and Ben's handwritten notes. Keisha had even drawn an overview of *Kandu* which roughed out the cockpit and the wheel, the forward hatch, the stairway going below and even the positions of the sails.

Ben, as Hank had already instructed him, had gone to the offices of Tanner Associates to interview Maya Vereen. If Jason Cava were there, Ben could also report on how that young man was handling things after the death of his employer.

"Lieutenant." He heard his name called and turned from the white board. A uniformed officer was standing in the doorway holding a large manilla envelope and a see-through evidence bag.

"This just came up for you, Lt. Nightingale," Officer Lucy Estrada said.

"Thank you," Hank said, taking the material from her. One look at the bag told Hank it contained the murder weapon.

"Anything else, Lieutenant?" Estrada asked.

"No, thanks. Here, Sergeant," Hank said to Keisha. "Take a look at this." He lay the bagged knife on his desk, and she studied the weapon whose blade looked razor sharp. "Know what that is?"

"No, sir. It looks like a knife to me. That's all."

"It's a rigging knife. I've seen them lots of times on sailboats. If the lines foul, you can use one of these to cut them apart fast. It's open now, but it can be kept closed."

"*Foul?*"

"That's the nautical term for when the ropes get tangled."

"It looks lethal," Keisha said.

"It is, believe me. It's made to cut through anything." He grimaced. He'd never thought of using a knife like this on another human being.

"So would you have to be a sailor to know how to use it?" Keisha asked, still unable to take her eyes from the desk.

"No, a knife's a knife, I'm afraid. You don't need a user manual. But a sailor would definitely know how sharp it is."

"I don't suppose there were any fingerprints."

Hank opened the envelope and scanned the report inside. He shook his head.

"Wiped clean."

"We wouldn't be that lucky."

"No, but it tells us something." Keisha looked at him questioningly. "I'll take it with me to Rourke's Charters to see if Val Ainsley recognizes it. But I'm betting she will. No doubt she'll tell me that this knife was kept on *Kandu* in a scabbard attached to the binnacle." And before Keisha could ask, he added, "The binnacle is the stand in the cockpit that houses the wheel and the navigation instruments. The scabbard would be attached to it. That makes it handy to grab when you need a knife in an emergency."

Keisha's eyes met his. Neither said what they were thinking: *or when you need it as a murder weapon.*

When Jason arrived at the Tanner offices on Bellevue Avenue, he found Sgt. Ben Davies talking to Maya Vereen. He cursed himself for not anticipating this visit and coming in extra early on this of all days. There was no telling what Maya had already shared with the police about what she knew, or even imagined, about the firm's business dealings. Althea had been scrupulous in keeping Maya focused on the ordinary tasks needed to keep the office running. The unsophisticated administrative assistant answered the phone, greeted visitors, ran errands. She ordered supplies, scheduled service calls on the HVAC, wrote out checks for the usual expenses of utility bills and routine services like the alarm system and exterminator. Never had she been allowed to handle the client statements nor did her computer have access to the client's investment files. She did keep a mailing list of the clients' contact information which she used for inconsequential mailings like holiday cards and invitations.

Now she was talking with this police officer who no doubt had begun his questioning by acquainting her with the details of Althea's death. Not that Maya seemed especially upset over the news. Rather she appeared happy being the center of attention.

"Good morning, Maya," Jason said, interrupting Ben. "I apologize for not getting here sooner. I had wanted to tell you everything myself, but I see this policeman has beaten me to it."

It had been hard enough telling Eva Miller this morning about Althea's murder. The housekeeper had gotten positively hysterical and had to be put to bed sobbing. Jason had not believed that the woman had been so attached to Althea, but the more she whimpered the more he decided she was just an emotional personality type. At last he had left her, knowing that he had more on his plate today than babysitting Eva, who had a daughter living in Newport. He was sure that once the housekeeper recovered from the shock, the telephone call would be made to her offspring to share all the details of the crime for which her mother could claim a close connection.

"Oh, Jason," Maya said, now doing her best to look grief-stricken, "it's awful. Poor Althea. I really can't believe it."

"No, dear," he said. "No one can. I still can't believe it myself." He put on his grieving face as well.

"Mr. Cava," Ben said. "I've been telling Ms. Vereen that we need your client list."

"I didn't know if I should give it to him until I asked you," Maya said.

"Give him the information you have on your computer, Maya. You have the contact list in a file."

"O.K.," she said, turning to her screen and gripping her mouse. "I will print one out. Thank you. I was afraid I wasn't allowed to do that."

"It's fine," Jason said with a wave of his hand.

Sgt. Davies took the printed sheets from Maya and studied them. Jason swallowed and tried not to show his impatience. He needed to leave and it seemed forever before the policeman folded the papers and put them in his pocket.

"Is that all, Sergeant?" he inquired smoothly.

"Yes, for now. I'm sure Lt. Nightingale will have more questions as we go forward."

"Naturally. We'll do everything to help. You have to find out who did this." He heard Maya begin to sniffle.

"Who could do something like that?" she said miserably. "She was such a lovely person."

"Yes," Jason agreed. "Everyone thought so."

CHAPTER XXIII

"How was your trip?"

"How do you think it was, Jason? By the time I got to Penn Station this morning, there were no more business class tickets left for this train. I had to sit in coach. I was in the quiet car, but people were talking anyway. Some idiot woman had a ring tone for messages that sounded like a duck quacking."

Cameron Epsberg stood on the empty Kingston, Rhode Island station platform and looked distastefully at his surroundings. His fierce blue eyes were flashing displeasure.

"And I'm hungry," Epsberg added. "Where can you get something decent around here? I was in no mood for the muck they had on that train."

"There's a nice little Italian place out on Route One. I thought we'd give it a try," Jason said, looking at his watch. "It's almost noon."

"Do they have a bar?" Cameron asked.

"Yes, they do." Jason had checked. He knew Cameron's tastes.

"Let's go then. I've got a ticket for the 2:42 back to Manhattan. Thank God it's business class, although what passes for class on Amtrak I hate to have to contemplate."

Since Jason had begun working for Tanner Associates he and Cameron had frequent meetings to discuss the inside information which the lawyer obtained through his work at his law firm. But it was always Jason who took Amtrak's Northeast Corridor train down to Manhattan to have lunch with Cameron to discuss the tips. Events in Newport had made Jason's leaving town for more than two hours today impossible, and so Epsberg had reluctantly agreed that it should be he who traveled north for an emergency conference.

So here the two men were in Kingston, which had the closest Amtrak train stop to Newport. The station building was a quaint gingerbread Victorian structure painted a sad yellow, the historic color used on railroad stations in the nineteenth century. Jason was sure that whoever the official was who had made the decision to use this shade of paint must have been either color blind or a melancholy lunatic.

Cameron stared glumly out of the car as they drove the few miles on Route 128 to the restaurant. The main road in this part of Rhode Island, far from Interstate 95 had changed little in the last fifty years. The rural scenery offered an old-fashioned view of modest houses, a white clapboard church, and farms with picturesque old barns and silos. Green fields were planted for the coming summer's harvest of corn, peaches and vegetables. There were few commercial properties beyond antiquated gas stations, craft galleries and small cafes.

Jason turned south onto Route One toward Westerly, and Cameron frowned when he saw two modern retail shopping plazas. Jason held back from apologizing for the area's limited choice of restaurants. He wouldn't give Epsberg the satisfaction that he cared. Because of Althea's death both of their lives could turn into dog shit, and Jason found it infuriating that his peevish companion was finding time to worry about the quality of the *osso bucco*.

The decor of the Italian restaurant was basic but colorfully decorated. Red and white checkered tablecloths paired with bright green napkins on blond wood tables. Travel posters for Italy hung on the stone-colored walls.

"It doesn't look like that," Cameron said, pointing to the poster advertising vacations in Tuscany. Under an arbor, heavy with bunches of fat purple grapes, a table was set for a meal with a large bottle of wine at its center. In the background was a sunny field with the image of the Italian tricolor flag floating in a cloudless blue sky.

"I wouldn't know," Jason said.

Cameron relaxed after his first Grey Goose martini. The menu offered the usual catalog of Italian specialties, and both men decided on an arugula salad followed by pasta. Jason had his with red clam sauce and shook his head as Cameron chose a concoction of eggplant, spinach, pancetta and wild mushrooms. Jason hadn't ordered alcohol initially but changed his mind and asked the waiter for a glass of red wine. He was served a warm glass of Chianti which he chilled by adding an ice cube from his water glass.

"You should never do that," Cameron lectured him.

"The wine is too warm."

"Send it back."

"You're kidding me, aren't you?"

"No."

They sat in silence. Finally Jason spoke.

"You don't seem very upset that Althea's dead."

"I did my grieving last night." He met Jason's eyes. "Did you kill her?"

"What? I don't have a motive."

"Who did then? You were there. What the hell happened?"

"The police are investigating. We have to be careful."

"You're scared. Admit it."

"Of course I'm scared. We're in a very vulnerable position here. Maybe you don't follow the news, but the feds don't take too kindly to what we have been doing. Bernie Madoff's secretary got six years in prison for falsifying records of stock trades. That's what I've been doing."

Jason sighed heavily. Did he need this in his life? Maybe it was time to get out. He wasn't as greedy as the rest of them.

"Yes, yes," Cameron answered impatiently. He put his empty glass down and leaned across the table toward the other man. "But I'm also a lawyer, and a pretty damned good one. So I know that we have been careful to provide the feds with no evidence with which to connect us to of any crimes. None." He sat back, looking satisfied, then turned to signal the waiter to bring him another drink before he continued.

"There are no emails, no written communications, no recordings, no phone calls they can trace. Just prepaid phones we throw away. You and I meet from time to time in Manhattan. That's all. Maybe we have a gay relationship. Who knows? I'm an attractive man. Don't forget that I met you when you were the lead accountant for that brokerage firm selling its clearing house business. We could have gotten hot and heavy way back then." He smiled. "Would you be willing to swear to that to avoid going to jail?"

Jason felt his head spinning. It was true that he and Cameron had connected during his assignment with the law firm to work out the details of the sale. During that period they had played squash together, had a few drinks afterwards. And the accountant had revealed his larcenous heart to the lawyer over steaks and cigars.

When Althea had proposed her fraudulent investing scheme in Bermuda, Jason Cava had been the first person Cameron thought of as the ideal crony to provide the financial expertise to fabricate the books of Tanner's investment accounts and deceive her investors, and he had readily joined in.

"All right," Jason conceded as the waiter brought their arugula. "What happens next?"

Cameron waited until the waiter was out of earshot before he spoke. "The first thing is not to panic." He took a forkful of salad. "Fresh. Not bad."

Jason hadn't been able to eat breakfast. He took a slow, deep breath and began on his salad, hoping he could digest his lunch. "Not panic," he repeated. "And what's the second thing?"

"I've been giving that some thought." Epsberg looked pleased. "We have to convince the investors that you can take over from Althea."

"Me?" The chewed pieces of salad half way down Jason's throat caught as he began to choke.

"Drink some water," Cameron advised. "And then think about what I am saying. You've been with Althea for what? Nine years now. Going on ten. The clients know you."

"It's Althea who gave them confidence, Cameron. Not me."

"You've got to convince them that Althea had the confidence in you. That she was grooming you to take her place."

"They'd never believe that she was doing that. Besides she was too young to think about retiring."

"Tell them she had some mid-life crisis. Wanted to go to Fiji and paint seascapes. Get away from the stress. You lived with her, man. Everyone knows that. It was no secret. She's been confiding in you for some time... the last year or so... plotting her escape. Who can contradict you?"

"I don't know, Cameron," Jason said. Running was going to be difficult. Staying in place was so much simpler.

"Remember what I said." The lawyer finished his salad. "What's the evidence *against* your saying that Althea was retiring? Is there anybody who witnessed another version of the story? Whatever you say happened, happened, Jason. Althea's dead. It's only Jason Cava who's alive to tell what was said between the two of you. Now, do you think you can do that?"

CHAPTER XXIV

Hank brought back a bag of sandwiches with him when he returned to the station after his visit to Val's office. Lunch would be a working session for him, Ben and Keisha. It was time to take stock of the case.

His trip to the charter office had confirmed that the murder weapon was her knife.

"You're exactly right, Lt. Nightingale," Val had said. "That's the knife I normally have on the binnacle in the cockpit." She shook her head sadly. "I couldn't ever imagine it being used to kill someone. It's unbelievable."

"When's the last time you saw this knife, Ms. Ainsley?"

Val thought before she answered. "I know it was onboard where it should be when I was checking the boat around five o'clock." She sighed. "The problem is I'm so used to seeing it there, I can't remember if it was in the scabbard or even if I particularly looked there during the trip. Someone could have taken it when they first came onboard, I suppose. There were a lot of people, it was very busy that night."

"Your brother knew you had the knife onboard."

"Of course. Teddy and I have been sailing together all our lives. We both know boats."

"That night, did anybody ask you about the rigging knife? What's it for? Why do you have it there?"

"No." She shook her head.

"I understand Mr. Seeger and Mr. Vargoff were in the cockpit for a time."

"Yes, Seeger asked to take the wheel. He said he was an experienced sailor."

"Was he?" Val nodded. "Any of the other guests want a turn?"

"No, but his friend stayed in the cockpit with him."

"Anyone else in the cockpit during the trip?"

"People were near the cockpit. I got a few questions about the boat. People always want to know about the America's Cup and Newport."

"Who do you remember specifically talking to you?"

Val looked disheartened. "I wish I could help you, Lieutenant. Honest I do. But as I told you last night when you interviewed me, I was concentrating on my job of keeping all those passengers safe. You're a sailor. You know that you can't be too careful that somebody doesn't fall overboard, especially when there is drinking going on."

"Yes. I know it's a big responsibility."

"And I have my reputation."

"Did you know of any other people onboard with sailing experience?"

"Scott Forsythe. He has his own sailboat. It's bigger than *Kandu* and much more luxurious. He named it *Invictus*."

"Really? So he's an experienced sailor? Knows his way around boats."

"Yes, he had the boat built in Costa Rica. You must know about those deluxe boats that are built by wealthy boaters these days. They can cost millions. Scott got a naval architect to design one to his specifications." Hank found it hard to hide his admiration. "Yeah," Val added. "It's a terrific vessel. No problem for him to take it around the world if he wants. I know he's sailed down to Bermuda."

"Tell me why you left the cockpit," Hank said.

"Well," Val began. Hank could see she was forming her answer before she spoke. " I usually give Matt some time at the helm. He was in the Caribbean this winter working with a charter company down there. I've been meaning to speak to Scott about him. He's good crew."

"When you gave Matt the wheel, you went to talk to your brother Teddy?"

"That's right. I hadn't spoken with him all night."

"I've been told that you and he looked upset... while you were talking together."

"We were upset? Who said that?"

"Did he tell you about the argument he had with Althea Tanner?"

Val stared at him. Again, he could see the wheels moving. What was she hiding?

"We know that Teddy wanted to take money from the investment account your family has with Tanner Associates. Ms. Tanner told him that he had to be patient until she could make the funds available to him."

Val was still silent.

"Your brother was impatient, couldn't wait, and so he threatened her," Hank prodded her.

"No! He did no such thing."

"I have two witnesses who say otherwise."

"If you think my brother killed Althea, you're wrong. Teddy isn't a murderer."

"No matter if Althea Tanner provoked him?" Val was glowering at him now, but he continued. "I think he took the knife when he came onboard because he might use it to threaten her when he asked her for his money. She rebuffed him, he lost his cool." He paused. "And he saw his chance to use it!"

"No," Val cried. "Teddy did not harm Althea. You don't know him. He wouldn't harm anyone." He thought she was close to tears. "I know him. He wouldn't...he couldn't."

But experience had taught Hank that the opinions of friends and family members were the last people to rely on when it came to knowing who was capable of murder.

CHAPTER XXV

"Is it possible that somebody was hiding in the head, Lieutenant?" Ben asked. He was holding a roast beef sandwich in one hand and a can of soda in the other while examining the drawing that Keisha had made of the deck of *Kandu*. "I mean, here we are trying to figure out who went down those stairs between the time Althea Tanner and Teddy Ainsley had their argument and when the body was discovered. Maybe someone was already there." He took a bite of the sandwich and turned around for Hank's and Keisha's reactions.

"When did this person come back upstairs?" Keisha asked. She had finished her turkey wrap and was sipping a bottle of water. "No one was in the head when the body was found. We haven't found anyone who can say for certain that they either saw someone go down the stairs after Teddy came back up, or they saw someone come *up* the stairs after he did. I've been all over the statements. There's nothing."

"So all we are sure of," Hank said, "is that Teddy came back up. The waiter Nick Dargis saw Teddy on deck talking to his sister." He studied the white board, his half eaten sandwich ignored on his desk. "Where were they standing?"

"Mrs. Kent saw them, too," Keisha said, "so they were forward, not aft." She looked pleased with herself as she said *aft*. His sergeant was working on her sailing vocabulary.

"Can we account for everyone else during that time?" Ben persisted. "Is there someone missing above deck? That's the person who could have been hiding in the head."

"This is what we have," Keisha said. "Mrs. Kent was with Mr. Granger during the whole relevant time." Hank hid his annoyance that Caroline had been in the gigolo's company for such a long period. "Mr. and Mrs. Seeger were speaking with each other. That is before he had to use the head. The doctor was sitting on the deck

89

with his wife. They were having something to eat."

"When did Ms. Ainsley turn over the wheel to Matt Williams?" Hank asked.

"She said it was about five minutes before she started talking to her brother."

"Five minutes," Ben repeated. "Did she look at her watch?"

"She estimated the time based on where the boat was."

"So what was she doing for five minutes?" Hank asked.

"She said she was watching the crew handle the boat."

"We should check that further," Hank said. "Would it register with anyone on the boat if the captain went below?"

"Good point, Lieutenant," Ben said.

"O.K., who else? Tristan Marchand, the art dealer's son. I think we need to look some more into Marchand. Something about him didn't ring right with me." He remembered the middle-aged man's bored demeanor during his interview. Hank had thought Marchand's answers surprisingly dismissive given the fact that he was being questioned by the police as part of a murder investigation.

"My father set up the account with her firm," Marchand had said as casually as if he were talking about the landscaper's bills instead of ten million dollars, "and now I'm happy to collect the quarterly checks. Althea Tanner does a good job for me. I don't have much contact with her."

"And he doesn't run the father's business now," Keisha observed.

"No," Ben answered. "Our Tristan doesn't seem to do much of anything." He looked at Hank. "He did seem reluctant to tell us about himself. He couldn't be the romantic interest in Althea Tanner's life, could he?"

"Neither Jason Cava nor Maya Vereen said they knew who she might be involved with."

"If anybody." This from Keisha, and both men looked at her. "Not every woman has to have a man."

Ben shook his head. "With her looks, there had to be someone. My money's always been on Cava."

Now it was Keisha's turn to shake her head. "Beautiful women require men?"

"Come on, Keisha," Ben said.

"O.K., O.K.." Hank held up his hand. "Here's something else I want to explore. Not all of Althea's clients were on the boat."

"Maybe they all wouldn't fit," Keisha pointed out. "Or maybe she picked the most prominent ones... the richest ones maybe. She had to invite Seeger because he was recommending the new people."

"Marchand could be the lover," Ben said, still on his line of inquiry, "but what about that Scott Forsythe? He looks like a ladies' man if there ever was one."

"Forsythe said that he became a client of Tanner when she went on her own after John Ainsley died," Hank said. "He never said what his occupation was, only that he was 'an investor.' Where was he around the time of the murder?"

"Talking to Melody Granger," Keisha said.

"For the entire time?"

"They had parted company before the murder was discovered, but she wasn't sure and he can't remember."

"Terrific," Hank said. "Forsythe's a sailor by the way. He would have definitely known that the rigging knife was sharp enough to kill someone."

"I think we can eliminate Mr. and Mrs. Dalworthy," Ben contributed.

"Too old, do you think, Ben?"

"No, sir," he said with a quick glance at Keisha. "I don't want it said that I think older women can't be murderers. They can."

"Yes," Keisha said, ignoring the look. "But the Dalworthys do alibi each other."

"What about Selena Dawson?" Hank asked.

"Now she's another client who has been with Tanner from the get-go," Keisha said. "Her husband Charles was a friend of John Ainsley. Invested his money with Althea, died a few years later, and the widow continues with the firm."

"What did you think of her, Lieutenant?" Ben asked. "I couldn't get an angle on her."

"She didn't make much of an impression on me either, but I think she was genuinely upset at what happened on the boat. Selena Dawson must have been a lot younger than her husband if we can assume that he was a contemporary of John Ainsley."

"So we need to look at her a little closer," Ben said. "Along with Marchand." He paused. "Maybe the two of them match up... as a couple. That's why they got invites."

"I think it's more likely what Keisha said, that Althea was trying to impress Dr. Tompkins and Leo Vargoff by having them meet these old money types on her client list."

"But that Alex Seeger isn't an old money type, is he, Lieutenant? You know him from your Tai Chi class. He owns some businesses over in Providence. Hardly an old Newport family with Gilded Age money."

"You're right, Ben. The Seegers moved here six years ago. They also live in a big place out on Ocean Drive. New money. Could be worth looking into how he made it."

"Well, if we're looking at new money versus old," Keisha said, "don't you think it's odd that the two new clients Althea wanted to recruit aren't from an old Newport family either? That doctor and his wife are Seeger's relatives. And what about Leo Vargoff?"

"He invited me on his boat that he keeps on Jamestown. While it sounds like he's got money, it's also the new kind. He's a developer. What's his alibi for the murder time by the way?"

"None," Keisha answered. "He said he didn't talk much to the other guests. Do you suppose he's shy?"

"He could have been happy enjoying the view. He is a boater, as I said, but not a sailor." Hank looked thoughtful. "Jason Cava's movements don't seem precise either, do they? He was in a lot of places."

"The Dalworthys were talking to him just as Seeger came up the stairs screaming," Keisha added.

"There's more to Jason Cava than meets the eye," Ben said. "He's very evasive about the details of that investment firm. He is the financial guy who keeps the books. Do you suppose he was stealing and Althea caught him at it and he had to do away with her?"

Keisha frowned. "Why would he suddenly decide to kill her last night on a boat full of people? Wouldn't it be easier to murder her at their home they shared and blame it on a burglary gone wrong? Some faked violence like that makes more sense."

"Can we at least eliminate the crew?" Hank asked irritably.

"Matt was at the helm, and Jill was trimming the sails," Keisha said. "If you believe Val Ainsley, she was on deck watching both of them."

"Dargis seems out of the frame, Lieutenant," Ben said. "He came back on deck when Althea told him to leave. Teddy can corroborate that. Besides, what would be his motive?"

"What is anybody's motive, Ben? That's the most puzzling aspect of this case. Althea Tanner was making money for everyone. Two new clients were eager to join the club. Everybody was happy. Who would want her dead? Who benefits by her death?" He turned to Ben. "We'll need a copy of her will. Get Cava to tell us who her lawyer is. Let's hope he knows that about her at least."

"Right, Lieutenant."

"Let's focus on the crime itself," Hank said. "It wasn't premeditated. Something happened on that boat that caused someone to go over the edge. They had their opportunity when they saw that rigging knife, and they used it to put an end to Althea Tanner's life."

"Well, we know one thing that happened on the boat, Lieutenant, that could make someone snap."

"Yes, Ben, and it's the only thing we have that makes sense - the argument between Althea and Teddy Ainsley. That encounter was unplanned and we know that Teddy got very angry because of it."

"He would know about the rigging knife, how useful it could be" Keisha said.

"Yes, he's been sailing since he was a child." Hank sighed. "We keep coming back to Teddy Ainsley. Let's get him in here this afternoon."

"O.K., Lieutenant," Ben said.

"I've got a lot more questions for him. Right now of all the people who were on that boat last night, Teddy Ainsley has got to be our number one suspect."

Caroline was looking pleased as she stared at the summer reservations calendar that afternoon on her computer's screen. She liked seeing all those days colored in the blue which indicated there were no rooms left to reserve. Of course there were prospective guests who would be disappointed, but she hoped they were looking at alternative dates which were still free. This year could be the inn's most profitable one yet, and Caroline hoped her optimism wasn't misplaced. She loved living at Kenwood, and keeping the house as a sought after hotel was her one hope of continuing to do so.

Caroline's office was in the original smoking room of Kenwood, and it was a cozy space with its old brown leather chairs and dark paneled walls which were covered with Kent family photographs. There were several of Reed as a child and then a young adult. His amiable, smiling face watched her from around the room, and it was always a comfort to her to look at these pictures of Reed. Almost all of them had been taken before Caroline had met him, and she often found herself thinking of what he must have been like in his youth. Happy, to judge from his facial expressions, and she often wished that she had known him as a child the way Teddy and Val had.

A knock at the door jolted her from her thoughts. Louise would never knock.

"Come in," Caroline called, and the door opened.

"Mrs. Kent?" Caroline heard the voice of Lindsay Ames, one of the inn's staff, as she entered the room. She was a friendly dark-haired woman, one of the students from Salve Regina University whom the inn routinely employed. "There's someone here to see you."

"Who is it?" Caroline asked. She wasn't expecting a visitor.

"His name is Jonathan Granger," Lindsay read from a calling card in her hand.

"Jon?"

"Yes. I didn't tell him you were here. I said that I would see if you were, in case you didn't want to see him."

"No," Caroline said, rising from the desk. "Of course I'll talk to him. Where is he?"

"He's waiting in the foyer. Was it all right to leave him there? Or should I have put him in the morning room? I wasn't sure."

"Bring him back here, Lindsay. We can talk in the office."

"Sure thing," she answered and was gone. After a minute or so, she reappeared followed by Jon, who seemed bursting at the seams with news.

"Caroline," he exclaimed. "Caroline, I wanted you to be the first to hear this."

"Hear wh--" Caroline began, but she was quickly silenced.

"I know who the killer is!"

CHAPTER XXVI

Lindsay Ames was staring at Jon with wide frightened eyes.

"Lindsay," Caroline said with a warning glance at Jonathan Granger. "It's all right. You can go. This is nothing you need to hear."

"But, Mrs. Kent, is he talking about that murder on the boat last night? The one where you were?"

"Lindsay, please. I'll sort this out. Now would you please get back to your work."

"All right, I just hope you're going to be O.K.," the young woman answered as she reluctantly left the room. As soon as Lindsay had gone, Jon shut the heavy wooden door behind her.

"Caroline," he said excitedly, "I mean it. I absolutely know who killed Althea."

"Jon, can you calm down a little?"

"But I saw him."

"You saw who murdered Althea Tanner? Why didn't you tell the police? Wait a minute, how could you? You were with me when she was killed. You couldn't have seen anything. Jon, you're not making any sense."

"I know, I know. But, it really is too exciting." He finally blew out a breath and looked at Caroline with the decided grin of the Cheshire Cat.

"Sit down, why don't you. Here." She pointed to one of the leather arm chairs. Jon looked unsure of what he wanted to do, but finally dropped into the chair. He was wearing black jeans and a powder blue polo shirt. Caroline took the chair across from him. "Now, start from the beginning. Who did you see? What's happened?"

"That's just it, something did happen today. I can't believe I was there." He blew out another breath.

"Go on," she coaxed.

"All right. This morning Melody asked me to drop off something for her at the Newport Art Museum. She's on some committee."

"All right,"

"I took the envelope into the museum. You know where they are on Bellevue Avenue next to the Redwood Library. Then I came out and got in my car and started back home when I passed Althea's office. There was a police car parked out front." Caroline nodded. "So I thought, what's that all about?" He grinned again. "So I parked across from the building and watched."

"You had nothing else to do?" Caroline couldn't help asking the question.

"Not really anything on tap during the day. We've got some dinner party to go to tonight, but it doesn't start until eight. Anyway, there I was outside her office. Well, not hers anymore, is it?"

"Tanner," Caroline declared, "is still the name of the company." She was getting impatient with Jon.

"A police officer came out, not the Inspector but the other one who was asking the questions with the Inspector last night."

"Sgt. Davies."

"Yes," Jonathan answered with a pleased look on his face. "Right. So this Davies bobbie comes out and gets in his car, drives away. So I'm thinking if no one's going to be arrested I may as well go home. Then my phone rang, it was Melody. Wanted to know if I was coming home for lunch, and I was about to say yes when I saw Jason Cava's car come down the driveway from the parking lot behind that building. He came out of the driveway and turned left. So before I knew what I was doing, I told Melody something had come up and I wouldn't be home for lunch and I started following Jason."

"What on earth made you want to follow his car?"

"He turned left. Don't you get it? Away from town. It didn't make a lot of sense for him to go in that direction. I was curious where he was going."

"And you followed him."

"Yes, and it's a good thing I did. He drove across the Newport Bridge and went out of town."

"And he didn't notice that you were following him?"

Jon looked astonished at the question. "I was driving the Lexus SUV. He's used to seeing Melody's Mercedes. Besides he didn't seem interested in anything but driving as fast as he could. That car has some power."

"Where did he go?"

"I followed him all the way to the train station in Kingston."

"Kingston? Did he get on the train?"

"No, he collected a bloke getting off of the train."

"Did you recognize who it was?"

"No, never saw him before. But he and Cava knew one another all right."

"How do you know that?"

"From the way they greeted one another," Jon said with satisfaction. "They were all serious business, not even a hello handshake. And from the looks of it, that bloke from the train was not happy to be there."

"What did this man look like?"

"I've seen the shoes at Brooks Brothers. The suit was Armani."

"What did he look like, Jon? His face."

"Oh, bloody handsome. Greying hair, but premature I'd say. Light eyes. Square jaw."

"What happened then?"

"They got in Cava's car, and I followed them to an Italian restaurant somewhere south of the train station in the direction of Westerly. The restaurant wasn't the kind of place to take such a well-dressed chap. But the two of them went inside. I waited in the parking lot outside, and they stayed for about forty-five minutes. So they must have eaten the food." He grimaced.

"They wanted to talk where no one from Newport would see them," Caroline said thoughtfully.

"That's what I've been trying to tell you. Don't you see how suspicious this is?"

"And what did they do after lunch?"

"Cava took the other bloke back to the Kingston station."

"What did you do?"

"I almost got on the train myself. I knew that if I followed him I could find out who he is."

"Naturally," Caroline said. She'd seen that scene in more than a few movies.

"He wouldn't know who I am," Jon pointed out, "even if I sat on the seat next to him. I've never seen him, he's never seen me."

"But you didn't get on the train with him?"

"No," Granger shook his head regretfully. "We have that dinner tonight, and Melody would have my head if I was off train riding when I should have been home in time to change."

"Jon, could you see in which direction the train was going, the one this man took?"

"It was on the westbound side. Toward New York City. And from his clothes, I'd say that our chap is from the city."

"But you did keep following Jason." Granger nodded. "Did he return to Newport?"

He nodded again. "He drove like a fury and went straight home."

"Where does he live?"

"Oh, that's right. You wouldn't know, would you? He and Althea lived together."

"Really?" Caroline was taken aback by this information.

"Everybody knew it, Caroline. Althea didn't hide it. The funny thing was that there didn't seem to be anything going on between them except for the fact that they lived together."

"Where is the house?"

"It's one of those modern places out on the Drive. It's smashing. One thing you can say - could say - about Althea is that she had superb taste in everything."

"And now you think that what you saw today tells you who Althea Tanner's killer is?"

"Caroline, it's Jason Cava. It's got to be. Those two chaps are in it together. You should have seen their guilty faces when they met."

"I wish I had."

"Last night Jason killed Althea. Today he meets secretly with his partner in crime. They couldn't take a chance and talk to each other on the phone."

"Why not?"

"The phones could be tapped."

"Oh, Jon, that's what happens in films. Not real life. You have to get a court order to tap a phone. The murder only took place last night. The police couldn't be that far along in their investigation."

"Well Cava wouldn't know that, would he?"

"I don't know what he would know. But I agree with you. This meeting today was extremely suspicious."

Jon leaned forward in his chair. "Caroline, I know it's Cava. But everything the police know points them toward Teddy Ainsley. He is the one who argued with Althea last night over money. Trust me," he said, looking grave. "That Inspector will arrest Teddy before you can say 'Sherlock Holmes and Dr. Watson.' The law isn't brilliant, you know."

Caroline held back the urge to say that, to the contrary, she knew that Lt. Hank Nightingale of the Newport Police Department was brilliant. What's more, he needed to hear about this new development in the case.

"You don't believe that Teddy is the killer," Caroline said, liking Jon all the more for his defense of Teddy Ainsley.

"Of course not. The man couldn't kill a rabbit." He paused again. "So it's up to us."

"Us?"

"You and I have to prove that Jason Cava is the killer."

"We do?"

"Of course, Caroline. The police aren't going to be of any help. They are bound to accuse the wrong man. They don't have a bloody clue as to who really committed this murder."

CHAPTER XXVII

After Jonathan Granger left, Caroline sat in her office quietly mulling over everything he had said. On one hand she was relieved that Jon was so sure that Teddy Ainsley had not killed Althea Tanner. There she agreed with him. It was his strong contention that the identity of the killer was Althea's colleague Jason Cava which interested her.

Last night Althea had introduced Cava to Caroline shortly after she had boarded *Kandu*. He had appeared polite but made no real attempt to engage her in conversation. He had to have known that Caroline wasn't a prospective Tanner client, merely a guest whom Althea had invited on a whim when they had first met in Val's office.

So Caroline had missed the opportunity to talk with Jason and learn something about him. All she had were her first impressions of a diminutive man with an air of intensity, curiously dressed all in unnautical black. If she had not known his actual occupation Caroline might have supposed that Jason Cava was a fellow actor. His moves were practiced, his words sounding rehearsed. She remembered watching him as he had talked about the stock market with Mr. and Mrs. Dalworthy. Cava could have been reading lines from a play. He had all the right inflections and facial expressions complete with timing the appropriate laugh.

Did he look so rehearsed because he needed to mask his real purpose in coming onboard - to commit murder?

Caroline let her mind turn over the question. If she assumed, like Jon, that Cava was the killer then the next question had to be: what was his motive?

The only fact Caroline knew was that Jason and Althea lived in the same house. Jon had insisted that there was no physical relationship between the two, but how could he know that? Who could know what went on in the privacy of that house out on the Drive? How much of Cava's intensity was driven by sexual energy?

Althea Tanner was a very physically attractive woman. Perhaps she had tired of Jason and had given him an ultimatum to leave their house, which Caroline had to assume belonged to the wealthy financial advisor. And even further damaging to Cava, Althea had decided to terminate his decidedly lucrative employment with her firm.

To continue with the hypothesis, Caroline tried putting herself in Jason's place. Planning for the murder to take place on the sailing cruise would have been tricky, but it did allow Jason the ability to hide among a dozen or so potential killers onboard. Stabbing Althea could appear to be a sudden decision by one of them. Her heated argument with Teddy was a Godsend to Jason, framing a very convincing suspect with an obvious motive. Caroline knew enough about sailing to know that knives were always found on boats. That an angry Teddy Ainsley had grabbed a knife he saw lying in the cabin and stabbed Althea over her balking at his request for money would be the working theory of the subsequent investigation into her death.

And how simple this solution to the crime would appear to the police, which despite her faith in Hank's intelligence, Caroline knew the detective would have to consider.

But if you could move away from consideration of Teddy as the killer and turn your attention to Jason, when was Cava's opportunity? There had been very little time between the argument and the finding of the body.

Hank would be able to determine where Jason was during that period once he had interviewed everyone on the boat. If Jason had no alibi for the time of the murder, then a case against him could be made. Caroline had her early suspicion that the killer could have gotten down into the cabin by dropping through the hatch at the forward end of the boat. After Teddy came up from below, Jason saw *his* chance and slid down through the opening. Certainly his small frame could have managed this maneuver.

Cava's initial plan might have been to strangle his victim. But the presence of the knife onboard had presented itself as a much quicker weapon to use. One thrust and Althea's life was over. Caroline shuddered as she pictured the crime being committed, her belief growing that Jon was on the right track with his suspicions. Jason Cava could be the killer.

CHAPTER XXVIII

As soon as Jon had left, Caroline went to look or Louise. She found her in the rose garden, which was located in a restful spot on the rear lawn which bordered the Cliff Walk. She was deep in conversation with one of the current guests, Cynde Lawson.

"Hello," Caroline said as she approached the two women. "Are you two gardeners sharing tips?"

"Louise has some wonderful roses here," Cynde said. She was a tall middle-aged woman with a mass of brown curls framing her friendly face. "We can't grow many of these varieties in New Hampshire. We're not that far from Newport, but your climate near the water is so much better than ours for roses."

"It takes a lot of work to achieve this," Caroline said, sweeping her hand around the spacious circular bed. "Louise has done wonders since we have lived here. You should have seen it before that."

"Our gardener George helps me a great deal," Louise said. "Preparing the soil is hard work. I'm afraid I'm not as hardy *as I once was.*"

"Oh, I'm sure you do just fine, Mrs. Kent."

"She does," seconded Caroline.

"Oh, look at the time," Cynde said. "I promised Ken we'd go over to Jamestown this evening. Yesterday we went for a cruise on that boat called the *Rum Runner*, and he loved all the stories about Prohibition and hiding in the coves over there. Have you ever taken that tour, Caroline?"

"No, but I've heard it is a fascinating trip."

"Have a wonderful time," Louise said.

"I'm sure we will," Cynde said, and she started back toward the house.

"Boats," Louise said when their guest was out of earshot.

"I don't want to go on another for a very long time," Caroline said.

"No, I shouldn't imagine you would."

"Let's go sit in the gazebo. I want to talk to you about the latest development."

"In the murder?"

"Yes."

They followed the shrubbery at the back of the property in the direction of the perennial garden, also a center of Louise's horticultural endeavors. Beyond this garden was the gazebo. As they entered the small summer house, Caroline was reminded of the first murder she had encountered. She still shivered at the thought of finding that lifeless body right here in the gazebo. She could never have foreseen that Maurice Hargreave's death would be the first of several mysteries she would come to investigate. Now Jonathan Granger had asked her to solve another mysterious death. Could she? Should she? Perhaps it was time to leave the investigating to Hank, a proper police detective.

"Do you know Melody Granger, Louise?" Caroline asked as they sat down. Caroline noticed that Louise had chosen a long chair in order to elevate her feet.

"I knew her as Melody Nickerson."

"Before she married Jon?"

"Yes. I haven't met this new husband. It was her first one, Alfred Nickerson, whom I knew."

"What happened to him?"

"He ran off with a waitress from the restaurant at the old Canfield House."

"Her husband what?" Caroline asked.

"Yes. Alfie and Melody used to go there every Sunday night for dinner. It's closed now, of course, but Melody used to love the place. I expect she meant the decor and the food. Little did she know that Alfie was going for the service."

"Louise," Caroline chided. "You are a scandal."

"Well, Alfie was no looker, but he was very rich. A nice catch for some enterprising young woman."

"And Melody did very well in the divorce, I imagine."

"Naturally. She was no fool. Deserved everything she could get, in my opinion."

"And then she went ahead and found a young spouse of her own. Where did they meet? Do you know?"

"In New York. Probably at some fashion show, I understand he's a model. Melody always went down to Manhattan for Fashion Week. She loves clothes."

"Even if they make her look like a sunflower."

"I beg your pardon, Caroline."

"Oh, just something Jon said. I met him on the boat last night. He and Melody were there. She, and I'm guessing Alfie, had their money invested with Althea Tanner."

"I suppose that makes sense. What did you think of this... John, did you call him?"

"Jonathan, Jon. He was charming. We had quite a long chat."

"Well, I'm glad he's charming. I'd hate to think of Melody stuck with a rake."

"I think he honestly is fond of her."

"That's good to hear."

"But he's also latched on to me as a friend."

"Really?"

"Yes, and he doesn't even know my history of detecting."

Louise raised one eyebrow. "Is he what you want to talk to me about?"

"Yes. It appears that young Mr. Granger has decided to play detective himself." She told Louise about Jon's following Jason Cava and the unknown man from the train. "He believes that all this is so suspicious that it must mean that Jason is Althea's killer."

"It does have to be one of the people who was on the boat. That much we do know. Do you think that Melody's husband could have actually solved the murder?" Louise asked. "I still don't understand why any of her clients would want to kill her."

"It is possible what Jon found out does point to Althea's assistant. I certainly don't want it to be Teddy."

"No. We don't want that."

"I'd like to talk to Hank about it." Caroline paused. "But I'm not sure of the right way to tell him about Jon's activities. I can't help but think he'll laugh."

"It does sound rather cloak and dagger."

"Yes, but don't get the impression that Jon is a silly man. He realizes that the obvious suspect is Teddy, and he told me unequivocally that he knows Teddy couldn't be the killer."

"Well, then he does have some intelligence."

"Yes, Louise. And he also believes that the police investigation will lead them right to Teddy. He's the obvious suspect because of the argument he had with Althea. And also the threat he made." Caroline shook her head. "Motive, opportunity. It's all there."

"I'm so sorry Teddy threatened Ms. Tanner, Caroline. He was foolish to do that."

"Of course. But Jon thinks that he and I should work together to prove that the killer is Jason Cava."

"You *and* he working together to solve the case? What would Hank's reaction to that be?"

"Exactly. It's one thing for me to show an interest in his case. But a total stranger?"

"What are you going to do?"

"I don't know yet. Maybe I should just put my faith in Hank's ability to get to the bottom of this and believe that he will not jump to the conclusion that the killer is Teddy. The evidence against him is only circumstantial."

"Yes," Louise said thoughtfully, "but can Hank look beyond it?" She shook her head. "I'm sorry, but I think you should try to help to save Teddy even if it means interfering in Hank's case."

CHAPTER XXIX

"Althea was alive when I left her below," Teddy declared. "Why are you asking me about all this?"

Hank and his two sergeants were sitting across from Teddy Ainsley in an interview room in the Newport police station. Hank pointed out that there was only Teddy's word for that statement.

"But she *was* alive," Ainsley insisted.

"Then who killed her?" Ben asked.

"How should I know? Isn't it your job as policemen to find that out?"

Hank winced. Police officers did not have magical powers which let them see who committed crimes. They developed the facts and focused on the evidence which presented itself to them.

"You were heard to threaten Ms. Tanner," Keisha reminded Teddy.

"What threat are you talking about?" Ainsley seemed genuinely puzzled.

"We have two witnesses who heard you say that you would make her pay if she didn't release your invested money to you."

"What witnesses? No one else was with us."

"We have two witnesses," Hank repeated.

"I don't remember what I said to Althea. I was upset. She upset me." Teddy looked unhappy now, his face that of a disappointed child.

"Maybe you don't remember killing her," Ben said.

"I didn't kill anyone," Teddy said vehemently. "Least of all Althea. She was a friend of my father."

"Who let you down," Hank reminded him. "You told her that she wouldn't have treated you like that if your father had still been alive."

"Did I?"

"You don't remember that either, do you?" Ben asked.

"No," Teddy shrugged. "I said I was upset. I need my money for the music center." He looked directly at all three detectives. "It means everything to me. I've got to buy Laurel Hill."

"Mr. Ainsley," Hank began. "I'd like you to understand--"

"No," Teddy said angrily. "You have to understand. Somebody might buy that house before I can get my money. They could take it away from me. I can't have that."

"No," Hank said. "I can see that. And now you should see why we think you murdered the one person who stood in your way of getting what you want."

"No, that's not what happened." Teddy beat his hands on the table.

"I think it did. And your anger now is not giving us any reason to believe otherwise."

Teddy slumped in his chair. Hank watched him, waiting, but finally deciding that there was nothing else to be gained from this interview. He motioned to Keisha to remain while he and Ben left the room.

"He's guilty, Lieutenant." Ben said when they reached the hallway. "I don't think he meant to do it, though. Do you think he could plead temporary insanity?"

"I don't know, Ben. That's not our call. I only wish we had some hard evidence. But there are no fingerprints on the knife, no blood on his clothes. He stood close enough to her, I expect, for some DNA to be on her. We'll see from the report when it comes in."

"Ms. Tanner was all over that boat talking to people. The body will have lots of hair and fibers. She probably kissed every last person on that boat." Ben sighed. "What do you want to do with him?"

"Let's hold him overnight. We've got enough to do that. Maybe he'll remember more about what happened after he has had a night in the cells to think about it. We'll talk to him again in the morning."

"Right."

"You and Keisha take him down. Look stern. I want him to see the seriousness of this. I'm not sure he quite realizes that." Hank shook his head. "He was there. He had the opportunity. He certainly has the motive."

"And conveniently, he knew about the murder weapon and had access to it."

"Yes, Ben. It does look bad for Mr. Teddy Ainsley."

CHAPTER XXX

When the telephone rang in the kitchen of Kenwood the following morning, Mattie had unaccountably let the two eggs she was poaching for Cynde Lawson overcook and Caroline had just realized that she had forgotten to make the decaf coffee for her husband.

"I hope this is important," Caroline said as she put down the carafe of water she had been ready to pour. As she walked across the room to answer the phone, Louise came into the kitchen, and Caroline gave her mother-in-law hand signals to finish making the coffee. Louise nodded and took up the task.

"Hello, The Inn At Kenwood Court," Caroline said in as pleasant a voice as she could muster. "How may I help you?"

"Is this Caroline?" an agitated voice asked. Caroline frowned. She wasn't sure who was on the line.

"Yes," she answered. "Who's speaking?"

"Caroline, it's Val. Val Ainsley."

"Of course. Val. I'm sorry. It's a little hectic here, and I couldn't quite make out--"

"They've arrested Teddy!"

"Teddy?" Caroline glanced across the room at Louise who had turned toward her with a questioning look.

"He didn't murder Althea, Caroline. I know he didn't. You know he couldn't do it."

"Yes, Val, I know. But start from the beginning. Tell me what's happened to Teddy."

"He's in jail. They are keeping him in jail. A police officer came to Bellehurst yesterday and said he wanted Teddy to come with him to the station to answer some questions. Teddy left with him, and then they didn't let him come back home last night."

"But is he actually arrested, did they charge him with the murder?"

Louise had hurried to the phone. Caroline put the receiver on speaker phone.

"I don't know what they've done, but he can't leave the jail," Val's voice came on in the kitchen. "Doesn't that mean he's been arrested?"

"Not necessarily. I think they can hold someone for twenty-four hours without charging him. Have you been able to talk to Teddy?"

"He was able to call last night. He said that they told him they will have more questions for him today. Why didn't they ask him all the questions they had yesterday? What else can he possibly tell them?"

"But is he charged yet?" Caroline asked again.

"I really don't know," Val said, sounding worn and dispirited. "I don't understand what any of it means. I've called our family lawyer."

"Good. You need to get legal advice immediately."

"Lewis Crenshaw is not a criminal lawyer."

"Teddy needs someone to protect his interests now, Val. I'm sure Mr. Crenshaw can do something right away. Is he going to the police station today? I know it's Saturday."

"He said he would, but I don't know how soon he will get over there. Mother is really overwrought. I don't know what to say to her to calm her down."

"I'm sure your mother is very upset." Caroline looked at Louise. "What do you want us to do?"

Louise began to say, "I can come--", but Val cut her off.

"You know the police detective in charge of the investigation, Caroline, that Lt. Nightingale. You told me you were going to bring him to Althea's party. Can you call him and find out what is going on?"

"I'm not sure what he will tell me, Val." Caroline didn't admit that she had been planning to do that very thing later that day.

"You've got to make him realize that Teddy didn't do it," Val continued. "There's no way he killed Althea. It's just impossible. Ask Louise. She's known Teddy all his life."

"Val, it's Louise. Caroline will do all she can to help Teddy. Please tell Margaret that Caroline will do everything she can."

Caroline shook her head. "I can't promise anything."

"Don't worry, Val," Louise said. "I'm sure Hank will listen to Caroline."

"Please. Caroline, you've got to help Teddy."

"Yes, Val," Caroline said. "I'll see if I can reach Lt. Nightingale."

"Thank you," Val said, and she quickly broke off the connection. The sound of the dial tone buzzed from other end of the phone.

Caroline carefully reset the receiver in the cradle and stared at Louise. "I don't know if I should call Hank this morning. Or should I let him finish talking to Teddy first? Val could be overreacting to this. Once Hank is done with his interview, Teddy could be released."

"A night in jail is quite serious, Caroline," Louise said. "I don't like the sound of this at all."

"It's exactly what we feared would happen," Caroline said. "You don't think that Hank has found evidence, something that we don't know about? Suppose there is evidence that connects Teddy to the murder." Caroline stared hard at Louise. "Could we have been wrong? Could Teddy have done something horrible?"

"No," Louise said firmly. "We are not wrong. Teddy hasn't killed anybody. It's all some terrible mistake, and Hank will see that."

"So should I call him now?"

"Do you think he's at the station yet?"

Caroline looked at the kitchen clock. "It's only ten past eight. Maybe I can catch him awhile he's still at home."

She picked up the phone and called Hank's cell number. The call went right to voice mail, and Caroline left a message to call her when he had the opportunity.

CHAPTER XXXI

Teddy was duly questioned again early that morning. If Hank had hoped that the second interview would bring out more information than the first, that was far from the result. The questions Hank asked were similar to those he had posed on the previous afternoon. Teddy's answers were also the same familiar, vague responses. Hank's suspect did not offer any new details on his actions while he was below deck with Althea Tanner. It did not appear that Teddy knew as much about what had occurred as did the two witnesses who had overheard their argument.

Reluctantly, Hank had Teddy taken back to his cell. Ainsley looked surprised, almost confused. The detective began to wonder, like Ben, how much of what had happened on the boat was in Teddy's consciousness.

Now, sitting in his office and going over the evidence, Hank believed that he had little choice but to take his case to the prosecutor. He couldn't prove that Teddy had planned the crime ahead of time. Second degree murder seemed the likely charge.

But the Ainsley heir's actions strongly suggested that once onboard *Kandu*, his anger towards Althea Tanner had gotten the best of him. He had reacted with a vengeance, stabbing her with the handy rigging knife after she insisted that she could not hurry the release of his funds. Teddy would do anything rather than be thwarted in making an offer on the estate he wanted to buy, the only topic of which he had spoken in the interviews that appeared important to him.

Hank had no evidence to connect anyone else on the boat to the murder. He had gone over the statements, examined the timeline, even speculated as to who could have slipped below to attack Althea after Teddy had left her. There was nothing. It was Teddy who had argued with Althea, Teddy who threatened her, Teddy the last to see her alive. Teddy had to be her killer. Even if he didn't remember what happened.

So why did Hank have this nagging feeling of uneasiness?

Caroline. He knew that she would disagree with his conclusion because Teddy was a friend of the Kent family and had grown up with Reed. His widow wouldn't see that childhood friends of your husband could commit crimes, the same as anybody else on this earth.

He had seen Caroline's call on his cell phone. Hank didn't know what she wanted but he had a feeling that she had found out that Teddy was being held at police headquarters. No doubt his sister had called Kenwood with the information.

It was almost noon. The prosecutor would take the evidence and go before the judge sometime today to get the arrest warrant. Since it was the weekend, things could move slowly. The judge would certainly wait until Monday to set the bail hearing. It was going to be a stressful weekend for the Ainsley family.

Meanwhile he would have to go to Kenwood to see Caroline - in person, sometime today, before the news of the arrest leaked out.

The murder of Althea Tanner was a high profile case, and the Ainsleys were prominent in Newport. The media would like nothing better than to give Teddy's arrest twenty-four hour coverage. Such a sensational story would drive the news cycle for the foreseeable future. Hank was happy not to be the Newport PD's press officer. Sgt. Mark Mathews would earn his pay this month.

Since arriving in Newport, Jason Cava had grown to love living so close to the ocean. His previous exposure to the Atlantic Ocean had been confined to childhood trips to Brooklyn's Coney Island and New Jersey's Atlantic City. But the busy commercial boardwalks and crowds of people only served as a picture frame around the water. Jason had never imagined how splendid living so close to such a powerful force of nature could be. Once in Newport, the former New Yorker had never tired of sitting outdoors, enjoying the water view from *Di Sole's* terrace. He could stare endlessly at the sparkles of light shining on the heavy, lumbering ocean waves and the solemn blue sky over them. The sight of the massive, worn grey rocks rimming the Newport coastline thrilled his body so much that there were times when he felt he actually understood what the world was all about. It was a feeling better than using the most expensive designer drug he had ever tried.

During the two days since Althea's death, Jason often went out onto the terrace and sat by himself. He couldn't get out of his mind that he would soon have to leave *Di Sole*.

He should have been worrying about more important matters such as what would happen to Tanner Associates without Althea at its head. Could Jason pull off Cameron Epsberg's daring scheme of reassuring the investors that he could take charge of their investments? And the larger question of how much longer he and Cameron and Scott could continue duping Tanner's investors into believing that their profits came from actual shares they owned in the stock market, not from manipulating the insider trading of huge blocks of shares.

For several months now Jason had experienced a gnawing feeling that it was time for their luck to run out. He had seen how Althea had become much too cavalier with her approach to the business. The easy profits from the insider trades were all she needed to be successful now. Jason wondered what John Ainsley would have made of the disintegration of his protégé's skills. Maybe they had been overrated to begin with.

"People are sheep, Jason," she had told him on more than one occasion. "Where I lead them, they will follow." It sounded almost Biblical.

But so far she had been right. And that had only served to support her boldness in dealing with the clients who trusted her without question. As long as the generous quarterly checks arrived, no one wanted to know what went on behind the scenes to manufacture the profits. Did no one really wonder why Tanner's investment results were so much better than what was offered by other firms? In order to meet Teddy Ainsley's request for a big withdrawal from his family's account, Althea was going to get the money to pay him from the two new investors, Leo Vargoff and Richard Tompkins. Jason had expected that the two men would want more than a handshake to fork over ten million dollars. Yet neither seemed to question the stability of Tanner Associates to safeguard their money. Perhaps that was Biblical as well, like the miracle of the loaves and fishes which had fed thousands on the mountainside. That food had all multiplied from the five loaves of bread and two fishes brought by a young boy.

CHAPTER XXXII

Later that same Saturday afternoon Jason left *Di Sole* and walked purposefully across Ocean Drive to the other side of the road. He found an empty seat on one of the benches on the grassy strip facing the ocean. It was a public space where people brought chairs and blankets and picnic lunches, stretching out in the sun to enjoy the hazy warmth of its rays. Children played happily on the rocks below, climbing and jumping, ignoring the shouted admonitions from their adult minders to be careful, not to go too close to the water.

Today's sky was its usual bright blue, the sun overhead warm, and the wind coming off the ocean waves brushed Jason's cheek like the soft caress of a woman. With his eyes closed against the brightness of the sun, he let his mind drift off into space, his worries left behind on earth. When someone slid onto the bench next to him, Jason felt the presence without opening his eyes. He had been dreading this meeting since the text came this morning.

"Are you asleep?" the newcomer asked.

"No," Jason said, opening his eyes and straightening his back. The brightness of the sun was a shock to his eyes. He had forgotten his sunglasses.

Scott Forsythe was wearing his sunglasses, also a grey baseball cap that said *Key West*. His tanned legs stretched out from under dark canvas shorts, and he was wearing a white pullover sweater. On his feet were grey sailing sandals.

"Have you been out sailing this morning?" Jason asked.

Scott shook his head. "Later today I'll take the boat out for a run. I can relax out there, get away from all this. The wind is perfect today," he said with satisfaction.

Jason resisted the urge to close his eyes again. "I've met with Cameron," he announced, staring ahead.

"I thought you would. What is he saying about all this?"

"He seems happy with us going ahead as if nothing had

114

happened. Like Althea's not dead. He's amazing."

"I wouldn't know. I've never met him."

"Some days I wish I never had."

"Then you wouldn't have your share of the money."

"And what good is that to me?"

"I don't know. What do you do with it?"

"Most of it's socked away so one day I can do whatever the hell I want with my life. To tell you the truth, I'd been thinking a lot lately about getting out. I mean even before this happened."

"Make sure the money's in a place far away where the feds can't find it."

"It is. Don't worry."

"So are you getting out? This would be the time."

Jason turned to study Scott's face. Was he joking?

"Are you joking with me?"

"No. It's your life, man. Disappear. It's been done before."

"What about you if this whole thing falls apart? What would you do if the feds get on to us?"

"Get on my boat, move to my island and continue doing what I do now - make lots of money for myself. I'd still do the day trading, which is how I can camouflage the insider stock trades I've been doing for Tanner. My part in all this has always been for my own amusement."

"Oh, I see. You've been having fun."

"You do know that I'm filthy rich?"

"I assumed so," Jason said. "Well, good for you."

"This money I make from Tanner is for my caprices."

"Your caprices," Jason repeated. "I have to remember that one."

"I like to enjoy life. Althea understood that."

"There's one problem about all this. The thing that keeps me tethered. We've been breaking the law."

"But so far no one knows it."

"They'd certainly find out if Tanner went out of business. All the clients would want their money back. It's not all there anymore."

"But you've saved your profits. And in a manner of speaking, I could come up with mine."

"What about all the money Althea and Cameron have taken as their 30% shares?"

Scott sighed. "Definitely not there, I suppose."

"Althea has been living very well. Cameron, too. That's why he wants to keep everything going the way it is."

"How is he planning to do that?"

"He wants me to assume Althea's role. I'd tell the clients I can be the new stock picker."

"You?"

"Cameron said the clients would believe me if I said that Althea taught me all her secrets. She planned to retire while she was still young and groomed me to continue on in her place."

"And you're thinking of this, are you?"

"I haven't had time to consider it," Jason lied.

"I don't know. It seems a stretch."

"Then how do you think we're going to be able to keep going without Althea as Newport's guru of investing?"

"You know, Cameron's plan has just given me an idea." Scott looked pleased. "Suppose we make it look as if Althea was the only perpetrator in this. You could re-cook the books, couldn't you?"

"Pretend I didn't know anything about it? That Althea stole millions from the investors, and I didn't notice?"

"She is dead. We could blame anything on her."

CHAPTER XXXIII

Jason sat upright and looked directly at the other man. "You know, you and Cameron really take the cake. I know for a fact that both of you had affairs with Althea." Cava paused. "Probably yours was still current." Scott looked away. "I thought so. You were happy to enjoy that creamy body of hers. She probably even thought you had real affection for her. And now it appears you would step down hard on her memory and trash her reputation."

"You are forgetting that if all this comes out, her reputation and memory are going to be trashed anyway. So why should we all suffer along with her?"

"I don't believe this."

"Come on, Jason. She wouldn't have done the same to us? If one us was murdered the other night?"

"No, I really don't think so." When Scott didn't answer, Jason said, "Let me ask you a question."

"What?"

"Who do you think killed Althea?"

"I don't know. It didn't make any sense to me."

"You don't think somebody is on to us, do you?"

"Who?"

"One of the investors."

Scott contemplated the idea. "If that's the case, that would mean the killer ought to be going after all of us."

"Maybe we should watch our backs."

"Nah," Scott said, shaking his head. "How would anybody figure this out? One of us would have had to talk. And we didn't."

"No, I'm sure of that." Jason was quiet. His head was beginning to throb from staring into the sun. Maybe he should go for a drive in the convertible later to clear his mind.

"We do need to have a plan," he continued. "The clients have to be managed so they don't get nervous. The first few days after

Althea's death... well, people are going to be respectful, aren't they? But after this week, I'll be the one to have to be ready with some answers. Nobody knows that you and Cameron have any part in this."

"The answer you give them is that Althea always has had her investing plan with a year's projections. It's only May now, so it's going to be good until the end of the year. You can lay it all out in writing. Work up an executive summary." He smacked his hands together. "Rich people love to get executive summaries. Trends in the markets, economic forecasts. The kind of crap I heard you bullshitting people with the other night on the boat."

"I could certainly do that report," Jason said, now eager to have a task that he could begin on Monday at the office.

"I can reach out to the other investors." Scott's voice was excited now. "They all believe I've got my money invested with Tanner. And I wouldn't leave it there if I felt it wasn't safe. I'll call Melody Granger and put the bug in her ear. She's always trusted my advice since Alfie died. I'll tell her I've talked to you and you have everything under control. I'll insist that I have confidence in you to execute what Althea was planning to do."

"Thanks," Jason said sarcastically.

"I'll also remind her how much I know Althea relied on you."

"That's good of you."

"Come on, Jason," Scott said, patting the other man's arm. "You and I need each other if we don't want to start making plans to leave the country anytime soon. We need to buy ourselves some time."

"I'd like a little breathing room."

"We'll get it, don't worry. We shouldn't make any decisions in haste. Meanwhile I'll call Hamilton Dalworthy, too. Take him out to lunch at the club. Ham trusts my judgement when it comes to money, too. I'll be able to convince him that if I'm not worried about my investments, he shouldn't be either. Meanwhile you write that report and circulate it among the investors. Put it in a fancy folder with lots of charts and have it hand delivered to their houses. You watch. I bet the geese will swallow it."

"The geese?"

"Oh, just an expression Althea used the other night when we were walking over to *Kandu*. We'd just had a drink at the Clarke Cooke House. It's not important. I don't know why I thought of it."

Scott stopped and looked sad. "She was a fantastic woman. She meant a lot to me, and I'm sorry about what I said before. I am going to miss her."

"Good."

"You will, too. Isn't it lonely in that house all by yourself?"

"Kind of. The housekeeper went to stay with her daughter for the weekend. Eva was pretty upset. Besides everything else that's going on, I need to start thinking about moving out."

"Why would you want to do that?"

"Because it's Althea's house."

"Not anymore."

"Yeah, now it belongs to whoever inherited it from her." When Jason saw that Scott looked genuinely surprised, he asked, "Why are you looking at me like that?"

"Because I thought you knew. Althea left *Di Sole* to you."

Jason's heart skipped a beat. Did she realize how much he loved the house? "It can't be true."

"Oh, it is, my young friend."

"You know the terms of her will?"

"I know you get the house. As far as all the other assets, most of it goes to her niece."

"Her niece? I never heard her mention a niece."

"Her brother's daughter. He and Althea didn't get on, she thought he was an asshole. But he has a daughter. She'd be in high school now. Althea planned to send her to college. The kid wants to be a doctor. Someone who works in Africa in the poor villages."

"That's admirable. Do you think this niece will be able to see any of the money?"

"It depends where it is."

"Who would know about all this?"

"Her lawyer. He drew everything up for her. That's how you come to get the house. The niece would be living in Africa so Althea figured why not leave it to someone who lived in Newport. I've already got a big house so she thought of you."

"That was generous of her."

"Yeah, you could say that."

"Who's her lawyer?"

"Lewis Crenshaw. He was John Ainsley's lawyer so Althea always went to him, too. I'm sure he'll be contacting you soon enough to discuss the disposition of the house. I don't even think it has a mortgage. Very soon, Mr. Cava, you should own your very own Newport mansion free and clear."

CHAPTER XXXIV

It was approaching five o'clock in the afternoon when Hank Nightingale drove through the ornate iron gates of Kenwood. Despite its reincarnation as the Inn At Kenwood Court, a simple stone marker continued to identify the estate with its original one word name. Although Hank understood how Caroline would choose to manufacture a new, fancier one to appeal to potential guests, he much preferred the original: Kenwood. But he knew that people expected Newport to be a fancy place. The tourists came to see the mansions after all, and he supposed lodging at a *Court* had a palatial sound to it.

The grove of elderly beech trees, their spring leaves already open and their branches hanging low to the ground, stood to the left of the expansive front lawn. To his right was the old stone gatehouse, now unused. As Hank turned up the winding drive he could see Louise pruning the plantings along the front of the house. There were several varieties of green shrubbery, the only one which he recognized being some holly bushes which he always associated with winter. Stone planters on either side of the front steps were filled with the cheery shapes of tulips. White, yellow and red heralds of the current season.

The detective parked the car on the gravel drive and got out.

"Hank, hello" Louise called. "I was hoping we would catch up with you today."

"I know you've been anxious to hear an update about the case. This is the first chance I've had all day since I got Caroline's phone message this morning. I figured I'd better come and deliver my news in person."

"That means it's not good." She looked anxiously up at him.

"I'm afraid not, Louise. We've charged Teddy Ainsley."

"Oh, dear. Hank, are you sure?"

"Everything points in that direction. He had motive.

Opportunity. And there was so little time elapsed between when he and Althea Tanner were overheard arguing and then when the body was discovered." He looked at her, hoping she understood. "We had no choice, Louise. The warrant was issued today. That means a judge believes our case is strong."

"Yes, I see your point of view, Hank. But you don't know Teddy. If you did, you wouldn't believe him capable of murder."

"Caroline has said much the same thing." He shook his head ruefully. "But you see I don't know Teddy. I only know my evidence."

Louise remained silent. Hank was sorry to cause her anguish, but he had to do what he saw to be his duty.

"Is Caroline inside?" he finally asked.

"Yes. Last I saw her she was in the library."

"I'd better go and find her and get this over with. She's not going to be happy with me."

"Be patient with her, Hank. She cares deeply for her friends. She's loyal to them." Then she smiled at him. "As you well know."

"Yes, I wish I could come up with another suspect, but I can't. It is interesting, this case. That it's resolved itself so quickly. There's been no chance for her to use her detecting skills. I missed sharing things with her."

"You still can. She wants to find the real murderer."

"Has she suggested anything to you?"

Louise looked at him carefully. "You'd better ask her that question yourself."

Hank pondered the meaning of Louise's parting remark as he opened the front door of Kenwood. The library was to the right down a hallway beyond the morning room. The house was a grand affair, but to his liking as the decoration and furnishings were not as ornate as many of the famous mansions in Newport. There were marble floors and rich gold colors on the walls, but the inn had a lived-in look that welcomed its guests.

When he reached the door to the library, he could hear Caroline talking.

"Help yourself to the drinks' cabinet, Mr. Talbot. Ice is in that small refrigerator behind the paneled door, and glasses are up here. Please make yourself at home."

Hank stepped back into the hallway. Since he assumed Caroline wouldn't be sitting down with Mr. Talbot for cocktails, he would wait for her to come out of the room.

His prediction was correct, and within a few minutes Caroline strode purposefully out into the hallway. Hank stepped forward and startled, she lurched against the wall.

"Caroline, I didn't mean to surprise you. I heard you talking to someone about a drink, and I thought I'd wait for you out here."

She looked at him warily, and the reaction he dreaded her having was clear on her face. This conversation was going to be difficult.

"Can we go to your office? Or maybe upstairs?" He meant the sitting room in the family quarters.

"Upstairs is fine." She studied his face. "It looks like I need to offer you a drink."

"It wouldn't be turned down," he said appreciatively. "It is that time of the day."

He followed her back to the front foyer and up the grand staircase which led to the second floor. Upstairs they crossed the gallery and went into the family sitting room. He knew she kept a drinks' cabinet there as well as the large one downstairs for the inn's guests.

"I can't be seen raiding my own drinks' cabinet in the library," she had once told him. "I don't think it makes the best impression on the guests."

"What can I get you?" Caroline asked as Hank stood waiting in the middle of the room.

"Vodka. On the rocks."

She opened a small cabinet door and he heard the familiar tinkle of ice cubes.

"Sit down, Hank," she directed him.

He sat on one of the upholstered chairs near the open window. The family quarters overlooked the Cliff Walk and the ocean beyond it. The air inside the room had the smell of the sea air drifting in from outside.

"Here," she said, putting a rock glass filled with ice and clear liquid on the table in front of him. She was holding a tall gin and tonic. He took a long drink while she settled herself on the sofa.

"Tell me what has been happening."

Hank took in a deep breath and looked directly at her. "You're not going to like it, but we've had to arrest Teddy Ainsley." He stopped to watch Caroline's reaction which was not as dramatic as he thought it might be. She'd had the whole day to prepare herself for bad news.

"What happens now?" she asked, her voice betraying no emotion. "Does he get out on bail?"

"The hearing will be Monday. I expect the judge to set bail. Teddy is not a risk to flee. The charge is second degree murder, not first."

"You've notified the family."

"Yes. They sent their lawyer to the station earlier today, and he made sure we did things according to the book. It's unfortunate this is the weekend and they have to wait until Monday for the bail hearing, but there's nothing we can do about that."

"How is Teddy?"

"He's confused, if I had to say what my impression is. Caroline, he doesn't seem to remember everything about what happened on that boat, the argument and what happened afterwards."

"What does that mean?"

"I'm sorry, Caroline, but you have to consider the possibility that Ainsley killed Althea Tanner and doesn't realize it."

CHAPTER XXXV

"That's impossible," Caroline said angrily. "You're manufacturing a scenario you don't have evidence to prove." Caroline paused, staring at him with wide eyes. "Do you? Have any evidence."

"I have him arguing with Althea. That you know firsthand. Then I have him the last to see Althea alive."

"You've eliminated everyone else on that boat. No one went below after Teddy?"

"It doesn't appear that way."

"Appear? That doesn't sound as if you are completely certain."

"What else can I do?"

"Look at other suspects. Other people had motives."

"They did?" he asked, surprised at the statement. "Tell me a motive and who had it."

"Well," she began, her voice wavering slightly. "I have some information for you."

"Yes?" he asked, leaning forward in his chair. "New information?"

Now she took a drink from her glass. He wondered what she was girding herself to say.

"You know Jonathan Granger, right?"

"The gigolo?"

"The what? Hank, what are you talking about?"

"I'm sorry," he said, quickly regretting the spoken comment that had escaped his thoughts. "It's only something somebody said. Forget I repeated it. Go on."

Caroline frowned at him. "It's something that occurred yesterday... the day after the murder." Hank was listening intently. "Jon happened to see Jason Cava doing something very suspicious."

"What was it?"

"He, Jon that is, happened to be on Bellevue Avenue near the

Tanner office. He saw Jason driving away from there in his car."

"If Mr. Granger saw something, he should have come to me. I gather instead, he came to see you."

"That's right," she said uneasily.

"Because you two became such good friends on the boat Thursday night."

"Hank, that's not fair! Jon and I talked for a while. He's a very friendly young man. And a *married* man I might add."

"You seemed to have spent a lot of time in his company. You overheard the argument between Teddy and Althea while you were together. Then you were standing near the stairs when Alex Seeger ran up... together."

"You seem to know a lot about what I did on that boat." Her face flushed.

"I took statements from the witnesses, don't forget."

"About me and Jonathan Granger?" She stood up and walked away from him across the room. "You know if you had been there, I would have been talking to you."

"Caroline," Hank said in as calm a voice as he could manage, "you said you had information that could help Teddy. Why don't you tell me what it is? Then if it seems relevant, I'll go to see Mr. Granger."

Caroline turned to face him. She squared her shoulders and began talking briskly. "Here it is. Jon followed Jason Cava out of Newport to the train station at Kingston."

"Why would Granger do that?" When he saw her face darken, he said, "It doesn't matter. Tell me what happened."

"The fact is that Jason Cava picked up a man from the train at Kingston yesterday around noontime. Then the two of them went to a restaurant to have lunch. After lunch Jason put the man back on the train."

"That's it?"

"Why? Ask yourself why."

"Maybe he's a client of Tanner who had some concerns after the death of the head of the company that manages all his money. He was looking for some reassurances about his investments." He sat back in the chair. "I'm sorry but I don't see the significance of this at all."

"You don't think the man from the train could be a co-

conspirator in the murder?"

"That's a big leap. Is that what Granger thinks, too?"

"As a matter of fact, he does. And I agree with him that the whole business is extremely suspicious. Why didn't this man come to the Tanner office in Newport? Why did he and Jason Cava have to have lunch in an out of the way place where no one would see them?"

"For any number of perfectly good reasons."

While Caroline looked querulous, Hank continued. "One, this man's time was limited. He's a very busy person. He had to catch the train to get back to where he came from."

"New York."

"He came from New York?"

"We think so."

"*We do?*" he asked evenly.

"Yes, we do, Hank," Caroline said firmly. "This is a clue, and I'm surprised you can't see it. It means something."

"But what?"

"That's what you need to investigate. We think this meeting connects Jason to Althea's death."

"We do?" he asked again. This time his tone had hardened.

"Hank, I can see that you don't like Jon, but don't let that cloud your judgement."

"I'll try. But what is the bigger picture here?" Caroline glowered at him. "O.K.," he said raising his hands in a defensive motion. "You said that we need another motive. Tell me. Why do you think that Jason Cava would have murdered Althea Tanner?"

"It could be something to do with the business. Perhaps he was... stealing? Could it be as simple as that? Althea found out he was stealing money from the investors."

"Nothing so far has led us in that direction. But I suppose we could look into the state of the business. We have forensic accountants who can do that, but it's tough to get one quickly. They work for the state, and there's a waiting list to get them assigned to cases."

"Even a murder case?"

"I'll talk to the chief. That could give us priority. But I'd have to have something more than evidence of this story of a lunch to request an investigation into the finances of Tanner Associates."

"Hank, as I understand it, Tanner had tens of millions of dollars under management. The head of the firm is dead. Murdered. And who's running things now?" Hank waited for her answer. "Well, I'm guessing it has to be Jason Cava - who can now cover up anything he wants to."

CHAPTER XXXVI

As soon as Hank left Kenwood Caroline phoned Jonathan Granger to tell him about Teddy's arrest. Jon's reaction was what she had expected.

"I told you the police would jump to conclusions once they knew about the argument between Teddy and Althea."

"I've talked to Lt. Nightingale, Jon. It doesn't look like he's planning to look any further for suspects. Even though I told him what you saw when you followed Jason Cava to the train station in Kingston."

"You did?" Granger sounded surprised. "What was his reaction?"

"Well," Caroline began, unsure of how much criticism she wanted to level at Hank. "He said it wasn't evidence. A lunch between two men who could have had good reason to get together to talk about financial matters."

"In a restaurant where nobody would see that they were together," Jon scoffed. "Really, Caroline, I hope you're not agreeing with him now."

"No. Not at all." She explained about the forensic accountants which the department could call in if there was evidence to provide cause for suspicion. Hank would need some solid information before he could request such an investigation.

"So it's up to us to get some," Jon concluded.

"I know, but how?"

"I should be able to learn something. After all, Melody's got an account with Tanner. That's a start."

"Can you ask her about it?"

"I've never shown much interest in her investments before. I don't have a head for figures. But I could begin to show interest. After all, with Althea dead, Melody must be wondering what is going to happen next with the firm."

"Has she said anything?"

"Not to me, but I know she's been talking to Scott Forsythe. You know who he is, one of Tanner's other clients. He's rich as Croesus. Did you meet him Thursday night?"

"Yes, Althea introduced us."

"Scott telephoned earlier today and Melody had quite a long conversation with him. I can ask her about it tonight." He paused. "What about this? Melody loves to entertain. I can suggest that we have some of the other investors for a dinner party to talk about what's been happening. I'll get them talking about Cava, see what I can pick up from them."

"And you think Melody will do it?"

"Absolutely. She'll jump at the idea. Let's see now. Who we should invite? Forsythe, definitely. Tristan Marchand and Selena Dawson."

"What about Alex Seeger and his wife?"

"Melody doesn't really know them."

"I expect they are part of another social set."

"I'm afraid so."

"Leslie Seeger was quite friendly to me at the party. Maybe I can find an excuse to talk to her."

"Good idea, Caroline."

"Although I will say that she was extremely complimentary on Althea Tanner's skills as an investment advisor."

"Yes, but that doesn't mean something dodgy wasn't going on with Althea's trusted assistant."

"True. I only hope, for Teddy's sake, we can find out what it is."

"Keisha, I want you to do some research for me."

"Yes, Lieutenant, what about?"

"I'd like to have all you can find about Tanner Associates."

Hank had come out of his office early on Monday morning and was standing in front of his sergeant's desk.

"Anything in particular?" she asked, reaching for a pad and pen.

"I'd like to understand how the firm is run. How the clients' money is invested. How Tanner makes *its* money."

"Right," Keisha said, making notes.

"I assume you can get some idea from the Internet of how this kind of business is run. You know, how financial advisors work, how they are paid. I've heard they charge fees, a percentage of the money they manage. But I want to know exactly how they work. How Tanner might have worked."

"How it still works," Keisha said.

"Yes, you're right. How it will continue in business. Assuming it will."

"Should I get in touch with Mr. Cava and ask him for this information."

"No." Hank shook his head. "Not now. We will have a talk with him, but I want to know a lot more before we do."

"I understand, sir. I'll get right on it."

"Tanner Associates is a private company so you won't learn much about it online, but whatever you can come up with, I need."

"I'd like to go to Bellehurst today to see how Margaret Ainsley is doing," Louise said as she stacked breakfast plates on the kitchen table. "Do you think you can spare me this afternoon, Caroline? I know the bail hearing is this morning, but Teddy should be home afterwards, don't you think?"

Caroline, who was busy rearranging the contents of the big steel refrigerator, made a muffled sound.

"I'm sorry, dear," Louise said in a loud voice, although it was Caroline's response which had been hard to hear. "Did you say that was all right?"

"Yes," Caroline said equally loudly, withdrawing her head from the appliance's innards. She gave a distasteful look at the inside before she shut the heavy door. "Yes. By all means. I'm sure your visit will be appreciated, and I would like to hear some news of how the family is coping."

"Do you want to come with me?"

"No. I don't know Margaret well; you do. You go and comfort her and see how Teddy is doing."

"If you can only come up with something, Caroline, something to exonerate Teddy. Do you think it's possible?"

"I told you that Jon and I are working on the Jason Cava angle." Caroline thought for a minute. "Maybe you can do something for me while you are at Bellehurst."

"Yes, what is it?" Louise asked.

"See what Margaret Ainsley knows about Jason Cava, Althea's

employee. He's been with Tanner for several years and I'd like to know anything she can tell us about him. His background, where he came from."

"I'll do my best."

"Try to get her impression of him."

"What are you thinking, Caroline? That he could have killed Althea?"

"I'm not sure. But there is something suspicious about Jason Cava, and I mean to learn what it is he's hiding."

CHAPTER XXXVII

A few miles across town, in the offices of Tanner Associates on Bellevue Avenue, Jason Cava was busy working on the summary report which Scott Forsythe wanted delivered into the hands of every client of the firm. Writing was a skill which Jason possessed, and he was happy to be focused on the kind of project which came easy to him.

That morning, he had awoken with an entirely new appreciation of his surroundings. Where once Jason had considered himself fortunate to be living at *Di Sole* because of Althea's generosity, he now knew that he could live in the house because it was his. It belonged to him.

Walking into the bathroom, taking a shower, choosing his clothes from the closet. All these everyday activities took on new meaning. He was in his own home. A home which he loved and never wanted to leave.

Eva Miller had returned that morning, and Jason had barely listened to her chatter as she questioned him about the future management of the house, the status of her employment, and his plans for meals for the week. Nothing she said mattered. Smiling, he had taken his breakfast out onto the terrace, sat in his favorite chair and stared out at the ocean, at peace with his surroundings.

Jason read over the preliminary outline which he had made. This report would lay out the financial plan for the firm supposedly in place until the end of the year. If he could phrase his words correctly, the investors would believe that their money was safe and sound for at least seven more months. And if they became convinced of that, then he and Scott would have enough time to make their plans to continue the scheme for however long they wanted. Once the investors saw that they were receiving their quarterly checks as usual, they would soon forget that Althea Tanner had ever played a role in the company.

Typing quickly on his keyboard, he began by describing the blossoming industries whose undervalued stocks Althea had purchased for her clients' portfolios. *Fast growers with room to grow*, he typed boldly, explaining that before she died Althea had made certain that millions of clients' dollars were safely stowed in these profitable investment categories.

Charts and diagrams were constructed to show the history of rising share prices. He quoted leading economists who gave their stamp of approval to such a philosophy of investing as was being followed by Tanner. *Althea's investment playbook* as he termed it. At the report's end, there was a wildly optimistic forecast of how much profit investors could expect by year's end.

Jason paused and stared at the computer screen. He wanted to applaud himself. This was a masterpiece worthy of Jules Verne or H. G. Wells. Once the investors digested these statistics and studied these positive figures, how could anyone in their right mind think it was a smart idea to withdraw their money from Tanner Associates' management?

In addition, he was comforted by the fact that Teddy Ainsley's current difficulties with the law made his demand for his money a moot question. He was fighting a charge of murder. And if Teddy were to be convicted, there would be no more talk of using $30 million of the Ainsley family's money to buy a Newport estate to be turned into a classical music center.

Jason read the draft of the report on his screen. His confidence was growing that the whole enterprise would work as long as the remaining three participants wanted it to work. He could live in his house in Newport while Cameron Epsberg found ways for them to make money from insider trading and Scott Forsythe executed the necessary stock purchases.

And Jason would continue to send out the quarterly checks, write the glowing reports, and assure the investors that there was no better place for their money.

In investing, he typed with a flourish on the final page of the report, *discipline is critical. It is the first rule: ignore your emotions and stay the course.*

CHAPTER XXXVIII

Louise Kent had never been fond of Bellehurst, the Ainsley family's Newport *cottage*. The massive stone house was built of rough cut grey granite and always reminded her of a fortress. The broad front piazza overlooked gardens designed by Frederick Law Olmsted, the designer of Central Park, but to Louise's eye the landscaping did little to soften the structure's hard appearance.

The house had been constructed for an Ohio banking family in 1883 and subsequently purchased by John Ainsley's grandfather for his growing family in 1913. Its original appearance was masculine, and through successive generations of owners, that look had never changed.

A uniformed maid opened the door to Louise and took her into the library where Margaret Ainsley was sitting on a high-backed royal blue upholstered chair. She was a woman of ample proportions with a bun of white hair and serious blue eyes.

The room was gloomy, paneled in mahogany with a dark red Turkey carpet on the floor. Despite the warmth of the day, a fire burned in the grate of the ornate fireplace. Over the mantel hung a large portrait of Teddy Ainsley at the age of six, dressed in a white sailor suit. He was standing tall, his straight yellow hair neatly brushed and his pale hazel eyes solemn and resolute.

Louise looked carefully at the eyes of the boy which stared out from the painting. Did this image of the young Teddy reflect the adult of today? Had they all missed some signal during the years that Teddy had determination beneath that gentle exterior?

"He was a beautiful child," Margaret Ainsley said, following Louise's gaze. "I hated to see him grow up."

"I had a boy, too," Louise said softly. "I think about him at that age often."

"Sit down, Louise. I'm sorry not to stand, but my sciatica is troublesome today."

Louise bent and touched the other woman's cheek with a kiss. "Hello, Margaret. It's good to see you."

"Thank you for coming, Louise. We haven't seen each other for far too long. It's unfortunate that it took this to bring us together."

Louise sat down. "This room hasn't changed a bit."

"No," Margaret said with a rueful smile. "I've no interest in decorating anymore. Valerie could care less... when she's here, that is. And Teddy... well, Teddy has his own ideas of keeping busy."

"The music center."

"Yes. I was so pleased when he came to me with the idea. *Of course I encouraged him.* It would finally give his life purpose." She shook her head. "If only Althea Tanner had been more understanding. For the life of me, I can't understand why she fought Teddy to release our money."

"Caroline suggested that it was part of the agreement for the investors. There had to be a waiting period while she liquidated the funds."

"Ahh," Margaret said loudly. The sound was guttural. "What agreement? John allowed her to handle our money. There's never been any kind of an agreement beyond that. After he died I kept her on. I thought it was what he would have wanted." She sighed and grasped her hands together.

"Tell me about her, Margaret. What was Althea Tanner like? I never met her."

"John loved the stock market. He fancied himself like that fellow who makes all the profitable stock investments. Warren Buffet." She smiled. "John thought he was another Warren Buffet. When he met Althea at the bank he was taken with her, a woman. But a woman who knew her way around the market."

"And she was that good? That John could be impressed by her."

Margaret nodded. "When I first met her, she wasn't what I had expected. Some frumpy woman with glasses and no make-up. That's what I had expected. But instead she was slim and blond and perfectly dressed." Now she shook her head. "I can still remember the first time she came here. I could only stare at her. John should have prepared me."

"Were you jealous?"

"That's a good question. And I think the answer is yes. I had heard John sing her praises for so long and as I said, I had this picture of who he was talking about. Then I saw her, and I began to think."

"What did you think?"

"Oh, the worst of course. John was never perfect as you know, Louise. He had his reputation. And it was well-deserved. But I'll tell you this. I never saw anything between them when they were together that suggested something untoward."

"So you liked her?"

"I can't say that. I thought she was a bit full of herself. Especially after John died, and she took on other clients. I hadn't expected that. But I realized there was no reason why she couldn't start her own firm. Our portfolio seemed to be doing well. How could I complain?"

"Did you ever meet the man who worked for her? Jason Cava is his name."

Margaret Ainsley thought for a minute. "He came here with Althea once a few years ago. He didn't say much."

"So you didn't get an impression of him?"

"Why is that important, Louise?"

"It's something Caroline wanted to know. She's hoping to find other suspects for Althea's murder."

"Bless her. And she thinks this Jason Cava could have something to do with it?"

"She doesn't know for sure, but... well, she's working on one theory that he could have been dishonest."

"You mean stealing money?"

Louise swallowed hard. "I can't say anything definite. It's just something Caroline is trying to explore. After all, Margaret, someone did kill Althea Tanner."

"And we know it wasn't my son."

"But until we find that someone, Teddy is the one the police want convicted."

Margaret Ainsley's eyes began to fill with tears. Louise got up from her chair and went to her side.

"Oh, Louise. They can't believe my Teddy would do such a thing."

Louise took one of Margaret's hands in hers. "How is Teddy doing?"

"He thinks it will all work out. That the police are still looking for the real murderer."

"And they're not," Louise said with a grim expression. "But Caroline is. And you've got to have faith in her, Margaret. She's solved murders before, and I believe she can do it again."

CHAPTER XXXIX

"Lieutenant," Keisha said, coming into Hank's office, "I've got something I think you ought to see."

Happy for the interruption, Hank Nightingale looked up from the stack of paperwork on his desk.

"What do you have?"

"It's a curious thing, Lieutenant. I don't know exactly what to make of it."

"So tell me. Maybe we can figure it out together."

"Well, it's this, sir. I've been on the phone with the state. Rhode Island has a Department of Business Regulations, which in turn has a banking and securities division."

"And?"

Keisha drew in a breath and let it out before speaking. "They've never heard of Tanner Associates."

Hank cocked his head. "What does that mean?"

"What I said, sir. There is no record of the firm being registered with that department."

"What about other departments?"

"Nothing. No record of incorporation, no company tax records. It's like they don't exist."

"How can that be? We know they exist. They take people's money and invest it. There have to be records of that. Somebody must oversight an investment firm like Tanner Associates."

"That's just it. They should. Lots of government bodies should have records on them. But so far I've turned up nothing."

"You have to keep looking. This doesn't make any sense."

"No, sir, it doesn't."

"All right. It's getting late. Why don't you shut this down for the day? We can start again tomorrow. These company records must exist somewhere."

"All right."

"How did you do understanding the fee structure? How Tanner is paid. Did you have time to do any research on that?"

"I've started. There is a lot on the Internet on how a fee structure is set. They can charge management fees, administrative fees. That's how I got into the state web site. I wanted to see what the state has to stay about regulations for this kind of company. The thing is, sir. Now I'm not sure exactly what kind of company Tanner is. Are they investment advisors? Money managers or financial consultants? And what's the difference? Do you think we can talk to Jason Cava now? I'd like to ask him about all this."

"There's time for that later." Hank shook his head. "This doesn't make any damn sense. Some of the wealthiest people in Newport have given their money to Tanner to... do what? Manage their wealth for them, that's the impression I got from Cava in his initial interview? Let me go back and look at my notes."

"According to the state, if you manage client assets, you have to go through a licensing process. There are exams and everything. I think I understand that correctly."

"You talked to someone at the state?"

"Yes, a very knowledgeable woman who spent a lot of time on my request. But she got back to me with nothing. She was as mystified as I was. I'm thinking she's going to go further with this. Alert somebody that this firm exists." Keisha paused. "Do we know how much money Tanner has?"

"No, why?"

"Well Ms. Arden pointed out that if more than $110 million is under management, then the federal Securities and Exchange Commission has regulations for that as well."

"I seem to remember that Cava said that the minimum investment Tanner required was ten million. It wouldn't take too many investors to get to a hundred and ten." He shook his head again in amazement. "I think we've opened up something here."

"I agree, sir."

"The question is: what is it?"

The telephone call was a routine request for information on the availability of lodging. Caroline explained the choice of rooms available and the caller listened. Then he chose the most expensive room, which was the guest suite on the northeast corner of the inn facing the front. It had a large sitting room with a fireplace and a bedroom.

"I'll be in Newport on Wednesday," the male voice said. "What time is check-in?"

"Whenever you arrive, the room will be ready for you. There's no problem." The suite was currently unoccupied. "Will you be arriving by car?"

"Yes. I'll be driving up from New York City. I hope to get to Newport around noon. Do you serve lunch?"

"A full English breakfast is served in the dining room each morning. We do offer meal service for lunch and dinner if guests order it in advance. I should explain that the inn is not large. Most of our guests prefer to dine out. There are so many restaurants in town. I find that people are eager to try them all."

"I would like to order lunch. Something cold in case I get tied up in traffic getting out of the city."

"Of course. Do you have any food allergies? I've learned to ask."

"No, I'm fine on that score."

"Our cook does a lovely lobster salad plate."

"That sounds perfect for me. How is your cellar?"

"I can recommend a 2015 Muscadet."

"Muscadet? What an excellent suggestion. Have a bottle slightly chilled."

"All right," Caroline said. "We will have everything ready when you arrive. Now, can I get the name for the reservation?"

"Certainly. The name is Epsberg. Cameron Epsberg."

CHAPTER XL

Hank had been unsure whether he had the time to drive over to Easton's Beach for his lunchtime Tai Chi class on Tuesday. He was eager to be in the office to hear any new developments which Keisha might turn up with her research. But on second consideration, he decided that attending class would give him the opportunity to talk to Alex Seeger. He hadn't given up hope that Alex would remember something about the time just before he decided to go below to the head for the second time, whom he had seen, what they had been doing. He also wanted to ask him about Tanner Associates. The wealthy businessman must done some research into the company before committing at least $10 million of his money to their management.

As usual, despite his best attentions to be early, Hank arrived at class a few minutes after it had begun. He quickly began the stretching exercises and tried to clear his mind of the case and all the questions he had. It was amazing to him, but he was able to do just that. For forty minutes he moved and breathed in sync with the other participants, enjoying the bracing ocean air.

When the final Temple Exercises were complete, Hank closed his eyes and savored his body's feeling of contentment. Why couldn't he feel like this all the time? What was it about modern life that tied your neck and back into knots?

But he knew full well what it was: modern life itself. You couldn't get away from the tension and pressures of daily living. And he had read that there were even some theories that claimed such stress was good for you. Didn't famous actors throw up before they went on stage? Athletes, too, whose stomachs were a bowl of jelly before game time. And police officers also felt anxiety as they worked to bring justice to an often unjust world.

"Hank, I was hoping you'd come today."

Hank turned to see Leo Vargoff. He was dressed in the familiar

142

black fleece jacket and had already put his gold watch back on his wrist. Hank thought it interesting that the weight of it must interfere with the movements of Tai Chi. He strained for a look at it. He was determined to know the brand.

"Leo, hello. How are you?"

"I'm still reeling from Thursday night. I see you already made an arrest." Hank nodded. "Not who I would have suspected of doing a murder, but who knows what makes people snap. I mean, the Ainsleys are a prominent old family in Newport. Who would have thought one of them could be a murderer?"

"I've learned to keep an open mind about that kind of thing."

"I bet Ainsley's got a big time criminal lawyer."

"Yes, Christina Gaimo. Maybe you know the name. Her office is in Providence. You've got business interests over there, haven't you?"

"Sure, but I don't know her. I'll have to Google her."

"I think you can look for a lot of publicity about this case. The victim had notoriety as well."

"That's for sure."

"Can I ask you? Purely for professional reasons. Are you still interested in becoming a client of Tanner Associates?"

"Oh, no," Leo said, looking shocked. "I wouldn't go near the place now. I mean with all this going on. I wonder if there will be a firm after this."

"I wondered the same thing. But let me ask you this. How did you come to be interested in Tanner in the first place? As part of my investigation I've been looking into how they attract their clients."

"Alex. He was always bragging about how well he was doing in the markets. I don't know how well you know Alex, but he has to be number one in everything. He loved to boast to anyone who would listen about his investments doing so well with his firm of financial advisors. It definitely caught my attention, I can tell you. We both belong to the Chamber of Commerce over in Providence. Most of the members are always complaining about interest rates and bond prices, that kind of thing. No place safe to put your money these days. The market is up and down. But Alex always laughed and said he never had to worry about that."

"Because of Althea Tanner?"

"To hear him talk, that woman walked on water."

"And none of the other Chamber members expressed interest in going with her firm?"

"The threshold is a bit rich for most people, Hank. Ms. Tanner wouldn't even talk to you unless you could bring ten million to the table."

"And you're good with that?"

"I don't have a wife or children, Hank. Not even alimony to pay any exes. So I've been able to keep a lot of what I make."

"But you treated yourself to a nice watch," Hank said, gesturing toward the gold timepiece.

Leo held up his left wrist. He looked slightly embarrassed. "A fortieth birthday present to myself."

Hank looked at the watch's face closely now. Patek Philippe. Even Hank recognized the name of that brand.

"Well, I wish you luck finding a new investment advisor."

"Yeah. I have some ideas about that. And don't forget, Hank. You're coming out on my boat. Let me know a date when you're free. Hey, what about this weekend? Is that good?"

"Maybe Saturday. Can I get back to you on that?"

"Sure," Leo said, reaching into his pocket. "Let me give you my card. Call me at this number."

After Leo walked toward the parking lot, Hank made his way over to Alex Seeger. The instructor was talking to one of the other class participants, and Hank stood patiently waiting until the conversation was over.

"I saw," Alex said without preamble, "that you made an arrest."

"I see everybody reads the papers."

"Of course I'm following the case. After my part in it, I'd want to know how everything turned out. Teddy Ainsley... I never would have suspected him. I guess you're quite the copper after all."

Hank smiled. "I do my job."

"And you've got a strong case?" When Hank didn't reply, Seeger added, "Otherwise you wouldn't have arrested him. I guess I've answered my own question."

"It's in the hands of the prosecutor now."

"Can I expect a visit from Ainsley's lawyers? Because I was the one who found the body."

"Yes. But there's no need to be nervous about it. They'll ask you some questions. You could be a witness for the defense."

Alex was taken aback. "I don't want to be involved. I'd like to forget the entire thing ever happened." He shook his head. "It's not every day you find a dead body. Especially someone you know."

"No, it's not," Hank said sympathetically. "Listen, do you have a few minutes to talk?"

"Sure, Hank. What's up?"

"We're tying up some loose ends in the case, and I've been wondering about Tanner Associates. Specifically how they operate. You must know. You've been a client of theirs, for how long? Six years did you tell me?"

"Five."

"Five. Well, what did you know about Tanner when you first signed on with them? I remember your saying in the interview the night of the murder that your results with them were so much better than your previous advisor. Is that what you call these people, by the way? Advisors?"

"Yeah. They advise you on what to do with your money."

"But then they manage it for you?"

"Yeah."

"And you were satisfied they were... well, honest. Everything above board?"

"What are you suggesting, Hank? I'm not sure where you're going with this."

"I'm not sure myself, Alex. It's just that Tanner doesn't seem to be a conventional financial operation. I don't know the difference between advising, managing, consulting. Did you check out the background of the firm? If they were registered with the state, for example?"

"No, actually I didn't think it was necessary to check with the state. I knew from talking to one of their clients what their record for results was."

"Who was that? Can I ask?"

"Rupert Harlow. He wasn't one of the people on the boat last Thursday. Leslie was on a fund raising committee with him for the Fort Adams sailing museum. I got talking to him at one of their events and he recommended Althea Tanner. Said she was the best."

"And that was good enough for you."

"Yes."

"Do you plan on staying with the firm after what's happened?"

"As a matter of fact, something was delivered to the house this morning from Tanner. A glowing report on what to expect for the rest of the year."

"Really?" Hank's eyebrows rose. "That's quick work."

"Not really. The money Althea invested is still invested. The report lays out what the results of those investments are expected to be for this year."

"So the firm is going to carry on?"

"Yes."

"Under whose management? Jason Cava?"

"He signed the report. For the present he'll oversee the money the same way that Althea set everything up."

"That's interesting. And you think he'll do a good job?"

"Well, I have some time to decide, don't I? I'd hate to move too quickly. The report promises we won't be at a disadvantage. Our money is still where Althea put it so we should be able to anticipate the same results as always."

"Jason Cava must be an extremely talented young man."

"Althea had confidence in him. She ran that whole operation with only herself and him. He had to know everything about what she was doing."

"That's interesting," Hank said. "That's very interesting."

CHAPTER XLI

Wearing a dark suit and one of his few ties, Jason sat stiffly in the waiting room of Crenshaw, Howard & Dance. Ever since the morning phone call from Lewis Crenshaw's secretary asking him to set up an appointment, he had been on pins and needles waiting for the late afternoon meeting to take place. Although nothing had been said about Althea's will, he was sure that was the reason for the summons. The anticipation of hearing Althea's attorney confirm that he was in fact the owner of her home was so exciting that he had been unable to eat any food all day.

Lewis Crenshaw was a dry, humorless man of average height and weight with thinning blonde hair combed carefully across the top of his head in an effort to cover the pale white skin underneath it. The attorney was wearing a navy blue suit, white shirt and a dark purple tie peppered with tiny white shapes that looked like wheel gears. Jason studied the peculiar shapes as he sat across the big oak desk from the older man.

There were no pleasantries exchanged, no expressions of sympathy on the loss of Jason's employer. Instead Crenshaw delivered the details of Althea's will which pertained to him and swiftly affirmed that Jason was indeed the present owner of *Di Sole*.

"Title passed to you immediately on Althea's death," Crenshaw said in his laconic tone.

Jason allowed himself to smile. "Do I own the property free and clear? Are there any mortgages?"

"None. You may, of course, want to mortgage the property yourself."

Jason had no intention of doing that. He couldn't imagine the bank scrutiny which that decision would release on his financial affairs.

"I'm fine for now," he said.

There were documents to sign and Jason sat patiently as the

lawyer re-examined the papers before passing them to Jason for his signature. Then Crenshaw carefully studied each again as if some change could have been made during the time in which the document was out of his hands. Finally when everything was completed to his satisfaction, he put copies for Jason into a large white envelope.

"I appreciate your help in all this," Jason said as he accepted the envelope. "I had no idea I was to inherit the house. Althea never said."

"She was a young woman, Mr. Cava. If she had decided to marry, her testamentary affairs would have changed."

Jason had never seen Althea as the marrying type. She was too independent to share. "Of course," was all he said aloud.

"But unfortunately Ms. Tanner is gone." Was there finally a hint of sadness in Althea's lawyer's voice over the loss of his client? "Such a tragic business."

"She was so alive," Jason said. He'd found that this assessment of Althea was one that everyone seemed to agree with. "No one can replace her."

First thing on Wednesday morning, Caroline went into Cameron Epsberg's suite. She liked to put the finishing touches in the inn's rooms so that when the guests arrived, they felt as if they had arrived to stay at the Kents' home, not at a commercial lodging.

Lindsay had already carried up vases of fresh flowers. Once they were strategically placed, Caroline made a trip down to the library to select some books. Not knowing Cameron Epsberg's tastes in literature, she decided on some American history volumes, a biography of Cole Porter, and two recent best selling novels. She added a copy of Thornton Wilder's *Theophilus North*, a work of fiction which takes place in Newport in the summer of 1926. On the coffee table she arranged several issues of *Newport Life* magazines and a large picture book on Newport estates.

In the bedroom, on a tray on the dresser, Caroline put a tin of cookies and a box of chocolates. She usually put out a decanter of sherry and glasses but something told her that Mr. Epsberg, with his taste for French wine, was not a sherry drinker. After giving it some thought, she decided that she would wait until he arrived and then determine what might be an appropriate late night drink.

When the suite met with her approval, Caroline went down to

the kitchen to see how Mattie was coming along with preparations for lunch.

The cook had four steaming red lobsters cooling on the kitchen counter. Louise had gone early that morning to the Newport Lobster Shack, the fishermen's co-op on Long Wharf, to buy the fresh shellfish. Not only would Mattie use some of the succulent lobster meat for the luncheon salad, but she would use the rest to make lobster pie for their own dinner that evening. Caroline felt hungry just thinking about the sauce which was similar to Lobster Newburg and scandalously delicious. The dish was one of Mattie's best, and Caroline decided to see if Hank was free to join them that evening.

And that relaxing dinner would be just the occasion for her to learn more about his case.

CHAPTER XLII

Cameron Epsberg arrived at a few minutes before one. Caroline had been periodically checking the driveway from the front facing windows in the dining room since noon, and she was relieved when she finally saw a big black BMW sedan moving slowly up the gravel drive. As she headed toward the front door, Caroline called for Lindsay to go to the kitchen to let Mattie know that their guest was here.

The man who got out of the BMW was handsome and confident-looking. A smiling Caroline came down the steps to greet him, introducing herself and thanking him for coming to stay. Epsberg was wearing grey slacks and a dark blue blazer, his cream dress shirt open at the neck to reveal a generous swath of white chest hair. As his crystal blue eyes ran a practiced gaze over her, Caroline hardened her smile and asked about his luggage.

"I've only brought an overnight bag. I can manage it." He was looking at the house. "Lovely place you've got here. What's its history?"

"Kenwood was designed by Richard Morris Hunt in the 1880s. It has been in my late husband's family since then. After his death I began running the inn." She paused and then decided to add, "With my mother-in-law's help."

"I see," Cameron said gravely. He seemed unable to think of anything to say in response so he opened the trunk and took out a small Louis Vuitton Keepall traveling bag.

"Let's go inside," Caroline said. "I'm sure you'll be wanting your lunch after your drive. Did you run into traffic?"

"No," Epsberg said as he followed her up the steps and into the foyer. "After all my good intentions of being on the road by eight, I was delayed by things at the office."

Cameron stood in the foyer, appraising the inside of the house. Lindsay appeared and took his bag.

"The weather is pleasant today, Mr. Epsberg," Caroline said. "I thought you might like to eat out on the veranda. No one else is in for lunch today so the dining room might be a bit lonely. The view is wonderful from the rear of the house. It faces the ocean."

"Sounds fine. And call me Cameron by the way."

"Yes, certainly. Now, there's a powder room just there." She pointed to a door off the foyer. "To get out to the veranda, just walk past these stairs, go through the great hall and then to the right into the salon. The French doors at the back of the room lead out to the veranda." Cameron nodded. "Is there anything else I can do for you?"

"No," he answered. "I'm still admiring your house. Perhaps later I can see all of it."

"Most of the ground floor is open to the guests for their use. There is the library, a conservatory, and the morning room in the west wing. The billiard room is at the back of the house." Epsberg's eyebrows went up. "Do you play?" She knew she ought to have said *Do you play, Cameron?*

"I have. Does the billiard room have the original furnishings?"

"Yes, everything is quite original. We can see all the rooms after lunch if you like."

"Yes, but I think later this afternoon if you don't mind."

"Of course. I'm sure you want to get settled in your room after lunch. Lindsay's taken your bag up. There's no hurry to see the house. I'll be here whenever you are ready."

Caroline smiled graciously and didn't wait to see if Epsberg needed the powder room. She turned toward the east wing, went into the dining room and on through to the kitchen.

"What the hell is he doing here?"

"Please don't get upset. That's not what we need now."

"Was this your idea, Jason?"

"No, Scott, it wasn't. He decided all on his own."

"But why? I thought we had long agreed that he and I were never to meet. No connection between us. Lord knows you take enough precautions when there is communication between the two of you."

"I think he's nervous about going forward."

"Is that what he said?"

"No, but I could hear it in his voice. He wants to be reassured that I - we - can handle things from this end."

"Everyone on this end is very reassured. I've been talking to the clients, and no one shows any signs of withdrawing their investments. Did you tell him about the report you sent out?"

"The conversation was short. It always is."

"So what's the plan?"

"We'll meet him this afternoon. I've got a place picked out."

"We'll be seen."

"Don't worry," Jason said into the telephone receiver and explained the plan.

CHAPTER XLIII

Once luncheon had been served to Cameron Epsberg on the veranda, Caroline went into her office hoping to do some research online into some ideas she had on restoring the loggia, the open air room on the second floor which had fallen into disrepair. The furniture was shabby and the awning had long been removed, its mechanism rusted. While Caroline and Louise sometimes sat out there in the evening, the space was off limits to guests. Caroline had gotten tired of apologizing for the loggia's poor condition and had been hoping to set some money aside this summer for the work needed to make the room both welcoming and safe.

She was studying several house design web sites when the door was flung open and Jon Granger strode into the room.

"Caroline," he said, "sorry for the interruption, but your maid said you were in here. I knew where to come so I told her not to bother showing me."

Caroline, deep in concentration on ironwork lights and patterned tile, stared up at him.

"I hope you're not too busy to talk. It really is important." He sighed loudly. "I spent all morning with Melody at a lecture at the Preservation Society. God you wouldn't believe how boring Consuelo Vanderbilt really was!"

"Jon," Caroline said, "sit down. I hate when you pace."

"Yes, yes. But really Caroline, when you hear what I've come to tell you, you'll start pacing as well."

"Have you learned something important?"

Granger exhaled deeply without sitting down. As if he found the room's walls confining, Jon's long legs moved in the direction of the windows which looked out onto the back lawn.

"Last night Melody gave her dinner party, the one where we invited some of the other Tanner investors," he began.

"I didn't know it was last night."

"I should have told you, but really, getting it together on short notice was mountains of work, and she had me running around." He stopped for a breath. "But you don't want to hear about that."

"Jon, I want to hear your news."

"This is it. And I think you will see that we have found our motive."

Caroline's heart began to pound. "The motive?" she repeated.

"Jason Cava inherits Althea's house," Granger declared with triumph in his voice. "And it's all his."

"You mean it's paid for?"

"There's no mortgage, if that's what you mean."

"Is it worth a great deal of money? I don't know the house."

"Millions. Six, seven. Maybe more. It's stunning. I adore it. Motive for murder most definitely."

"How did you find this out?"

"Scott Forsythe. After he had a few drinks last night, and he started telling everyone how things were going to be absolutely smashing with Jason Cava in charge because he would do everything in the manner Althea had been doing. He had her financial plan and all that rubbish. Cava wrote up some report that made everything seem too good to be true. He sent it around to all the investors. Melody thought it was wonderful."

"I'd like to read it."

"It's a waste of time," Jon said, waving his hand to dismiss it. "Anyway, someone at the party asked if Jason would want to stay on in Newport. Scott said surely he would now that he owned *Di Sole*... that's what Althea called the house, you know."

"All our speculation about Jason's stealing money and afraid of being caught. Well, that's not his motive then, is it? Tanner's finances don't have anything to do with the murder. "

"It's the house. The bloody house." He grinned. "We have him now, Caroline."

"It does make sense," she agreed.

"Caroline?" Jon shrieked. "Who is that man?"

"What man?" Caroline asked, confused by the abrupt turn in the conversation. "Jon, what are you talking about?"

Granger was pointing out the window. "There's a man walking across your lawn. Who is he? Where did he come from?"

Caroline joined him at the window. "Oh, that's one of the guests who arrived today. He must be having a walk around the grounds."

Jon grabbed Caroline hard by the arm. She squealed in pain, but he ignored her and began dragging her toward the door. "How do we get out there?"

As they struggled through the office doorway together, Caroline pointed to an exit door by the back stairs. Wriggling free of Jon's grasp, she started rubbing her arm.

"Caroline!" Jon shouted, grabbing her arm again. "What is his name?"

"That's Cameron Epsberg. I told you, Jon. He's a guest. That's all."

"He's no bloody guest. That's the man from the train."

CHAPTER XLIV

"Jon, what are we doing?" Caroline demanded as they came outside onto the back lawn.

"We've got to know where he's going."

Epsberg was walking down the path which led through the shrubbery and onto the Cliff Walk.

"That's the way to the Cliff Walk," Caroline answered. "It looks to me like he's taking a walk after lunch for some exercise. He's been cooped up in a car all morning, driving up from New York."

"Quick. Get your skates on. We've got to see which way he goes."

"Are you sure it's the same man you saw, Jon?" Caroline asked as she hurried to keep up with Granger's long strides.

"Yes, and he's going to meet Cava. I know it."

As they reached the opening in the shrubbery, they saw Cameron Epsberg walking in the direction of The Breakers, the Vanderbilts' Italian Renaissance-style mansion, whose back lawn also abutted the Cliff Walk.

"And we're going to follow him?" Caroline asked skeptically.

"We are," Jon said. "Come on. Look like this is your first trip to Newport."

Following a safe distance behind their target, the couple's demeanor became that of two tourists, turning their heads from side to side, pretending to be awed by the sight of The Breakers and the ocean opposite it. Caroline wished they could have had sunglasses and hats to shield their identity.

"Can you still see him?" she asked.

"Yes. That blue blazer is distinctive. Everyone else is in standard day tripper garb." And as he said that, a hard breathing runner clad in shorts and a yellow Nike T-shirt pushed past them. "Bloody hell," Jon shouted at him. "Watch out for the rest of us."

They were passing Ochre Court, designed by Richard Morris

Hunt a few years after his work on Kenwood, which was once the home of the Goelet family. Now the building served as the administration offices for Salve Regina University and was the core of its vast campus in Newport.

"He's stopping. Look," Caroline pointed.

"Do you see Cava?"

"No," Caroline said with a smile. "But I think I know where Cameron's meeting him, if indeed that's what he's planning to do."

"Where?"

"The Forty Steps."

The Forty Steps were originally 40 wooden steps which led down from the Cliff Walk to the deep water below. They were constructed in the 1830s to give nearby residents access to the water's edge. During the Gilded Age they had become a popular meeting place for the mansions' servants to gather in their free time. In the 1990s the entire structure was restored by a charitable initiative with new steps made of granite with a sturdy rock wall encasing them on both sides. At the bottom was a wide enclosed stone platform jutting out toward the ocean where now it was the tourists who gathered there.

Jason Cava was standing at the bottom of the steps, his slim body nestled in a far corner of the thick rock wall which encircled the platform overlooking the water. As always, any view of the Atlantic Ocean pleased him, and Jason was content to stare dreamily out to sea. If only he didn't have to share this time with Scott and Cameron. But there was business to be taken care of, and he was pleased at how pragmatic he had become in the days following Althea's death. Now his head was full of plans, full of ways in which he would cement his place as managing director of Tanner Associates. For that was indeed the title he had bestowed upon himself in his new responsibility. That morning he had instructed Maya to have new business cards printed to formalize his promotion.

The first order of business with his partners today was to remake the profit split. His original ten per cent now had to be a full third of the take. Jason didn't think either Cameron or Scott would balk at this request, but nevertheless the issue had to be raised. It was too bad they couldn't meet at the office to discuss these things in a businesslike fashion. But there were still precautions which needed to be taken. Cameron's coming to Newport was reason enough to remain careful, but Jason was sure that a casual meeting of the three men at this, one of the most famous tourist attractions in Newport, would be noticed by no one. The people around him were too busy taking selfies, caring only about which mansions to visit and where to eat.

Scott Forsythe, his *Key West* cap shading his eyes, came jauntily down the steps. He smiled at a young couple holding their cell phone at arm's length to take their own photograph.

"Do you remember," he said to Jason as he joined him, "when you saw a couple like that and you would ask if they wanted you to take their picture together?" Jason nodded. "Now they don't need you to do that." He shook his head. "Another example of how we are isolated in today's world. No one needs anybody for anything anymore." He watched the couple taking another shot of themselves from a different angle. "We're all islands."

Jason frowned. He hated when Scott got all phony philosophical. It must be the arrogance that came with all that money. Perhaps, with any luck, he'd have it himself one day.

"Cameron should be here soon. He said two o'clock," Cava said.

"It's ten after."

"Yes, and may I point out that you're late."

"What exactly are we meeting for again?" Scott asked. The question irritated Jason.

"I think he wants to take his measure of you, quite frankly."

"Me? I've always done my part. Does he have any complaints?" Scott pursed his lips in a sour expression. "You know I've never thought I would like him."

"As I told you the other day. He likes his current lifestyle. He wants to be sure the money train doesn't come to a stop."

"It won't because of me."

"Oh, there on the top step. That looks like him."

"He's the one wearing the blue blazer?"

"Yeah, that's Epsberg."

"I see he doesn't want to stand out in the crowd," Scott said dryly.

"Do me a favor, Scott. Keep this friendly. Your two egos could be a problem."

"Oh, really? I see someone's getting his feet comfortable in the boss's shoes."

"Yes, and I believe those are the very ones you gave me to wear."

"Can you see the bottom of the steps, Caroline? Is Cava there?"

They had reached the top of the Forty Steps and were peering down. Cameron Epsberg was making his way carefully down the granite steps, his leather soled shoes not ideal for the task.

"Yes, I think that's Jason in the corner. See the man with the bald head there on the left."

"Right. And wait a sec. The man next to him. In the grey cap. Bloody hell. That's Forsythe!" Jon stared incredulously. "What's he doing here?"

Caroline strained to see the figure who was wearing the baseball hat. The man standing next to Jason Cava did seem to resemble Scott Forsythe.

"Why do you think Scott came here with Jason? It doesn't fit," Caroline said.

"Maybe it does. I thought Scott was a little too effusive last night with his praise of Cava. I'd never heard him sing his praises before. It was bloody suspicious." He fidgeted next to her. "I wish we could get closer to hear what they are saying."

"There's no way we could go down the steps without being seen. I'm afraid they picked a good spot to talk without being overheard."

"I hate standing here helpless," Jon said.

"Jon," Caroline said thoughtfully. "Why would Scott Forsythe help Jason Cava to get possession of Althea's house?"

"I don't know yet."

"There is a reason. There has to be."

"So what should we do now?"

"I don't think there's much we can do. We could wait to see how long they chat. But once they are done and decide to come back up the steps, we've got to be out of here. There's no place to conceal ourselves," Caroline said, looking around. "This is a very open stretch of the pathway along here."

"Do you want to head back?"

"We probably should. I promised Cameron Epsberg a tour of the house this afternoon. He was very interested in the history. I should be there when he returns."

"Try to find out why he came to Newport. And I'm curious as to why he is staying at your inn of all places in town."

"We are a five star hotel. He probably found us online. Most people do. I wouldn't read anything into that."

They had reached Kenwood.

"I'd better leave you to it, Caroline," Jon said. "You'll get better results if he sees that you are alone. I'm sure you can charm some information out of him."

"Of course I will." She gave him a conspiratorial smile.

CHAPTER XLV

"I thought that went well," Jason said as he and Scott climbed the steps back up to the Cliff Walk path. They had given Cameron a few minutes' head start so they all wouldn't be noticed together.

"Yeah," Forsythe said, "and I was right. I don't like him. Pompous prick."

"You don't have to like him. If you want, you never have to see him again."

"I didn't want to see him this time. I'm offended he had to check me out. What does he think I am? Some shady witness in one of his legal cases?"

"I told you. This was to make him comfortable. Now he can go back to New York, and we can get on with our job up here. There is a lot of money at stake, don't forget. Just because the investors are happy this week doesn't mean we can relax."

"I know. I do hope that media stock he shorted can be sold soon. It would be nice to get that money back in the kitty."

"We're fine for this quarter's payout."

"What about Teddy Ainsley's money?"

"He's in no position to be thinking about buying that estate he wants for his music center. Have you forgotten the man has been charged with murder?"

"No, although I try not to think about it. I still can't wrap my head around believing that he killed Althea. He doesn't seem the murdering type."

"Who does seem to be?" Jason asked curiously.

"I don't know," Scott answered, his face creasing into a frown. "I've thought about the people on that boat that night. Last night at Melody Granger's house, I looked at everyone who was there, thinking *did you kill Althea*."

"And?"

"I couldn't see it in anyone's face."

"Guilt? Do you think killers walk around looking guilty?"

"No, I don't. I don't know what I mean," Forsythe sighed. "I'm sorry things have changed. I realize now I liked everything the way it was."

Jason could have said *me, too* but he didn't. Because he wasn't sure now what he was feeling. Instead he stared ahead as they left the Cliff Walk and walked up Narragansett Avenue toward their cars.

"I'll be in touch," Scott said.

"Yeah. Call me if you want to. You're a Tanner investor, we can always talk. But I think we can low key things for a while. No news is good news."

"Yeah," Scott said, his tone sounding bitter. "That's what they say."

"I'll let you know if I hear anything from Cameron about the media stock."

"Yeah. You do that."

As soon as Jon went to his car, Caroline hurried to the gazebo. From inside the summer house she would have a clear view through the window to see Cameron Epsberg's return from the Forty Steps. After waiting about ten minutes she saw his figure emerge through the shrubbery. Timing her exit from the gazebo with the precision she once used in her stage career she came out onto the path and nearly collided with him.

"Cameron! I didn't see you there. I'm so sorry."

"Mrs. Kent," Epsberg exclaimed. "You startled me." She thought his face showed a trace of guilt.

"I've been in the gazebo. It's a popular spot for the guests and I need to check it from time to time. Empty drinks glasses, somebody's forgotten cell phone." She gave him her friendliest smile. "And you should call me Caroline."

"Caroline. Yes, I will," he said, recovering his composure.

"Have you been on the Cliff Walk?"

"Yes. I'd read about it. I wanted to see it."

"And how was your lunch?"

"Excellent. My compliments to your chef."

"And the wine?"

"A good vintage. You made an excellent choice."

"I'm glad you enjoyed everything, Cameron. Now shall I take

you up to your suite?"

"Please," he said.

"Unless that is, you would like that tour of the house first."

"Uh... not at the moment. I need to make a few business calls now."

"Of course."

Caroline led the way toward the door from which she and Jon had recently exited the house. Once inside she pointed out the doorway to the billiard room. Epsberg looked at it absently and said nothing.

"How long do you plan to stay in Newport?" Caroline asked while they ascended the stairs to the second floor. "You're only booked for the one night."

"I'm leaving tomorrow," Cameron said. "I'm afraid my business requires me to return to New York."

She would have liked to ask what his business was, but Caroline knew that was too forward a question put to a guest. Instead she asked if this was his first trip to Newport.

"Yes."

"Well you must come again."

"Perhaps I may return," he said. "And I'd enjoy staying at your inn a second time, Caroline."

She unlocked the door to the suite and Epsberg followed her inside. "You'll get the morning sun on this side of the house," she explained.

"Charming," Epsberg said, surveying the space.

"How did you find out about our inn, Cameron? It helps me to know how people hear of us."

"My assistant researched it online. I told her I wanted to stay in the best place in Newport."

"That's flattering to hear."

"I haven't been disappointed."

"Will you be in for dinner tonight?"

"No. A colleague gave me some recommendations for restaurants, and I think I'll try one of them."

"Do you need me to make a reservation for you?"

"No thanks," he said. "I can do that for myself."

Caroline couldn't come up with any more ploys to stay and talk. So she instructed Cameron to let her know when he needed anything and left him to unpack his bag.

"So do you know where Mr. Epsberg was going to dinner?" Louise asked Caroline while they set the small dining table in their sitting room. Since Hank had accepted her invitation to dine with them, there were three places at the table.

"No," Caroline answered. "I saw him leaving earlier but I couldn't think of any excuse to intercept him. We never did have that tour of the house he had been so insistent on having when he first arrived. I'm afraid I haven't been very successful in getting any facts about the mysterious Mr. Epsberg."

She was looking forward to seeing Hank this evening. Caroline couldn't wait to tell him everything that had happened today. First, there was the information which Jon had discovered about Althea's will and Jason Cava's inheriting her house. It sounded very much like motive for murder to her.

Also, Cameron Epsberg, the man from the train, was in Newport with the apparent purpose of meeting with Cava and Scott Forsythe. What was the common interest that would bring these three men together? And what was so vital to discuss that their conversation had to be done in person and in a place where they wouldn't be overheard?

Althea's will and the meeting on the Forty Steps were two disparate puzzle pieces, and Caroline couldn't yet see how they fit together. Would Hank be able to make sense of these new developments?

And, if so, would he finally come to the conclusion that the reason Althea Tanner had met her death was because of something entirely different from her argument with Teddy Ainsley onboard *Kandu*?

CHAPTER XLVI

"What do you think it this means, Hank?" Caroline asked as they sat down for cocktails in their upstairs sitting room. While Louise was mixing martinis, Caroline had taken the opportunity to tell Hank all her news. He absorbed it without comment, and Caroline was impatient waiting for his reaction. She hoped that the detecting role which Jonathan Granger had played was not keeping him from an honest assessment of the information's value.

"Are you having one of these, Hank?" Louise called from the sideboard. "Or do you want your usual?"

"Vodka is fine for me, Louise. On the rocks, please."

"Coming up."

"Louise enjoys bartending," Hank said. He looked relaxed now, and Caroline realized how much his official responsibilities continually weighed on his mind. Perhaps he had anticipated a dinner invitation that didn't involve thinking about work. She was sorry that she had to bring him back to the case, but she knew that he needed to hear what she and Jon had learned.

Louise brought forward a silver tray holding the rock glass with Hank's drink and two long stemmed martini glasses, the glimpse of a large green olive visible through the icy surface of each of the chilled glasses. Everyone settled in with their drinks before conversation was resumed.

It was Louise who spoke first. "This Mr. Epsberg is an intriguing figure, don't you think, Hank? It's strange that he would come here for only one night. What do you think his purpose is?"

"Frankly, Louise, I don't know. As Caroline said, it is a puzzling development."

"Yes," Caroline said eagerly. A bit too enthusiastically she knew, but she couldn't stop herself. "What is the connection between him and Cava and Forsythe?"

"I said last week, after you told me about Granger and the train incident, that this Epsberg could be a Tanner investor. Meeting with those two, well... that would be logical, wouldn't it? Apparently one manages the company now, and the other is a sizable investor."

"But, Hank. Why meet on the Forty Steps? Why not go to Tanner's office? Cameron Epsberg seems awfully fond of unusual meeting places."

"Maybe, as you said yourself, this Cameron wanted some exercise after his car trip. He's staying right next to the Cliff Walk--"

"You can't believe that for a minute, Hank," Caroline interrupted. "Not after I saw where he went and who he met up with. He's leaving Newport tomorrow morning. Can't you interview him before he goes?"

"What reason would I give for wanting to talk to him?"

"As a witness in the case. If he's a Tanner investor, he has a connection to Althea."

"I'd want to know more about him before I talked to him. And we know we can find him in Manhattan anytime we need him. Besides I'm much more interested in what Jonathan Granger learned about Althea's will. You know, I admit that I slipped up on that. Ben asked Jason about her will, but Cava said he didn't even know the name of Althea's attorney. Insisted that they stayed away from sharing information about their personal lives. I'm afraid I didn't follow up any further." He shrugged. "We did have Ainsley as our chief suspect at that point."

"You couldn't see past the argument on the boat." Caroline was still dissatisfied with Hank's responses.

"Hank," Louise broke in before Caroline's irritation became more evident, "does this change your mind about Teddy's guilt? It does seem that Mr. Cava had a real motive for wanting Ms. Tanner dead."

"I agree, and I intend to find Althea's lawyer and speak to him. Once I'm on firm ground with the details of Althea Tanner's will, I plan to talk to Jason Cava again."

"You remember my theory, Hank," Caroline said. The detective raised his eyebrows quizzically. "What I said on the night of the murder, about someone who could have crawled through the front hatch on *Kandu* and slipped down into the cabin after Teddy left. *That* was the person who committed the murder. You didn't think much of what I said at the time, but Cava has such a slim figure, and he's young and fit. Most of the guests were clustered at the back of the boat. Suppose there was a time when no one was near that hatch. Then nobody would have seen him going below."

"If Cava is the murderer, then yes, he had to be in the cabin at sometime. I'll go over the witness statements and see about questioning some of the guests again. Sometimes people do remember things days afterwards that didn't make an impression on them originally. It's possible that Mr. and Mrs. Dalworthy might have been confused about the several times they were speaking with him."

"Yes," Louise added. "People my age aren't looking at their watches all the time. They might not remember things exactly." She smiled at Caroline. "I do get forgetful myself sometimes."

"Not you, Louise," Caroline said affectionately. "You always know what's going on."

"Thank you, dear, and I do think the thing that should be going on now is our dinner. Let's feed this hungry man we've invited."

"I was promised a rather special dinner," Hank said, looking relieved to be able to stop talking about the case. "Something about a lobster pie. One of Mattie's specialties."

"Yes," Caroline said, "and I have a perfect wine to go with it. A 2015 Muscadet."

"Muscadet?" Hank repeated. "That sounds familiar. We've had it before, I think. Is it a white wine?"

"Yes, and I had a very good review of this vintage earlier today from our Mr. Epsberg."

"I won't forget him, Caroline. I promise I'll follow up on him tomorrow, too. Now, will you please feed me?"

Hank had made a conscious decision not to share what Keisha had discovered about Tanner Associates with Caroline and Louise that evening. It was not that he didn't trust their discretion with this confidential material, it was rather that he was yet to understand it all himself.

He had already begun thinking about how to question Jason Cava about Tanner's lack of transparency and regulatory accountability. Now Hank wanted to know how much Cava knew about the terms of Althea's will and why he may have lied to Ben about not knowing her lawyer's identity. Hank knew that someone who lied about one thing almost always lied about other things.

Getting Cava to clarify Tanner's business practices was going to be difficult. The possibility of being fooled by a practiced liar in an area where the police detective was a novice concerned him more than he wanted to admit.

Hank had no background in money matters. He had his police pension for his old age, and that was the extent of his financial planning. There was a savings account at the same bank where his paycheck was deposited into his checking account, and he regularly transferred funds to it after his bills were paid. But the saved money had grown very slowly. His apartment was rented so he had no home equity. There were still payments to be made on his car. He would have been embarrassed to make any claims on his renters insurance if he were robbed since his possessions were of such little value. Perhaps the work on this case was a message that the time had come to start planning for his financial future.

Right now, however, his job was to prepare himself to conduct an intelligent interview with the employee who was now managing Tanner Associates. Tomorrow Hank would sit in his office with the door closed and take out one of his yellow legal pads and begin writing down everything he knew about the firm and its business. From his experience in other investigations, the detective expected a pattern to emerge. It almost always did. And in this pattern he would see the questions which needed answers and the possibility of a new interpretation of the case.

He knew that Louise Kent was right to ask if he was changing his mind about Teddy Ainsley's guilt. Because what Caroline had told him this evening about Jason's inheritance had begun to open his mind to there being another solution to the murder.

CHAPTER XLVII

"I'm sorry you're not staying on in Newport, Cameron."

"I wish I could, Caroline, but I find that I do need to get back to New York today."

"If you plan to come again, I hope you'll give us a call." Caroline took one of the inn's business cards from the table in the front foyer and handed it to him.

Epsberg took the card and put it in his jacket pocket. He smiled, picked up his overnight bag and started toward the door. Caroline opened it for him and as he stepped out, she followed. Was it her imagination or did he stiffen?

"I may well return, Caroline," Cameron said. "I'm considering buying a house here."

"Really?"

"Yes, that's why I drove up. A colleague has been touting the place. His parents have a second home here. I figured I'd take a look around to see if it's to my liking."

"And it was, I hope."

"Oh, yes. Newport's reputation is well-deserved." He put his bag in the BMW's trunk and unlocked the car's door. "I can't afford anything as grand as Kenwood. But I'm sure a good realtor can put me on to some suitable properties."

"Are you interested in traditional or modern houses? There are some lovely modern houses out on Ocean Drive."

"I don't know that area," he said, getting into the driver's seat.

"I thought perhaps you did," she said, hoping to catch some reaction on his face. But there was none.

"Good-by," Cameron said as he started the engine. "If I decide to look at property, I'll be back."

"I'll look forward to seeing you."

Epsberg smiled and nudged the car across the gravel so as not to disturb the smooth surface. Caroline watched him, her disappointment growing. House hunting. She didn't believe it for an instant.

Before Hank began working on his notes that morning he called Ben into his office.

"We need to follow up on Althea Tanner's will," Hank told the sergeant, explaining how he'd found out that Jason Cava was a beneficiary.

"Mrs. Kent can be a pretty good detective."

"She does have an instinct for this, I'd be the first to admit. So let's see if Cava can tell you Althea's attorney's name now. He or she must have already contacted him about that house coming into his possession. Lawyers are pretty good at dotting the i's. Otherwise we're going to have to start making inquiries. Which could take a long time."

"Anything else?"

"Yeah," Hank said. "Alex Seeger told me that Cava wrote some report to the Tanner investors that detailed what returns to expect for the coming year. Said it was extremely positive. See if you can get a copy of it."

"A report?"

"It went out earlier this week. It was signed by Cava."

"O.K., I'll check it out."

"You're up to date on what Keisha found out from the state about Tanner?"

"Yes, it sounds crazy. Managing all that money and nobody knows about them. I thought there were so many regulations nowadays."

"There are."

"Then why aren't they following them?"

"That's exactly what I'd like to know myself."

Hank was pleased with how quickly his yellow pad filled up with notes. Althea Tanner's operation had been in existence since 2006. She had attracted wealthy investors who, he would have imagined, were smart enough to be careful about who they let manage their money. Alex Seeger said he was pleased with the glowing results he got from Tanner. Presumably all Althea's clients would say the same. There had never been any question that she was a successful money manager. The state would have had a record if there were complaints filed against her by disgruntled investors, and Keisha had found none.

If her track record was so outstanding, why had Althea Tanner steered clear of the regulatory authorities? Why had she operated in a dark corner of Newport? If you didn't count Maya Vereen, Althea did everything with only one employee, Jason Cava. That lone wolf operation had raised red flags for him earlier in the investigation. Cava had said all they needed was Althea's brains and a few computers. Her young assistant had downplayed his role as financial officer, the man who kept the books. But if Jason's contribution to the firm's success was so small compared to Althea's, why had Cava so easily slid into managing the firm now that she was dead?

Arching his back, Hank stretched his stiff neck upwards to the ceiling. He needed a break from staring at the yellow sheets of paper stacked on his desk. It was time to *grind the corn.*

After about twenty minutes of Tai Chi exercises, Hank reluctantly returned to his chair. He decided to follow up on Caroline's lead concerning Cameron Epsberg's stay at the inn. Hank did a quick search of the name in the data base. There was no police record for Cameron Epsberg. Next he Googled him.

"Hmmn," he said, looking at the screen. "That's very interesting. Can this mean something in our mystery?"

CHAPTER XLVIII

Had Hank been able to use some long range, infrared Defense Department camera that traveled across miles and penetrated walls, the detective would have seen Caroline in her office at the inn, engaged in exactly the same Google search that he was doing.

"Wow," she said, staring at the information on her laptop's screen. "I knew there had to be a big reason why Epsberg and Cava needed to see one another in such secret agent style encounters. I wonder if I've found how they're connected." She frowned. "But how Scott Forsythe comes into this triangle, I can't quite figure out yet. But this has got to be a start in working things out."

She hit *Print* and began collecting the paper as it ejected from the printer.

Hank showed Keisha what he had found in his online search. "I want everything you can get on Epsberg. Where he was born, every place he's worked. Where he went to law school, what property he owns. The name of his first pet."

"I'm still working on these licensing requirements and other things related to Tanner. The financial industry has its own regulatory authority. I've only started with their web site."

"Put that on hold for today. I'm going in to see Chief Williams in a little while. It's time he's brought up-to-date on everything we've learned."

"Yes, sir. I'll get my notes in order so you can show the chief what we have."

"Thanks. You're doing a good job on this, Sergeant. I'm not sure what we've got here, but it's damned important."

"It's exciting, sir. I've read about big financial fraud cases in the news. Do you think that's what we're on to here?"

"I don't know. So far no one's claimed to have lost any money." He shook his head. "Frankly, I'm not sure what the crime is that's taken place."

"Well, we know that Althea Tanner should have registered her firm with the state and the Securities and Exchange Commission. I'm sure of that."

"But why not do it?"

"There could be tax fraud," Keisha suggested.

"Perhaps."

"And what about one of those Ponzi schemes you read about? Like Bernie Madoff set up. Can you imagine something like that going on right here in Newport?"

"You're getting way ahead of me, Sergeant. Let's try to slow down."

"I'm sorry, Lieutenant." Keisha said, looking disappointed. "It's only what you said - it's a really important investigation."

"Which we're going to take one step at a time. It's imperative that we not give away what we are doing to the investors or anybody at Tanner. We don't want them to panic."

"No, sir."

"I've got an appointment with Jason Cava tomorrow morning." He patted his stack of yellow paper. "We'll see if he has some of the answers we want about what has been going on at Tanner Associates. I'd like you to come along. You've done the research. You can ask questions, too."

"Thank you, sir."

"Remember. We're asking the questions. He doesn't get any information from us."

"Yes, sir."

"Cava's the only one with the answers now at Tanner. He's got to explain why there's nothing on that firm with these government agencies."

Hank tried to smile, but he didn't feel confident. "I just hope we know how to ask the *right* questions."

CHAPTER XLIX

"Mergers and acquisitions, Louise. Think of the possibilities."

"I am, Caroline."

"Cameron Epsberg practices law with one of the biggest mergers and acquisitions specialist legal firms in the country. Imagine the inside information he has access to."

"I suppose that could be tempting. These days there seems so little regard for ethics."

"Was there ever, Louise? What has ever stopped speculators squeezing out other investors?" She stopped to think. "Is that what Scrooge did?"

"I thought he was a money lender. Which Dickens described in a much more genteel way."

"All I know is that at the end of the book Scrooge had to mend his ways."

"And what a wonderful story!"

"So what do you think Cameron Epsberg has been doing with Tanner Associates?" Caroline asked, looking deep in thought. "Something. I know it's something."

The two women were in the kitchen, surveying the meal on the counter which Mattie had left for them. There was vichyssoise, cold chicken and a green salad. Caroline ladled the soup into cups. Louise made two plates with chicken and salad. They took their dinner to the long wooden table and sat down. Caroline poured two glasses of wine from the bottle.

"Do you have everything?" she asked her mother-in-law.

"I'm fine, dear. Thank you. Let's eat."

They started on the soup, and Caroline reached for a piece of French bread from the basket on the table. "Delicious," she said. "Do you think we could get Mattie to write a cookbook? *Recipes from the Inn at Kenwood Court?*"

"No," Louise said firmly. "Never."

"Could we at least get her to write these recipes down?"

"You'd have a hard time. Your best bet is to watch how she does it."

"She'd never let me do that."

Louise savored her soup. "Then I'm afraid you'll never know."

"Then let's get back to Mr. Epsberg."

"What's your theory, Caroline? Is he involved in Althea's murder?"

"I'm not sure how he is connected to the murder. He was miles away from the boat when it happened. But if Jason is connected to the crime... we know Epsberg is connected to Jason."

"Does inheriting the house come into it?"

"I thought it did, but how does Jason's getting a valuable piece of real estate connect to Cameron Epsberg?"

"I don't see it, dear."

"Mergers and acquisitions," Caroline said slowly. "That connects more to Althea, don't you think? She was the financial guru. Picking stocks was her special talent. John Ainsley discovered her abilities and set her up as his advisor."

"Is that how she met Epsberg?"

"No, no," Caroline said with some sureness. "Epsberg came later. After John died, and Althea was getting clients of her own." She took a forkful of salad. "Louise, you've met Cameron Epsberg. What did you think of him?"

"I saw him in the dining room at breakfast. We only exchanged the usual pleasantries."

"He's an extremely attractive man, don't you think?"

"Yes," Louise agreed. "He's a definite type, a good example of the rugged look. His eyes are quite striking."

"He's not my type at all," Caroline said while pushing the image of Hank from her mind.. "But do you suppose he might have been Althea's?"

"Margaret Ainsley commented on how stunning Althea was in person. Margaret admitted to being jealous of Althea's relationship with John."

"Was there reason to be jealous?"

"Margaret said she couldn't be sure. She had to admit there might have been nothing between them but a business relationship."

"I met Althea on two occasions. First in Val's office, and then on *Kandu* the night she died. Both times she exuded unmistakable confidence. I could see her matching up with Cameron as a couple."

"How did they meet?" Louise asked.

"Althea might have gone down to Manhattan for business reasons, social events, even to shop. So she could have met him there. That is, if you believe Cameron's assertion that he'd never been in Newport until this week."

"I agree it's reasonable that Althea would spend time in New York, and their paths first crossed there."

"And how fortunate that Cameron's law work with large corporate mergers and acquisitions offered him access to privileged information."

"Yes," Louise said, her eyes brightening. "Inside information must be very helpful if your business is buying and selling stocks."

"Of course it is," Caroline said. "So let's ask ourselves the big question. Did Cameron Epsberg ever share insider information with Althea Tanner?"

"And if so, did she buy stock based on that information?"

"Because if she did, Louise, then I think we have the explanation of why Althea never disappointed her investors."

"And," Louise said, "how Jason Cava can now run Tanner Associates without the benefit of Althea's well known stock picking talent."

Caroline nodded her head in full agreement.

Althea Tanner might be gone from the picture, but it would seem that Tanner Associates with Jason Cava as its head must be planning on keeping its lucrative connection to Cameron Epsberg.

CHAPTER L

"When the police come, I'm going to take them into the conference room. Hold my calls."

"Yes, Jason."

"I don't want to be disturbed for any reason, Maya."

"I understand." Maya looked anxiously at him. "You're not still mad at me, are you? I mean I didn't know I wasn't supposed to give that policeman your investors' report. Last time the police were here and you told me to give them the client list, you made it sound like they could have whatever they asked for."

"I wish," Jason began evenly. He was trying to hold onto his composure. The last thing he needed this morning was a disagreement with Maya. "I only wish that you had asked me about it first."

"You weren't here. And I didn't want to get in trouble with the police."

"Yes, you said that. But we do have confidential information here. For the clients' eyes only."

"I didn't understand. I'm sorry. I won't do that again."

"Did you give that sergeant anything else?" Please say no he thought.

Maya looked uneasy.

"Maybe I shouldn't have told him."

"Yes?" he demanded impatiently.

"He asked me if I knew the name of Althea's lawyer."

"And you told him?" She nodded. "How did you know his name?"

"I had letters for him I had typed for Althea. Mr. Crenshaw. I remembered his name. He's here in Newport. I've passed his office."

"I suppose they could have found that out on their own," Jason said, forcing a smile. "The police probably want to know about the will."

"The will?" Maya looked interested.

"It's routine, Maya. I'm sure there's nothing in the will for you."

"Oh, I didn't expect it to be."

I bet you did, Jason thought. A few thousand for your service. Once he had a firm grip on running things around here he was going to replace her. Maya was too stupid to be trusted with anything about the business. Althea had prized that clueless quality, but there was too much of a risk with someone who was so brainless.

A man. He liked the idea of having a man as his assistant. A man wouldn't feel the need to talk all the time. A man would be discreet with private business matters.

"Anyway, Lt. Nightingale is coming here at ten." Jason looked at the clock. It was a few minutes until the hour. "I'll take him into the conference room."

"I thought they'd arrested Althea's killer. That Teddy Ainsley." Maya shuddered. "I still can't believe he is the murderer. I mean, the Ainsleys are so rich. Why would he kill Althea? I mean, she was keeping him rich, wasn't she?"

"Maya, that's enough chatter. I'm sure the police are coming here because they have some loose ends relating to Ainsley's guilt that they need to tie up."

But Jason knew there were no loose ends that he could help the police tie up. Not after the sergeant had come calling yesterday to get a copy of his report. How did the cops even know that he had written it? Who were the police talking to? He began to tick off the names of the people who had received the document. As a courtesy he had sent one to Margaret Ainsley. Had she read it and become suspicious? No, he couldn't see the older woman even reading the damned thing. In Mrs. Ainsley's dealings with Althea she had always been a very silent investor. The faith her husband had in Althea was unshakable, and his wife never questioned Althea's decisions.

No, there was another investor who was talking to the police. He'd better get on to Scott Forsythe to see what he knew.

But first he would have to deal with the police.

This was his first visit to Tanner's offices, and Hank had been interested to see the place where Althea Tanner had made her reputation. He approved of the interior, open and clean. The furnishings and other appointments were expensive. Even his untrained eye recognized quality. Two paintings on the wall were original oils, and he liked their modern look. Bold colors and hazy geometric shapes.

"Will you have coffee, Lieutenant?" Jason asked.

"No, thank you," Hank said. "We're both fine."

"I thought we'd be comfortable in the conference room. It's small, but we won't be disturbed." Jason's eyes met Maya, and he hoped she remembered his instructions.

Hank and Keisha followed Cava as he led the way through the outer office into the smaller room. A rectangular glass table gleamed in the sunshine, and six comfortable looking beige leather sling chairs were placed around it. This room had two framed art posters. One was an Andy Warhol with its subject The Rolling Stones. The other was a colorful psychedelic poster of Big Brother and the Holding Company featuring a very young Janis Joplin. The detective's curiosity as to their importance to Althea Tanner was roused.

Hank and Keisha took seats next to one another and Jason sat at the head of the table. Cava watched him as Hank put a thick folder from his case on the table and Keisha took out her notes as well.

"How can I help you today, Lt. Nightingale?" Cava asked. He leaned in toward the two police officers as if he were some television interviewer.

"Some points have arisen in our investigation which I hoped you could clarify, Mr. Cava."

"Certainly."

"In a case like this background is important. We have made an arrest and now we need to keep filling in the pieces around that arrest. Now we know that Mr. Ainsley argued with Ms. Tanner onboard *Kandu* the night she was killed, and the subject of that conversation was money."

"I didn't know about that," Jason said. "That wasn't reported in the press."

"No it wasn't. But we have a witness who overheard the argument. It appears that Mr. Ainsley wanted to withdraw a large portion of the money his family had invested with your firm. Are you aware of that fact?"

"Yes."

"And Ms. Tanner had informed him that she couldn't allow the withdrawal to take place immediately?"

"That's correct. Our agreement with our clients is structured. We have a minimum requirement of three months' notice for a withdrawal request to be processed."

"Why is that?"

"We are not liquid, Lieutenant. Our clients funds are fully invested. We couldn't function if we had to deal with constant demands for withdrawals." Jason met Hank's eyes. "Do you know much about a firm like ours?"

"No, and that's exactly why I am here, sir."

"Well," Jason said, leaning back in his chair now. "Our clients invest money with us long term. They are looking for both capital appreciation and yearly profits."

"I see," Hank said.

"Profit checks go out to our investors on a quarterly basis. With the large portfolios of stocks and bonds which our clients have, I am sure you can understand that given the rate of the returns Tanner offers, they receive generous checks. I expect many of them depend on the income for their living expenses. Some are retirees, of course. But others have no employment other than being investors."

"And so you explained to Teddy Ainsley that he had to wait for his request."

"Althea did. She handled the clients."

"And he was unhappy with this?"

"I didn't know for sure. But you tell me he was. That's why he murdered her, isn't it?"

"I can't comment on that."

Keisha cleared her throat, and Hank turned to her. "Do you have a question, Sergeant?"

"Yes, thank you, sir." She looked down at some papers on the table in front of her. "I've been looking into the regulatory filings of Tanner Associates, Mr. Cava." Jason frowned. "And the thing is, sir," she continued, looking up to stare into his anxious eyes. "There are none."

CHAPTER LI

Jason felt his heart skip a beat. He clenched his jaw and stared at the policewoman. How old was she? Little more than thirty, he guessed. And a sergeant. She must be clever. He would have to keep his head.

"Could you explain what you mean, Sergeant?" he asked, doing his best to sound vague.

"I've checked with the state. Rhode Island has no records of Tanner Associates. It's my understanding that they - and the SEC - would require your firm to be licensed. Tanner has large sums of money under management."

"In a way," Jason said.

"In what way?"

Jason brought his hands together in front of his chest. Carefully he pressed the tips of his fingers together in a steeple.

"It sounds as if you are under the impression that we are a firm of financial managers."

"Aren't you?"

"No."

"Are you saying you don't manage your clients' money? Invest it on their behalf?"

Jason looked at Hank. He tried to read Nightingale, but the man's face was giving nothing away.

"You'll need to explain," Nightingale said.

"I can see that." Jason sighed heavily. "If only Althea were here to do that."

"But she's not. And you are."

Jason swallowed. He tried to look apologetic. "This all has to do with the way she ran things. She called the shots. I hope you realize that I've only been an employee here."

"Yet presently you are sending out reports to the clients under your name, Mr. Cava. Reports which explain how the firm will continue in operation without Ms. Tanner."

"I thought it was the right thing to do. To reassure the investors." His tone bordered on being sympathetic. "They have so much money at stake. If you read the report, and I hope that you did, you will see that I am keeping things as Althea set them up. She had the investing philosophy and made the seminal decisions. I'm only following her guidelines."

"But, it still doesn't tell us why the company is not regulated. Then or now."

"Because we're a hedge fund," Jason said firmly.

"A hedge fund?"

He saw that Nightingale hadn't expected this. Did the man even know what a hedge fund was? He doubted it. Jason wasn't completely sure himself how a hedge fund operated. But he did know that they had no licensing requirements.

"Yes," Jason answered smoothly. "And if you know about the rules governing hedge funds, Lieutenant --" And here he allowed himself a glance at the sergeant. "-- well essentially there are none. You may disagree with it, as police officials, but the financial regulations aren't in place for us. We have no licensing requirements."

He saw Nightingale exchange a look with his subordinate. She appeared confused.

"A hedge fund," Nightingale repeated. "Nothing in that report you wrote alluded to the fact that this is a hedge fund. In fact, that description has never been mentioned before in our investigation. Has Tanner always been a hedge fund? The night Ms. Tanner died, during your interview, you led me to believe that she managed money."

Jason looked sheepish. At least he hoped he did. For some reason, he was having fun with this.

"Althea always ran things as a hedge fund. She just didn't explain to the clients that was what she was doing."

"Why?" the sergeant asked. "Why couldn't they know what they had given their money over to?"

"Our clients are very conservative. But at the same time they want high returns. Always demanding way above average gains. That puts a lot of pressure on an operation like Althea's. We know what's best to achieve their investment goals, but we can't always tell them what we are doing, how we get them those fantastic profits."

"Sounds very paternalistic," Nightingale said. "It also sounds dishonest."

Jason chuckled. "Believe me, Lieutenant. I understand your scruples. But--" He spread his hands apart and shrugged. "--in the world of high finance, wealthy investors look at things a little differently than you and me. Tanner Associates has been an extremely successful firm. We don't lose clients. *We gain them.*" He liked the sound of that. He'd save that phrase for his next investors' report.

"Hedge funds have no regulatory oversight," the sergeant stated skeptically. "None at all. What about FINRA?" She turned to Nightingale. "FINRA is the Financial Industry Regulatory Authority. It's independent. It's not part of the government. But it was set up by Congress to protect investors. You have to pass their exam."

"But we are not brokers, Sergeant. FINRA oversights brokers. And I believe investment advisors as well. But as I explained. Althea was neither."

"So you said," Nightingale said.

"I know your colleague has done a lot of research on this, Lieutenant, but I'm suggesting that perhaps she turn her attention to learning about hedge funds. Find out how we work."

Hank didn't like the direction this interview was heading. Jason Cava had ready answers for everything. But the detective wasn't convinced they were the correct answers. But the hedge fund declaration threw him. Since he needed time to process it, he would take his losses for the present and proceed in another direction.

"That's a good suggestion, Mr. Cava." He saw Jason's look of relief. A little premature. Hank still had the Cameron Epsberg card to play, but he wasn't ready to do that.

"I understand that Scott Forsythe is one of your clients." He saw Cava look wary. "His name was on your client list. Remember? You gave it to us last week."

"Yes. Of course."

"I believe that he is a very wealthy man." Cava nodded. "Does he know that this is a hedge fund?"

"Althea may have let someone like Scott Forsythe know more about how she was doing things than some of the less savvy investors. He would understand the risks involved in a hedge fund. We take long and short positions in the market. I've always suspected that Scott day trades for his own account. Enjoys the hunt so to speak. He wouldn't have been put off by the risks taken by a hedge fund... if they were paying off... which they were."

"I see," Hank said. He picked up the file from the table in front of him as if in preparation to leave. Keisha followed his lead and began to gather up her material.

"I hope I have helped you today, Lieutenant," Jason said. He rose from his chair. "If there is anything else, please let me know."

But Hank remained seated, and Jason was forced to stand, waiting.

"There is one other thing I wanted to ask you about."

"Yes?"

"Ms. Tanner's will." Jason stared at him, the look of wariness back. "I've spoken to her lawyer, Mr. Crenshaw. When there is murder, we always like to look at who profits by the victim's death."

"And you think I--" Jason's face reddened, and he almost spit out his words. "You think I killed her to get her money!"

"Oh I know you didn't inherit any money. Rather you received what I understand is a very substantial house. Congratulations on your good fortune."

"Now you wait a minute. I didn't know I was going to get her house."

"You didn't?" Hank asked, now standing and busily organizing the papers in his case. "You had no idea whatsoever?"

"No, I did not. I was as surprised as anybody. Althea never said a word to me. I swear, I didn't know I was going to get her house."

"Really?"

"No, even the lawyer said I wouldn't usually have been in line for something as much as her house. Althea wasn't married yet, you see. He said that she would have married eventually and then I would have been taken out of the will."

"Then what a stroke of good fortune that she died before she found a husband."

CHAPTER LII

Back in the car, Keisha drove and stared stonily ahead while Hank, sitting beside her, fumed. Finally he spoke.

"He's a damned slippery fellow. I'm more determined than ever to pin something on him. Mr. Cava's nowhere near as smart as he thinks he is."

"Do you want me to start researching hedge funds, Lieutenant?"

"No, I do not," Hank said, his voice sounding loud in the enclosed space of the car.

"Yes, sir," Keisha said.

"I'm sorry, Sergeant. I didn't mean to jump on you. He's lying. He pulled that hedge fund crap out of his--" He stopped before finishing the sentence. He needn't be unprofessional.

"I thought so, too, sir."

"The problem is that I'm out of my league here, and I'm the first to admit it." He was quiet for a minute. "I've an idea."

Keisha glanced sideways at him. "What is it, sir?"

"Let's go over to Bowen's Wharf and see if Val Ainsley is in her office."

"You think she can tell us about Tanner Associates, if it is a hedge fund?"

"We'll soon find out."

Keisha smiled. She was eager to be on the trail again. Swinging the car around into Washington Square, she headed them down toward the harbor. The day was a sunny one and there were visitors walking leisurely on the streets, looking in shop windows and scanning the posted menus outside the eating establishments.

"When we get back to the station I'll talk to the chief again," Hank said. "He's very interested in what we have come up with on Tanner. Now I've got to tell him this latest from Cava."

"Did Chief Williams think something illegal is going on?" Keisha asked. "Based on my research, I know they are supposed to be registered if they are managing all that money. *Which they are.*" She was still smarting over her lecture from Jason Cava.

"What you found is important," Hank said, wanting to reassure her. "I know you can't run a financial operation like Althea Tanner was running with no oversight by any regulators. And don't forget the fact that the investors don't seem to know what the hell is going on."

"That's hard to believe, Lieutenant. I check my bank statements all the time. And I don't have more than a few thousand dollars saved up. I want to make sure it's still all there."

Hank laughed. "You and me both."

"I wonder," Keisha said, as she turned into the narrow roadway off America's Cup Boulevard which led down into Bowen's Wharf, "are you sure Jason Cava did know what Althea Tanner was doing? She might not have told him."

"It's possible," Hank said frowning. "But his job was keeping the records. Wouldn't he know if things weren't being done according to industry standards? He had to account for the funds they had under management to the investors, didn't he? He had to send out those regular statements and checks. "

"Maybe he guessed and was looking the other way."

"Then that's a crime," Hank said.

"Have you decided that he's not a suspect in the murder?"

"No, I haven't. He gained substantially by her death. That's a hell of a motive in my book."

"So how do we prove it?"

"The usual way. Find some good, solid evidence."

Val Ainsley was typing on the keyboard of her computer when Hank and Keisha walked into her office. The bell on the door had jingled, but Val took several seconds before looking up. When she saw who her visitors were, she looked apprehensive.

"Good morning, Ms. Ainsley," Hank said. "We'd like to talk to you for a few minutes."

"Is this about my brother?" Val asked.

"Yes," Hank answered. "May we sit down?"

"Please. How can I help you?"

"This is Sgt. McAndrews," Hank said, gesturing toward Keisha. "And we're trying to understand the background of the argument your brother had with Ms. Tanner on the night she died."

"What about it?"

"I understand that it started because your brother wanted to withdraw funds from your family's account with Tanner. Is that correct?" Val nodded. "And these funds were to be used to purchase a house here in Newport, a rather large estate?"

"That's right. Laurel Hill. Teddy had big plans to develop it into an international music center."

"And what was the amount of the money Mr. Ainsley wished to withdraw?"

Val hesitated, and Hank smiled.

"Come now, Ms. Ainsley, we can get the information from Tanner, but why don't you cooperate? I think you'll find that being open with us may help your brother's case."

"How could that be? You lot think that Teddy killed Althea because she wouldn't give him the money."

"She would have done so eventually. It was only a matter of how soon he could receive the money, wasn't that right?"

"Yes. But Teddy wanted to put in a bid on the Laurel Hill estate now and he needed the cash on hand. He was afraid he would lose the property if he couldn't act quickly."

"And Ms. Tanner was indifferent to his plight. Seems a poor response to a member of your family. After all, wasn't she in business because of your father's support and patronage?"

"Which she soon forgot," Val said bitterly. "If my father were still alive--"

"Yes, I believe that's the very thing your brother said to her that night onboard *Kandu*."

Val swallowed. "I wish we'd never gone out on that damned cruise. Damn Althea. She caused her own demise."

"How much did Mr. Ainsley want to withdraw? Tell us."

"Thirty million. I'm sure that seems like a lot of money to you, and it is. But it is money that belongs to our family. Both my mother and I assured Althea that we wanted to have the funds released to Teddy."

"This music center was very important to him," Keisha said.

"Yes, and now look what's happened. My brother is charged with murder. His life is ruined."

"You assume that he will be convicted," Hank said.

"Won't he?"

"He is innocent until proven guilty," Keisha pointed out. "Why don't you have faith in the judicial system, Ms. Ainsley?"

CHAPTER LIII

Suddenly Val looked drained. "How does this help Teddy, Lt. Nightingale, to know how much money he needed? Doesn't it make it look more likely that he killed Althea over it?"

"It doesn't explain how he would get his money once Althea was out of the picture."

"What do you mean?"

"Killing her didn't get him the money any faster."

"Then why did you arrest him if it seems illogical that he killed her?"

"We believed he was angry, that he killed her in anger."

"You know, Lieutenant, that sounds more like me than Teddy."

"Did you kill Althea Tanner?"

"No, I did not. Although I think I could have. She had no right to treat Teddy the way she did."

"All right. Here's another question, and I'd like you to think carefully before answering it. Who could have gone down below after that argument and killed her - that is, if you brother did not?"

Val bit her lip, then shook her head unhappily. "I don't know."

"Did you see anyone go below?"

"I wish I had. I've racked my brain over what happened that night."

"What about the forward hatch?"

"The hatch?"

"Could someone have gone below without being noticed... by slipping down that hatch onto the V-berth?"

"Is that something you are considering could have happened?"

"It does explain the presence of a third person below."

"Who? Did anybody see something?"

"I'm afraid not," Hank said. "But you do agree that it's possible."

"Yes, but not helpful if you don't have a witness, is it?"

189

"No. Let's talk about something else."

"All right."

"How closely are you involved in your family's investments with Tanner Associates?"

"How do you mean?"

"I mean who in your family oversees the account you have?"

Val looked surprised. "Mother gets the statements. And the checks, of course. Everything comes quarterly."

"And you yourself don't go over the statements." Val shook her head. "Nor does your brother?" Val shook her head a second time. "But you and your mother and brother get your living from the checks which come quarterly?"

"Father left everything to Mother during her lifetime. It's all invested with Tanner. Mother has always supported Teddy and me. We don't have our own separate accounts, it's all in one for the family." She swept her hand around the office. "I also have the money I make from here. It's not a lot, but I have built the business up and I do have some income of my own." She thought for a minute. "But you're right that most of what we live off of comes from what Father left, which is held in our Tanner account."

"And that sum has grown handsomely over the years?"

"I think it has. Mother would know how much." Val looked puzzled. "What are you suggesting, Lt. Nightingale?"

"I'm trying to understand how Ms. Tanner conducted business at her firm. Did you ever hear Tanner Associates called a hedge fund?"

"A hedge fund? Why would it be called a hedge fund? Althea invested our money in stocks and bonds as far as I ever knew. Like Father always did. That doesn't mean it's a hedge fund, does it? I thought *hedge fund* meant something different. Hedging means, well, hedging bets, I would think. Althea keeps our money in our family's account and it's invested in stocks mostly. That's why she told Teddy she couldn't give him the money that quickly. She had to sell stocks and that takes time - to move large amounts of shares at the right price."

"Thirty million dollars worth of shares," Keisha said. "That would take three months' time?"

"That's what Althea said," Val answered, "but I didn't really understand why that would take three months to do." There was the sound of frustration in her voice. "But then I've never bothered to understand the markets."

"What is the status of your brother's request for the redemption now?" Hank asked. "Are you still expecting Tanner to release your money?"

"I haven't thought about it," Val said. "With everything that's going on with the lawyers and preparing Teddy's case, I really don't know what is being done about that money."

"Do you think your mother will be keeping her account open at Tanner?" Keisha asked.

"I haven't thought about that either. She could move it to another firm of advisors. After what's happened, I'm not sure that keeping our account at Althea's firm makes any sense now."

The last thing Caroline expected to see when she came into the kitchen at lunchtime was the sight of Jonathan Granger sitting at the table eating soup. Mattie was busy cutting the meat from what was left of last night's cold chicken and piling it onto thick slices of bread for sandwiches. Caroline watched the cook add a generous smear of mayonnaise and a spring of something green to each one.

"Caroline," Jon called when he saw her in the doorway. "Come have some of this soup. It's delicious. I've just been telling Mattie that the last time I tasted vichyssoise this good was at The Ivy restaurant in London a few years ago. Of course they add a bit of truffle, but you know. I don't think you need that." He pointed to his bowl. "This is tops."

"Jon, what are you doing here?" Caroline asked.

"I would have thought that was obvious, Caroline. I'm having lunch. Mattie has taken pity on a poor starving Englishman."

"Starving?" Caroline asked as she looked over at Mattie who was beaming from Jon's effusive praise.

"Yes. Melody went off to the club to lunch with friends, and I was loose on the world."

"So you came here in search of food?"

"No. I came here to talk to you. But when I found Mattie she insisted that I eat something."

"That was kind of Mattie. Louise and I had the soup last night. I agree. It is delicious. I'm glad you were able to find the way to the kitchen."

"You know," Jon said, finishing the last of the soup in his bowl. "I think Mattie ought to write a cookbook. She's been telling me about her favorite recipes, and she makes the kinds of things people want to prepare but they need plenty of guidance to do. I adore Beef Stroganoff, but our cook at Waverly makes a dog's breakfast of that. What do you think about a cookbook, Caroline? With lovely color pictures of these amazing dishes." He smiled cheerfully, ignoring Caroline's stunned expression. "I'd buy one for our cook for sure."

"I, uh, don't know what to say. Mattie, do you think you'd like to write a cookbook?"

If it was possible, Mattie was blushing. She turned her face away and recovered herself. Finally she said, "If Mr. Granger thinks so."

"Of course you can do it, Mattie. Why don't we sit down one afternoon and talk about it?"

"Yes, sir. That is if it's all right with Mrs. Kent."

"Of course it's fine with Mrs. Kent, isn't it Caroline?"

"I think Mattie means my mother-in-law, Jon."

"Oh, right. We don't want to upset mama, do we?" Louise's title came out as a veary British-sounding *ma-mah*.

"Well, this gives us food for thought," Caroline said lightly. "Now, Jon, are you going to have that sandwich and tell me why you've come to Kenwood?"

CHAPTER LIV

"Insider trading. Brilliant."

"You agree it makes sense, Jon?"

"Absolutely, Caroline."

Jon and Caroline had brought their sandwiches to the gazebo so that they could talk undisturbed. The day was a warm one, and the breeze blowing through the summerhouse windows hinted that summer was fast approaching. Caroline stretched out her legs on one of the long chairs and sipped from a glass of iced tea. She suddenly felt lazy, in need of a day free from her daily responsibilities.

"Caroline?" Jon repeated. "You look far away."

"I am," she admitted. "I was thinking of--" She laughed. --"a day on the beach in the sun with a good book to read. And nothing else to do."

"I'd go to Barbados," Jon said.

"I've never been to Barbados."

"You'd love it. Melody and I went there on our honeymoon. Friends of hers offered us their place, a fabulous house right on the beach. Complete with staff. That trip was an introduction to my new life as Melody's husband. When you married Reed Kent, did you think about the money changing your life?"

Caroline smiled ruefully. "There wasn't much money. I knew that Reed's father had lost most of it in bad investments years before. It was Reed's law work that supported him and Louise."

"But you had Kenwood."

"It was rented to pay the mortgage. Otherwise it would have been sold."

"You are kidding? I thought you did this for a lark." Caroline stared at him. "I mean it. I assumed you wanted to make a packet running this place as a hotel for the rich tourists. You know, like Diane von Furstenberg selling clothes. You'd look fabulous in one of her wrap dresses, by the way."

"I think I have one in my closet."

"Get it out. They never go out of style."

"Louise and I work hard to keep our guests happy, Jon. But it's by necessity, not choice."

"Melody told me that you used to be on Broadway."

"Broadway?" Caroline shook her head. "I did mostly roles in the small theaters. I never got to be famous... or rich."

A companionable silence followed while they finished their lunch. After several minutes, Jon returned to the topic of Cameron Epsberg and his role in the mystery the young Englishman was so eager to solve.

"Althea must have been using the information Epsberg knew about the deals his law firm was working on," he said. "It explains why she was always able to be making money in the stock market for her investors."

"There's no way that John Ainsley could have been involved in insider trading."

"No, Caroline, but he's been dead since... I think Melody said 2006."

"That sounds about right. But don't forget that the markets went through a bad time during the collapse of the economy in 2008. If Althea kept making money in stocks through that, well, isn't that a red flag?"

"Since 2008?" Jon whistled. "That's a long time."

"Do you think Melody would remember anything about that period?"

Jon shook his head. "She was still married to Alfie. He handled the money." He paused. "I think after the divorce is when she got so close to Scott Forsythe. He was walking her through her financial options. She came to rely on his advice, and of course ended up keeping her investments with Althea Tanner."

"Yes, and now we know that Forsythe is involved in whatever this scheme is as well."

"Scott's always portrayed himself as an investor with Tanner. But he's also got to be doing more in this than that."

"Do you think he's not as rich as he claims?" Caroline asked.

"No, he's got the money. I know his lifestyle. It takes a packet. Do you know he's bought an island in the Caribbean?" In spite of himself, Jon smiled in admiration.

"An island would cost a lot to buy and then a lot more to maintain."

"Forsythe needs a very steady stream of high income."

"And he gets it from the insider trading that Althea Tanner was doing? That Jason is still doing."

"The three of them are doing, Caroline. Don't forget Mr. Epsberg."

"Yes, all of them are in it. I wish I understood more about how it works."

"What's to understand? They're all bloody crooks."

"Yes, Jon, I understand that. But how did this lead to Althea's murder?"

"You're forgetting the house, Caroline. Cava gets the house."

"He had to know what was going on at Tanner. He kept the records. They had to pay him off to alter the books." She met Jon's eyes. "Why would he want that money to stop?"

"The house," Jon said stubbornly. "The bloody house."

"Then if there was a murder investigation..." Caroline was still thinking hard. "... well, then everything was bound to come out. Why would Cava take the chance?"

"You're assuming that Jason Cava has a brain. Maybe he didn't. Maybe he wanted the house and he did what he had to do to get it."

"I don't know, Jon. I'm having second thoughts about Jason as the killer."

CHAPTER LV

Hank Nightingale couldn't believe that he was having such an amazingly wonderful day. He had confirmed with Leo Vargoff that he was free to go boating on Saturday, and Leo had extended an invitation to 'bring your wife along.' Learning that Hank had no spouse, the other man had wondered if there was 'someone else you'd like to bring.'

Of course there was. Caroline. Hank had phoned her with all the expectation that she would decline to spend most of Saturday away from the anchor of her duties at the inn. To his surprise she had actually sounded pleased to be invited and had said yes immediately. And now here they were, strolling leisurely on sunny Block Island, returning to Leo's boat docked at New Harbor after a relaxing outdoor lunch.

Leo's yacht *Emma Lane* - named after his mother - was a large comfortable vessel. The boat had made the crossing from Newport to Block Island, across the choppy seas of the Atlantic Ocean, in two hours. Hank had sailed the route many times, often in races. He was pleased to take the yacht's wheel when Leo asked him to, but the leisurely pace of this boat lacked the challenge of ocean sailing.

Once on land the trio had walked the half a mile to the restaurant where they dined on fresh local swordfish. Their conversation centered on life in Newport. Leo was curious about the guests who came to stay at the Inn at Kenwood Court, and Caroline told a few stories about her experiences. Leo remembered the murders which had taken place when the inn had first opened, and Hank explained that was when he and Caroline first met. The murder scene where both Leo and Caroline had so recently found themselves was not mentioned. Hank waited for Leo, with his open inquisitiveness about Caroline's work, to introduce the topic. Hank knew Caroline well, and he was sure that she would be very eager to get the view of another passenger on the deadly cruise. Lunch, however, ended with Althea Tanner's name unspoken.

It was when they were out on the open sea that Caroline could no longer contain herself.

"After the last boat trip I took, I thought it would be sometime before I was ready to get on another boat. I have to thank you, Leo, for including me today. Otherwise it might have been as the old saying goes... about not getting back on a horse right away. The longer I waited, the harder it would become."

"Yes," Hank said. "And I appreciate it, too."

"I'm glad to have you both onboard," Leo said. "Hank's lucky to have found someone who enjoys boats. I'd like to find that somebody."

"I wish I could help you out," Hank said. "But the women I know who are into sailing aren't that crazy about powerboats."

"I know. I've met a few. Newport's a sailing town. Jamestown, too, for that matter."

"Have you ever tried sailing?" Caroline asked. "I saw you standing in the cockpit on *Kandu*, but I didn't think you took the wheel."

"No. I didn't feel comfortable, especially on such a big boat with all that history. I'm not experienced."

"Not like Alex Seeger," Caroline said. "He spent quite a bit of time piloting the boat."

"Yes, Val Ainsley let him bring the boat about. That's right, Hank. *About*? That's how you say it."

"Yes, that's exactly the way you say it. Alex is a good sailor, is he?"

"It seemed to me that he handled the boat very well. Val didn't have to give him much coaching."

"So you were in the cockpit for some time?" Hank asked.

"Half an hour, at least, I'd say."

"Let me ask you something. Did you happen to see a knife attached to the binnacle? The stand where the compass was?"

Leo stopped to think. Hank could see Caroline tense as she waited for his answer.

"Yeah," he finally said. "You're right. There was a knife there. In a scabbard. I did see it."

Caroline took in a very audible breath.

"When did you notice the knife, Leo?" Hank asked. "Think

before you answer. Was it when you first came into the cockpit... during the time you were there... or as you left to move about the boat?"

"I suppose when I first came into the cockpit and I looked at how the set up was. The sophisticated navigation instruments were what got my attention." His eyes narrowed. "But tell me, Hank. We're talking about the murder weapon, aren't we?"

"Yes, and it's important to know that the knife was there in the cockpit after the boat was under sail."

"I can see how that would make a difference." Leo frowned. "Does this make me a suspect, Hank?"

"What would your motive be?"

"None. That night was the first time I met Althea Tanner. Why would I kill someone I just met?"

Hank looked at Leo Vargoff, whose demeanor had shifted from sociable boater to guarded crime suspect. Had the detective misjudged his Tai Chi comrade? If he had, both he and Caroline were out in the middle of the Atlantic Ocean with a murderer.

"If not knowing a person before you killed them was some kind of rule, then a lot of murders couldn't get committed," Hank said.

There was an uncomfortable silence onboard the *Emma Lane*.

"Look, Leo. I'm sorry this came up. Maybe I shouldn't have accepted your invitation while the case is still going on."

"But you've arrested Teddy Ainsley, Hank. Your case isn't going on, is it?"

Hank saw the look on Caroline's face as she heard Leo's question, and he knew that she hoped the answer was yes. If only he could see another solution.

CHAPTER LVI

Caroline thought that Hank's apartment looked exceptionally neat. The last time she had visited there had been a pair of running shoes in front of the sofa and a week's worth of newspapers on the coffee table. A sweatshirt had been left draped on the back of one of the kitchen chairs, and that morning's coffee pot had the remnants of its last brew. Now the place was as tidy as a guest room at the inn, and she didn't have to look into the bedroom to know that the bed was made and all clothes hung tidily in the closet. She smiled and took it as a compliment. Hank was not a messy person by nature, but living alone did allow him to take some shortcuts in his daily housekeeping routine.

"Are you hungry?" Hank asked, turning on several lights. Had he dusted as well? "It's after five. How about a drink?"

"A drink would be lovely," she said. "Can we sit outside?"

"Whatever you want to do. Gin and tonic?"

"Gin and tonic will do nicely."

"Coming up," he said as he went into the kitchen where he kept his bar on the counter next to the coffee maker.

Caroline opened the sliding door and stepped onto the porch. "I don't see Delilah," she called back to Hank.

Delilah was a large black cat who could often be seen sunning herself on the porch railing. Her name had been given to her by Hank who didn't know to whom the cat belonged, let alone her real name. But he had taken an interest in her, and Caroline found it amusing that her very masculine detective liked the company of a soft, furry cat. She harbored the view that it would suit him to have his own cat to greet him when he came home at all hours of the day or night, but she had yet to suggest it.

Hank came out with two glasses. Caroline took hers and clinked it with Hank's.

"Cheers," she said. "To a wonderful day."

"Wasn't it," he said. "I still can't believe you left all your work behind on a Saturday afternoon. What's gotten into you? Next you'll be coming to Tai Chi with me."

"Spring fever, I think. I was telling Jon yesterday--" She stopped in mid-sentence when she saw the frown replacing the smile on Hank's face. "Oh, I've stepped in it, haven't I?"

Hank let out a breath and made an effort to look happy again. At least he probably thought he was looking happy. In truth, he looked as if he had just bit into a lemon. She couldn't help but laugh.

"What's funny?" he asked.

"You. Are you jealous of Jonathan Granger?"

"Of course I'm not. What makes you say that?"

"Every time his name is mentioned you look like the miserable loser on a TV awards' show when he doesn't know he's being caught on-camera."

"I just don't know what you see in that guy. He's got a pony tail, Caroline."

"Hank!"

"And I also don't know why he seems to see more of you than I do lately. Can you admit you spend a lot of time with him?"

There was truth to what Hank had said. "You know," she said thoughtfully, "this case seemed to solve itself rather quickly You arrested Teddy, even though I disagreed with that." When Hank opened his mouth to speak, she put up a warning hand. "Let me finish." He closed his mouth. "Jon was the person who agreed with me that we needed to keep searching for the real killer. Since I couldn't talk over the case with you... well, it's worked out that this time around... it's Jon and I who are discussing our theories. Not you and I." Before Hank could respond, she added, "And you are jealous."

"Me? Jealous?"

"Yes, you," she said taking his hand and kissing it lightly. "And I really don't mind."

"In fact, you like it," he said as he wrapped his arm around her and pulled her toward him. Caroline relaxed against the familiar broad chest, and their lips met.

"Hank, wake up," Caroline said in a soft voice as she tried to extricate herself from Hank's hold. "Hank, Hank. Try to wake up. I have to talk to you."

"Now?" he said sleepily as he tried to pull her down under the blanket. "What time is it?"

She looked at the bedside clock. 1:47. "Almost two o'clock."

"Are you going home now?" he asked. "I thought you were staying until morning."

"No, no, I'm not leaving. Listen to me."

"I'm listening, but I'd rather be sleeping." His voice was still groggy. "This is the first relaxing sleep I've had all week. What are you trying to do to me?" He reached for her again, but she grabbed his arm. His eyes opened in surprise.

"Hank, stop that and listen to me. I'm trying to tell you that I know how the murder was done."

CHAPTER LVII

"The coffee's ready, Hank. Can you get the eggs out of the fridge?"

"Sure. If you're going to scramble them, don't forget I like lots of butter."

"It's not good for you."

"Do you know how often I get scrambled eggs for breakfast? Usually it's coffee and a bagel. Sometimes I don't even have time to toast it."

"When's the last time you had your cholesterol checked?"

"My last annual check-up." He put the box of eggs on the kitchen counter along with an unopened stick of butter. "See, I never even unwrapped this. Probably been in there since New Year's."

Caroline smiled and set about making the eggs. Hank sliced a bagel and put the two halves in the toaster. He poured coffee and sighed contentedly as he watched Caroline stir the pan of eggs.

"This is how my life should be."

"Right. But I wouldn't get too used to it. We both have to go back to work. You tomorrow, and me later today."

Hank's face fell. "Today? Today's Sunday. I thought we might do something together this afternoon."

"I can't leave Louise alone for the entire weekend."

"I understand," he sighed. "I should count my blessings."

Caroline spooned eggs onto two plates. The bagel popped up in the toaster, and she added a half to each plate. "You don't seem to have any orange juice."

"Ran out. Sorry."

"Do you want butter on your bagel?"

"Can I?"

"They're not my arteries."

"Then I'll have butter."

They took their food to the kitchen table and began to eat.

"I didn't realize how hungry I was," Caroline said, taking a bite of the bagel. "And I have to admit that these eggs taste good with all that butter."

"We didn't get much sleep last night," Hank pointed out. "After you woke me up to tell me you had solved Althea's murder, who could go back to sleep?"

"What's next?" Caroline asked, her face now serious.

"Nothing can happen until I get some evidence."

"You think what I've explained is only a theory?"

"No, I can believe that's exactly how it happened. If you accept that Althea was alive when Teddy left her down below, then your explanation is the only one that fits. Remember what Sherlock Holmes said?"

"Once you eliminate the impossible, whatever remains, no matter how improbable, must be the truth."

"When did you first realize that's how the murder must have been committed?"

Caroline looked thoughtful. "I'm not sure how sure I was that anyone went down below after Teddy came up. And someone ought to have seen him... or her. Too many people were standing by the stairway not to have noticed something. And my supposition that someone climbed down through the hatch... well, that could only have been one or two people who had to be amazingly fit. And again, despite trying to make my theory work, someone going through the hatch... some of the guests would have paid attention to that. Or one of the crew... that waiter." She paused. "I like to think I would have seen that happening."

"And your friend Jon. You were standing together."

"Yes, my *friend* Jon."

"Are you planning to tell him about this?"

"No, I don't think that's wise right now. As you say, there is no evidence to support an arrest. You need some time to work on this." She looked unsure. "The motive still isn't clear to me at all."

"In police work, first we prove our case. Finding the motive is secondary. I've got to go back to look at the forensic evidence found on the body. See if we can match it to our killer. But the problem will be that so many other people are likely to have left traces on Althea. No doubt everyone was hugging and kissing in greeting."

"Yes, plus the boat, even though large, is a confined area. Lots of people were close to Althea Tanner during the trip. Me, included."

"Our killer is just one of many people she encountered."

"Oh, Hank, do you think you can prove this? Suppose you can't? Teddy is still going to have to go to trial for the murder. If you have no evidence to prove otherwise..." And despite her best intentions, Caroline's eyes filled with tears of frustration.

Hank jumped up and went across to her. She put her head against him and tried to regain control of her emotions.

"I want to help Teddy so much. He doesn't deserve to be tried for murder."

"And you have helped," the detective said, wrapping his arms around her. "I'll figure out a way to prove this case, Caroline. I won't let you down."

CHAPTER LVIII

"When will Miss Althea's funeral be, Mr. Jason?"

"How would I be expected to know that, Mrs. Miller?"

"Well, you living with her, I'd expect that you would be making the arrangements."

"I'm not her next of kin. Far from it. It's not my responsibility. Besides, the police haven't released her body. I understand that in these cases, it can take some time."

"But that's not right. She should be properly laid to rest. She deserves that much respect. Is she in one of those refrigerator things you see on the television? All cold and shriveling up."

Jason shuddered at the image. His breakfast was churning in his stomach, and he put down his coffee cup.

"The police will notify her lawyer when they are finished with her," he managed to say. "And then Mr. Crenshaw will be in touch with her family."

The housekeeper gave a disgusted grunt and turned back to clear the breakfast things from the table on the terrace. It was obvious that the police department of the City of Newport was a great disappointment to her sense of decorum.

"I only thought we would be having something here at the house after the service. I wanted to start preparing for it. I thought I'd get my daughter to help serve."

"Here?" Jason asked. "Why on earth would there be something here? Her family will want to bury her in Connecticut. For all I know, her will says that she is to be cremated."

"All her friends are in Newport. Miss Althea would want them all here for her lunch. To say good-by and all."

Lunch? How did the damned woman know it was to be a lunch? And why would Althea's so-called friends want to remember her all that fondly? Oh, this was too much. With everything going on, now Jason was to be tormented by a funeral service, lunch at his house, and God knows what else. Was he also to be writing the obituary? Maybe even delivering the eulogy at her funeral. No, there was to be nothing like that put on him. Crenshaw and that brother who never talked to her back in Connecticut were in charge of her now. That niece who gets all the cash could lend a hand as well.

"I'm just saying," Eva Miller said as she carried her tray toward the French doors. "I'm only saying she deserves a good send-off."

She made it sound as if Althea were getting ready to board the QMII for a cruise around the world.

A cruise around the world. Jason started forward in his chair. Why did the sound of that suddenly appeal to him? He looked around the comfortable grounds and forced his mind back to the present. He had intended to use this Sunday to plan his next moves. Despite his bravado in front of the two police officers on Friday he was far from sure of his position. That declaration made about Tanner's being a hedge fund. How long would it take them to realize he had been feeding them a line of crap?

Was he seriously in need of a Plan B? Jason loved *Di Sole*, but he had a practical side and he knew that he had to be ready to leave everything at a moment's notice. If the police or the feds showed they were getting anywhere close to the truth, he was gone. His money was safe offshore. Whether the house could be sold and the profits handed over to him was another matter. If the asset could be linked to a crime, it could be frozen. What funds had Althea used to buy the house? Could they be traced to her ill-gotten gains? His stomach resumed its churning.

Who knew when some smart investigator would begin to unravel the threads of the conspiracy? He must be ready.

"I can't believe it, Caroline," Louise said, hugging her daughter-in-law. "You are a genius. "You've saved Teddy. I'm so proud of you."

"I've just laid out the way the crime was done. Hank's the one who has to get the proof that it happened that way."

"But he can do that. I know he can." Louise wiped a tear from her eye. "Margaret will be so happy."

"You can't tell Margaret yet. I'm sorry, Louise, but you can't say anything about this to her until Hank says so. Once he has the evidence, he will make an arrest. We have to be patient."

"I understand. It's going to be hard to wait. I hope it doesn't take very long."

"I hope so, too," Caroline answered. But she wondered.

How long would it take to prove a murder that no one had witnessed and so far had provided no forensic evidence connected to the killer?

CHAPTER LIX

She knew she should have told Hank what she was planning, but Caroline had the idea that he wouldn't have been entirely pleased. True, she had joked with him about joining the Tai Chi class to help her relax and had even voiced interest when Hank and Leo had talked during lunch on Block Island about their mutual enjoyment of the exercise as a stress reducer in their busy lives.

Well, she had a busy life, and learning the discipline of Tai Chi ought to be good for her as well. So that Tuesday, while Louise worked in the garden and Jan cleaned her office, Caroline drove to First Beach. Unlike Hank's usual custom, she arrived early.

Alex Seeger was already on the beach staking out the area for the class. Several people who she assumed participated in the class stood waiting, chatting. Caroline didn't recognize anyone in the group so she lingered near the parking area, waiting for Leo to arrive. When she saw his now familiar black Mercedes sedan turning into the lot, she waved. He parked next to her own elderly BMW convertible.

"Caroline, what are you doing here?"

"I decided to join the class. You guys were so enthusiastic about its benefits the other day that I figured I'd give it a try. Registration's free so here I am."

"Terrific. Hank is pleased to have you, I bet."

"He doesn't know yet."

"What?"

"I didn't get a chance to tell him that I was coming today," she said.

"Should I read something into this?"

"No, no, not at all. It's... well he doesn't like surprises."

"And this is one?"

Caroline nodded.

"All right. You two work this one out. Come on. Let's get over there. Hank is always late. So no sense in waiting for him."

They walked across the sand. Alex watched their approach with a curious stare.

"Alex, we have a new member," Leo called. "You remember Caroline Kent. You met her -- " He paused. "Well, I think you remember meeting her."

Alex, still looking puzzled, nodded. "Of course. Not pleasant memory, but yes, hello, Caroline. Nice to see you again."

"I was hoping to join the class," she said, smiling. "Leo was telling me how much he enjoys it, and I think I need something like this."

"I didn't know that you and Leo knew one another."

"Yeah, we do," she said evasively. Suddenly she was wondering if this was such a great idea after all. She wished Hank would appear and she could get past his astonished looks as well. "I hope I can pick things up. I know I've missed the first several sessions."

"Oh, don't worry," Alex said. "I stand up in the front of the class. You all get in a line and follow my movements." He laughed. "Of course it's backwards. But be patient. You'll get the hang of it. One thing we don't do in Tai Chi is rush." Caroline nodded. "We do warm-up exercises in the beginning." He looked down at her feet. "You might want to take your shoes off."

"Oh, of course." She slipped off her canvas shoes and tossed them behind her. Leo stood on the end of the row, and she took her place next to him. "I'll follow you," she whispered. "I'm not sure about doing this backwards."

"We'll start with Temple Exercises," Alex said in a loud voice. "Everyone in Opening Position."

Caroline followed Leo's lead and tried to relax her shoulders and arms down as his were, with hands facing her thighs."

"Relax, sink, root," Alex said in a quiet voice. "Become part of your environment. Breathe in through your nose and out through your mouth."

Caroline followed directions and found her body already beginning to relax.

"Inhale deeply."

Suddenly her concentration was broken as Hank slid in the line next to her. Despite her efforts to stay focused on her position, she glanced sideways at him. His exasperated glare spoke volumes.

"Hello," she murmured. "I've decided to take up Tai Chi."

CHAPTER LX

"I think you could have told me you were coming today," Hank said as the class ended. He also would have hoped that Caroline might have left things to him for the present. The detective was a long way from getting the evidence he needed, and his nerves were unusually tight. Today's Tai Chi session hadn't helped much with that. Yet it was hard for him to stay annoyed with Caroline, and he forced a smile as he spoke to her.

"I didn't know I would be free until the last minute," she said lightly. He knew she was fudging the truth, but he nodded. She looked around the beach. "This is great. I see why you like it so much."

"So you'll be back next week?" he asked.

"If I can. Sure."

Suddenly they were startled as Leo came running toward them. They had last seen him on his way to the parking lot.

"Hank! I've got to talk to you right away."

"What's up?" Did he want to propose another lunch? Hank wanted to get back to the station.

"I've remembered," Vargoff said, his face looking incredulous. "It's all come back to me."

"What did you remember?" Caroline asked before Hank could speak.

"I remember--" And now Leo paused as Alex Seeger came toward them.

"How did you enjoy the class, Caroline?" the instructor asked as he joined them.

"I liked it a lot," she answered, glancing at Leo. "I'd like to return--"

"You took it," Leo said, grabbing Alex by his shoulders. "You! Why?"

"Wait a minute," Hank said, trying to separate the two men.

"Leo! Hold on."

"The knife, Hank," Leo exclaimed. "Alex took it. I know it was him."

"What are you talking about, Vargoff?" Alex asked, his face reddening. He twisted free of the taller man's grasp.

"You saw him take the rigging knife from the binnacle on *Kandu?*" Caroline asked excitedly.

"When we were together in the cockpit, I remember seeing the knife and then it wasn't there. At some point it wasn't there. I remember now." Leo reached for Alex again. "You must have taken it. I didn't see you, but--"

"See," Alex said, turning to Hank. "He doesn't know what he is talking about."

"He's talking about the murder weapon," Caroline said.

"Really?" Seeger asked with mock surprise. "So he could have taken it. He won't even say that he saw me take it. And why would I take it?"

"For a very simple reason," Hank answered. "To commit murder."

"You think *I* murdered Althea? That's crazy. Why would I murder Althea?"

"I don't know how you found out what they were doing," Caroline said. "But somehow you did, didn't you?"

"Find out what?" Alex had backed away from them.

"That Althea Tanner was cheating you. That she was cheating everybody. Stealing money from all her investors."

"That's a crazy story," Alex said angrily. "Who told you that?"

"There's been a conspiracy now for several years. Among Althea and Scott Forsythe and a man called Cameron Epsberg. They have been duping the Tanner investors."

"What?" Leo asked. "There was a conspiracy to defraud their investors?" He stared hard at Alex. "You encouraged me to become one of the Tanner investors."

"You mean become one of *the geese*, don't you," Alex said in a suddenly calm voice. "I can't believe that I actually encouraged my brother-in-law and my friend here to become geese."

"Geese," Hank repeated. "What does that mean?"

"That's what she called us, Hank. *The geese*. Dumb birds. I heard her say it."

"Althea?" Caroline asked. "When did you hear her say that?"

"That night on Bannister's Wharf before we got on the boat. Leslie and I had gotten there early. While she was shopping, I had to use the public men's room there. When I came out I had some time so I decided to look in that upstairs art gallery across from the Clarke Cooke House. I went over into the vestibule to take a closer look at a painting that was hanging there." He laughed incredulously. "I was thinking of buying it for my office. A huge sailboat, out on the ocean. A nice memento of that evening, don't you think, if I had?"

"But how did you hear Althea talking about... geese?" Caroline asked, sounding confused. "What does that even mean?"

"I saw her and Forsythe come out of the Clarke Cooke House. They must have been having a drink together before they went over to *Kandu*. I tried to catch up with them."

"But you didn't," Hank said, beginning to visualize the scene. "They never knew you were there."

"No. The wharf was too crowded. When I finally came up behind them, Forsythe was saying not to worry, that they would 'cover this quarter'... and that they would keep making 'this golden goose keep laying eggs'."

"But you just said that Althea was the one--" Caroline began.

"Yeah," Seeger said, his face furious. "It was what she said. And *how* she said it."

"How she said it?"

"Nobody talks about Alex Seeger like that and gets away with it."

"But what did she say, Alex?" Leo asked. "Tell us."

"Althea said to Forsythe: 'Let's go greet the geese'."

"The geese!" Alex shouted. "Don't you see. To her I was just a pathetic bird laying golden eggs for her." He glared at them, waiting for their anger to match his.

But instead of sharing Seeger's outrage, the look in his three companions' eyes was one of shock. Shock, as each realized that Althea's flippant description of her firm's clients was what had driven a man to think he had the right to end her life.

CHAPTER LXI

Once again a curious crowd of onlookers saw the police cars arrive in the case of the murder of Althea Tanner. On this occasion, their presence at Easton's Beach marked the arrest of her murderer. While Hank conferred with Ben and Keisha, the handcuffed prisoner was put into the back seat of one of the black and whites by a uniformed officer.

"I still don't understand it," Leo Vargoff said. He was standing beside Caroline as they both watched the scene unfolding in the beach parking lot. "I know Alex took the knife, but when did he kill her? Everyone thought that Teddy Ainsley had done it."

"We all thought that because Teddy was believed to be the last person to see Althea before she was found dead. No one else was seen down below with her before Alex supposedly needed to go to the head - and when he said that he *discovered* her body... or so he told us."

"But he had killed her first. My God, what an ingenious plan."

"Wasn't it? He must have been furious during the entire cruise, thinking of what Althea had said. The longer he waited, the angrier he felt. He took the knife while he was at the wheel of the boat, I think even before he had decided how he would use it."

"What a handy murder weapon."

"It sure was. You were right that he had taken it, even though you didn't see him slip the knife into his pocket. After he left the cockpit and started moving around the boat, we know he was talking to his wife, her sister and the doctor. Then he saw Althea and Teddy go below. If I heard Teddy and Althea arguing, I bet Alex did as well. When Teddy came up the stairs alone, the idea must have come in Alex's head. Go below, confront Althea." Caroline shook her head. "I can't believe Althea would have been eager to listen to Alex's complaints. Remember she had just been challenged by Teddy, demanding that she give him the money for his music center."

"Althea must have felt threatened from all sides."

"My guess is that she rebuffed an aggrieved Alex without a second thought."

"So he stabbed her," Leo said. "Alex has an enormous ego, Caroline. I'm sorry to say that I believe that he would be capable of doing what he did."

"Alex killed her and then rushed up the stairs, screaming that Althea was dead. It was quite a performance. I, for one, believed him."

"So did I. He maintained that stricken pose the entire time we were together in Val Ainsley's charter office while we were waiting to be questioned by Hank. That doctor hovered over him."

"No one at that point could have thought that he was the killer. He looked so in shock because he had discovered a body. I've never seen a better performance by a professional actor."

"What happens next, do you think? Will Alex be charged with first degree murder?"

"That's a good question, Leo. Was it premeditated or did he act in anger when Althea didn't respond to his humiliation about being called a goose?"

"That's amazing, isn't it? To be set off by name calling. And you say you began to suspect him? I wouldn't have guessed any of this."

"It was because I could never believe that Teddy Ainsley was the killer. I know him, you see. So I was sure it had to be someone else. And I finally I started coming around to the fact that it was Alex Seeger who was the very last person to see her."

"But we thought she was dead when he saw her, not alive." Leo shook his head slowly. "The audacity of it all is what gets me. How he could have pulled it off."

"It was the motive which perplexed me. I had no idea what it was that triggered Alex's rage. I was thinking of greed. Certainly not geese."

"Geese, they seem such harmless creatures," Leo said. "No, Caroline. You wouldn't think of them to be the cause of a murder."

The news of the arrest of Alex Seeger in Newport was on the evening TV news across the state of Rhode Island. The story reached Jason Cava when he arrived at *Di Sole*, and Eva Miller met him at the door. Not easily understood at first because she was overexcited, her words pouring out of her mouth in a jumble, the housekeeper at last managed to get across to her startled employer that a new suspect had been arrested in Althea's murder.

Jason brushed the older woman aside and ran upstairs to the privacy of his bedroom where he opened his laptop and searched the story on the Internet. He found it easily, quickly absorbing the meager details.

Alex Seeger.

Why did the police think Seeger killed Althea? Nothing in the story on the screen explained why he had been arrested. This made no sense. Teddy killing Althea made sense. Ainsley wanted his money, and Althea wasn't giving it to him. But Alex was happy, getting his profits every quarter. He'd just recommended two new investors to Tanner. And then Jason understood.

Alex knew. Somehow he knew.

How had he found out?

The ringing of his cell phone interrupted his thoughts.

"Hello," he said to his caller. "You've seen the news."

"Does Epsberg know?"

"I doubt it. I don't think this is a big news story in New York City."

"Why would Seeger kill Althea? What did she ever do to him?"

"I can't figure it out," Jason lied.

"We shouldn't talk on the phone. How about breakfast tomorrow? Come here."

"Is that wise?"

"I'm an investor. I need reassurance."

"Fine. I'll be there at eight."

Jason ended the call and sat motionless on the bed. The uncertainty that he heard in Scott's voice had made him uneasy.

He returned to the laptop. A few keystrokes and the screen offered the information he wanted. It was just as he remembered Kyle telling him. Croatia had no extradition treaty with the U.S.. Even better, U.S. citizens didn't need to get a visa ahead of time to travel there.

Jason walked across the room to his closet. In one corner sat several suitcases and traveling bags. He selected one of the smaller carry ons and began to fill it. It would be warm in Croatia in June.

*****

Louise had managed to reach Margaret Ainsley by telephone before the police department's announcement of Alex's arrest was released to the media. Margaret struggled to speak through her tears as she thanked Louise and begged her to thank Caroline for all her help.

"She's saved my son, Louise," Margaret said. "I thought he was lost to me."

"No," Louise answered. "You have him back."

The paperwork to drop the charges against Teddy had been filed and the arrest of Alex Seeger was completed by early evening. Hank sat alone in his office, the first quiet time he'd had all day. Everything had happened so fast. He could never have predicted the scene which had unfolded on Easton's Beach earlier that afternoon. The need for evidence with which to charge Alex Seeger, which the detective had found so elusive, suddenly appearing like that when Leo announced that he remembered seeing the knife go missing while he was in the cockpit. Seeger's dramatic confession in response to Leo's accusation was equally amazing. So much for the merits of good police work. Sometimes all it took was luck.

"Lieutenant," Keisha called, standing in the doorway.

"Come in," Hank motioned to her.

"Now that we know the motive for the murder, I'd like to keep digging into the structure of the Tanner investment firm. Mr. Seeger certainly corroborates that something shady has been going on there. For a long time."

Once at the police station, Alex Seeger had begun to talk freely. Despite Hank's warning that he could wait for his attorney to be present, the suspect could not contain the outburst of fury directed toward Althea Tanner.

"I was a fool to believe she was legit," he had shouted at Hank. "It was a Ponzi scheme from start to finish. And I fell for it."

"You don't know for sure," Hank had responded.

"What else could it have been? I was dazzled by all the money she fed us. I even recommended that my brother-in-law and Leo become investors. She made a fool of me. She used me. Nobody uses Alex Seeger."

"There'll be a full criminal investigation into her firm."

"What's to investigate? We were all geese laying golden eggs for her. I'm glad I killed her."

"Sir?" Keisha's voice interrupted Hank's thoughts. "Can I proceed?"

"Yes. Talk to Cava again. Go over there tomorrow and see if he knows anything about geese."

CHAPTER LXII

"He's gone, Lieutenant."

"Who is, Keisha?" Hank asked, looking up from the computer screen. The Tanner case notes were spread across his desk, and he had spent the morning struggling to write his report to Chief Williams outlining all they had concerning possible irregularities at Althea's firm. There were several threads to connect, including the suspicion of insider trading and an alleged Ponzi scheme.

"Cava. I think he's done a runner."

"Tell me," he sighed.

The story was a familiar one. Keisha had gone to the office of Tanner Associates to discover that Jason Cava had not come in to work that day. The assistant, Maya Vereen, had not heard from him.

"Did she call his home to find out where he was?"

"No, she didn't think it unusual that he would come in late. So I went on out to where he lives."

"And?"

"I talked to the housekeeper, Mrs. Miller. She was all over me, wanting details of the arrest. I had a time getting her to calm down. She lives in, but her rooms are in the back of the house off the kitchen. She doesn't hear much that goes on upstairs where the bedrooms are. It's a gigantic house. Cava has his own wing."

"He wasn't there?"

"No, not in his bedroom, not anywhere. His car was gone from the garage. Miller claimed she hadn't seen him since last night when he came home and she told him that we'd arrested Alex Seeger. She said Cava seem surprised and ran upstairs without saying much. Around seven she went up to tell him that she had dinner ready, and he told her that he was going out later for dinner."

"And she saw him go out?"

"She heard the car start in the garage. You can hear that from the kitchen. It's a high-powered sports car. Makes some noise."

"What time was this?"

"About 7:30."

"And he didn't return?"

Keisha shook her head.

"We went to check his closet. You know, to see if he had taken clothes. She couldn't tell if anything was missing. He has a lot of clothes. Very stylish dresser. There were a bunch of suitcases, so one of them could have been missing. But she wasn't sure."

"I think we can conclude that he's left town. The question is where would he go?"

"He moved up here from New York City. He could have gone back."

"O.K., let's check for family, a previous address."

"I can get on it, sir."

"We'd also better follow up with Scott Forsythe. I want to keep him in Newport. Tell Ben to get working on tracking down Cava. You and I are going over to pick up Forsythe and bring him in for questioning. We know *he* can tell us about the geese."

But when Hank and Keisha reached Forsythe's home on an elegant side street off Bellevue Avenue, the wealthy investor wasn't interested in talking to the police about geese or any other farm animals. He called his lawyer before casually getting in the police car where he remained silent for the journey across Newport to the station on Broadway.

Hank left him waiting for his attorney in the interview room with Keisha and went in search of the chief. The detective had a feeling that the time had come for people above his pay grade to take charge of this part of the investigation.

Caroline was in the morning room when she saw Teddy Ainsley park his blue Volvo sedan in front of the house. She watched from the window as he opened the door to the back seat and withdrew an enormous bouquet of flowers and what was obviously a magnum of champagne wrapped in gold foil and tied with a streaming purple ribbon.

She hurried to the door and greeted him with a hug.

He smiled his familiar boyish grin. "I'm glad I caught you at home."

"I work here, Teddy, remember."

"Yes, I know," he said, handing her the flowers. "For you, my savior."

"These are lovely, Teddy," she said, sniffing the fragrant top of the blossoms. "So many colors." There were purple and yellow iris, white and pink lilies, red roses. "Did you buy out the flower shop?"

"I tried to." Teddy held up the champagne. "And the wine shop."

"This is too much," Caroline said.

"No, Caroline, it's not nearly enough."

"Come inside." She led him into the foyer and through to the morning room where she set the bottle and flowers down on a table. "Sit down, won't you? I'm so glad to see you. You look terrific."

"I'll never be able to thank you for what you did for me, Caroline. I couldn't believe it when Mother told me that you had solved the case."

"I had the idea of how it was done, but the police did the rest."

"Yes, but until you came along, they were going to bring me to trial. And I don't mind telling you I was beginning to get nervous. It was starting to seem all too real. That lawyer had me terrified."

"I'm sorry you had to go through all that, Teddy. Thankfully, now it's over. You must feel that you have your life back."

"I do," he said, his face bright again. "And I am getting back to normal." He laughed. "Whatever that means for me, at least."

"What are your plans?"

"I'm going to buy Laurel Hill, of course. I'm meeting with my broker tomorrow to go over the bid for the estate. I can't wait to get started. You know I have an architect already working on some sketches? She's been wondering about the status of things, but now I can tell her we are full speed a – "

"Teddy," Caroline broke in. "Before you can do all that... well, I think you're going to have to be prepared for another setback."

"Caroline, Laurel Hill is going to be fabulous. I'd love for you to see it before we make all the changes. Will you come to see it with me one day soon?"

"Of course, Teddy, but you have to listen to me. There is something you need to know first. I'm sorry. I know Laurel Hill means a lot to you."

"Of course it does, Caroline. You know that."

"You see," she began, wishing it wasn't she who was breaking the news to Teddy. "It's that the motive for Alex Seeger's murdering Althea may relate to some financial irregularities that were going on at Tanner Associates."

"Irregularities?"

"I don't have all the details, but there will have to be an investigation of the financial state of the firm, what has been going on with the investors' accounts."

"But we can get our money, can't we? Mother has decided she wants to move her account to another firm of advisors. She's already talked to Mr. Crenshaw about doing that."

"Talking to your lawyer is a good idea, but you have to be prepared for delay. You need to understand that."

Teddy shook his head. "I can't wait. Someone else will bid on the property."

"After Althea died... well, you must have expected something to change. She was the principal in the firm. It was a small business after all, one person apparently handling everything."

"But our family's account - my mother's account - that's our money." Ainsley looked dejected. "I can't understand any of what you're saying. Father always trusted Althea."

"I'm sure the police will be contacting all the investors to explain things. In the meantime, talk to Mr. Crenshaw to see what he advises." Caroline reached across to take Teddy's hand. "The important thing is that you are a free man, Teddy. Concentrate on that."

CHAPTER LXIII

As a downcast Teddy Ainsley drove away from Kenwood, another car passed his coming up the drive.

"I was just about to call you," Caroline said as Jonathan Granger bounded up the steps. "Let's talk in the morning room."

The young man followed her, taking note of the flowers and champagne. "From Teddy?"

Caroline nodded. "He just left."

"I'm sure he's a happy chap."

"Partially," Caroline said. Jon raised his eyebrows. "Teddy might be free of the murder charge, but I had to tell him to expect bad news for Althea's investors coming out of the police investigation. His plans to finance the music center will have to be on hold until the authorities understand what's been going on at Tanner."

"I've been dreading having to explain all this to Melody. Do you know anything at all that the police have found out?" Anxiety clouded his boyish face.

"The police know what you and I had begun to suspect. There appears to be regular insider trading that's been funding the Tanner financial results. That the three principals have been skimming profits at the investors' expense also seems likely. But I think the police are a long way from unraveling it all. I expect this is a case now for the federal authorities."

"And Alex Seeger was able to find out about these crimes. Did your detective friend Hank tell you how he did that?"

"I was there when Alex Seeger confessed."

"You were what? Where?"

As Jon stared at her in amazement, Caroline explained what happened on the beach after the Tai Chi class.

"Geese," Jon said. "Geese. She called the investors 'geese.' And that was it?"

Caroline nodded. "It made a light bulb go on over Alex's head.

Amazing, isn't it? One word."

"Pretty sharp of him. But supposing that he was wrong, though... that Althea's business wasn't dodgy. 'Geese' might have meant something else."

"Alex didn't wait to find out."

"I don't know what to say."

"It's a lot to absorb."

"And I was absolutely sure the killer was Jason Cava."

"It did seem like a real possibility to me as well," Caroline agreed. "He seemed the most likely to have a motive." Caroline had decided not to explain to Jon how she had been able to work out how the murder was committed before even witnessing Alex's confession. Jon had been so pleased to be investigating the crime with her, it seemed unfair to tell him that she had been able to deduce the solution without his help.

"So where does Cava fit in all this?" Jon asked. "Will the police charge him in the fraud at least?"

"It depends on what the investigation comes up with. They always need airtight evidence."

"I don't know how I'm going to break all this to Melody, Caroline," Jon said unhappily. "This will devastate her."

"Does she have everything invested with Tanner?"

"I'm pretty sure she does. I think Scott Forsythe made sure of that."

"Oh, Jon, I am sorry." Caroline had some personal experience with Newport families losing their money.

"I'd better get going," Jon said, his look turning grim. "Melody deserves to know all this before the press gets a hold of it."

"Of course."

He looked squarely at Caroline. "If she's lost her money, it won't make any difference to me, you know. She's absolutely my wife whether or not she's rich."

"*For richer or for poorer,*" Caroline said, remembering her own wedding vows.

Jon allowed a rueful smile to form on his lips. "And now we'll see what that means, won't we?"

CHAPTER LXIV

The arrest of the new suspect in the murder of Althea Tanner brought the media's interest back to the original crime. Now attention centered on how Alex Seeger was able to convince the police that when he had found his victim she was already dead. There was no explanation offered for his motive, but one TV report speculated on a possible affair between him and Althea. The clearing of Teddy Ainsley's name was a minor part of the larger story.

Seeger himself was out on bail and secluded at his home on Ocean Drive. His legal team had not responded to requests for interviews or put out any statements.

Efforts by the media to solicit comments from the two employees of Tanner Associates had also met a dead end. Maya Vereen had refused to talk to any reporters when they appeared at the Tanner office the day after the arrest. Once rid of them, the young assistant had locked the door and gone home. Subsequent stories revealed that these same reporters had been unable to find Jason Cava. Eva Miller was uncharacteristically silent when cornered by the press at *Di Sole*, refusing to reveal anything about the whereabouts of her current employer.

In the days following Alex Seeger's arrest on Easton's Beach, Caroline heard little from Hank. His short texts indicated that he was busy with the case and would see her as soon as he had some free time. The letdown she felt was intense. She had solved the murder case and exonerated Teddy, but the satisfaction she should have felt from doing this was missing.

On Friday, three couples checked into the inn. They were traveling together and had booked their stay to include a formal dinner on both Friday and Saturday evenings. Caroline was happy to be busy in the kitchen with Mattie most of the weekend. When the guests departed on Sunday afternoon, Caroline was still disappointed not to be able to talk to Hank. If he would only tell her something.

Anything. The suspense was agonizing. She occupied her mind by making a list of chores that needed to be done around Kenwood. Her desk had never looked so neat and, to Louise's surprise, she even tried to help her with the gardening.

At last a telephone call came from Hank at the end of the week. Hearing his voice was a welcome relief from her anxiety, and Caroline made him an offer she knew he couldn't refuse: dinner. She even asked if there was anything special which Mattie could prepare. His answer was immediate. He'd love to have that lobster pie again.

The early June evening was one of the most pleasant so far of the spring season. Caroline set up drinks in the gazebo and carried out the brimming tray of hors d'oeuvres which Mattie had assembled.

"Are you sure you want me to have cocktails with you and Hank?" Louise asked. "You haven't had much time alone lately."

"No. Not at all. He's is going to talk about the case, and I know you want to hear about it as much as I do."

"I do," her mother-in-law admitted. "I only hope he is going to be able to tell us what's been happening."

Caroline looked at her watch. "He should be here about now. So we'll soon find out."

On cue, she saw Hank coming down the path toward the gazebo.

"It's so good to see you," she said, accepting his kiss.

Hank gave Louise an affectionate hug. "I see my favorite bartender is here. Thank you both for inviting me."

"Sit down," Louise said, indicating one of the wicker chairs. "I'll get your usual."

"Thanks," the detective said reaching for a smoked salmon canapé. "These look good, and I'm hungry."

"Then you know you came to the right place," Caroline said.

Louise passed out the drinks "You must be busy at work, Hank," she said. "We've been reading about your case in the newspapers."

"Yes," he said. "A lot has been going on."

"With the murder charge?" Caroline prompted.

"Yeah, but... other things as well."

"Hank," Caroline said with some exasperation. "Tell us what is going on."

The detective put down his drink. "Look, Caroline, I owe you for solving the murder. Believe me that I told the chief how it was you who first realized what really happened that night."

"But what about the motive? Is it true that Tanner Associates was involved in all the dodgy things we thought?"

"That's all being looked into."

"The insider trading?" Caroline asked, and Hank nodded. "What else? Fraud? What? Tell me," she pleaded.

"I'll try, but even I don't know the extent of it. Our department turned over all the information we had collected to both the state and federal authorities. Keisha has been doing a terrific job of research. She should get a commendation." He bit off the end a cheese straw. "I've been so busy this last week in meetings. I had to go over to Providence for two days." He grinned. "I'll admit, it's actually been exciting."

"I bet," Caroline said enviously.

"It's a very complicated investigation. And needless to say, what I'm telling you now can't leave this room." Both women nodded solemnly. "The insider trading comes under the jurisdiction of the U.S. Attorney's office and the SEC."

"Haven't there been a lot of insider trading cases in the last few years?" Caroline asked.

"Yes. Especially in New York. But some of the convictions have been overturned. The law, as I have learned, isn't clear on what defines insider trading. I've been reading up on all of this. It's a fascinating subject. There have been calls for Congress to make new laws to overhaul the existing laws which are weak. The amount of insider information about companies and their stocks that gets passed around behind the scenes is mind boggling. And most of the trading done on inside information is going undetected as far as I can see."

"I didn't realize that," Caroline said. "Could that mean Cameron Epsberg and Scott Forsythe will escape prosecution?"

"Not necessarily, but these cases can take years to bring to trial. Most are prosecuted as civil violations of security laws."

"Years," Louise said. "My goodness. That's not encouraging."

"I know," Hank said. "But on another front, I've been meeting with two lawyers from the Rhode Island Attorney General's office."

"Are they investigating the trades as well?" Caroline asked.

"No. They want to know if funds were being skimmed from the

investors' accounts by Althea and her colleagues. The geese angle. If they can find the evidence of fraud, the state would definitely prosecute this as a criminal case."

"Is this the same as a Ponzi scheme?" Louise asked.

"No one is calling it a Ponzi scheme yet, but they may eventually see it that way. Again, it's too soon to tell what we have."

"What about income tax evasion?" Caroline asked. "Maybe they didn't report their illegal profits."

"That, too, is a possibility. As I said, it's all early days."

Caroline shifted anxiously in her chair. The slow pace of these investigations didn't suit her sense of justice being served. She caught Louise's eye. Her mother-in-law was clearly unhappy with this aspect of the case as well.

CHAPTER LXV

"What about Jason Cava, Hank?" Caroline asked with exasperation. "Has he been found at least?"

"Now that's an interesting development I can tell you about," Hank answered with some relief in his voice. "He's left the country."

"I thought so," Caroline said triumphantly. "Where did he go?"

"Croatia."

"Croatia? What's in Croatia?"

"A country with no extradition treaty with the U.S.."

"I'm learning all kinds of things this evening."

"I didn't know about the extradition angle either. But we were able to determine his movements on the night he disappeared. We now know that he drove from Newport to Logan Airport in Boston where he left his car. He got there in time to make a Turkish Airlines flight to Zagreb that left around midnight."

"That's the capital of Croatia, right?"

"Yes. He could make a connection to Zagreb from Istanbul. Cava was safe and sound in Croatia by the next afternoon. Most likely his money is somewhere outside the U.S. so he can get to it easily. We don't know where inside Croatia he is, but the consensus is that he would be hiding in one of the beach resorts. There's a big tourist trade there now, you know." Hank shrugged his shoulders. "Although hiding is probably not what he's doing. He doesn't really have to."

"Does this mean that he may escape prosecution?" Louise asked.

"It's Epsberg the feds seem most interested in. Apparently his name came up in a previous insider trading investigation about ten years ago. There was insider information suspected of being used in the trading of the stock of a semi-conductor company that became a takeover target. On the day when the takeover plan was announced the stock jumped from four dollars a share to nine. Several people were the beneficiaries of some very profitable stock trades, including our friend Cameron Epsberg. Nobody but someone with inside information would have known that an offer to buy that company was going to be announced on that exact day."

"But he wasn't charged?"

"No, Louise. Two others were, but I guess they couldn't get what they needed on Epsberg. They'd love to get him now, and this time around the insider trading has been so flagrant it could result in criminal charges."

"What about Scott Forsythe?" Caroline asked.

"The feds are going on the assumption that it's been Forsythe who's been making the actual trades in his personal account. The profits were used to fund the quarterly checks to Tanner investors. How much was left for Epsberg, Forsythe, Althea and Jason is not known at this point."

"Wouldn't it be fairly easy to prove that it was Forsythe who made the trades?"

"He does have several stock trading accounts, and he makes a lot of trades in the market. Day trading, they call it. That's why he would have been perfect to camouflage the trades he made on Tanner's behalf inside his own accounts. But it will take some time and effort to separate all his transactions over the years to see who is benefitting from which ones. And where the money trail goes after that. Maybe Swiss banks, funneled to offshore accounts. The feds always want a lot of evidence before they charge people. They will take years sometime before they make their move. And don't forget that they'll also be looking for Althea's money as well."

"Years? I don't believe this." Caroline looked unhappy.

"There's a whole world of banks out there. Forsythe also owns some companies in Honduras. Shell companies where he can park the money."

Caroline slumped back in her chair. "This is so complicated."

"You can see why these investigations take years. The government has special accountants who go over all the data. It's painstaking."

"What about other evidence?" Caroline suddenly asked. "There must be phone calls, meetings... to discuss the insider information. I've read about phone calls being recorded."

"It's doubtful that kind of evidence exists in this case," Hank said. "They had to have taken precautions. Throwaway phones--"

"Meetings like that lunch near the Kingston train station," Caroline broke in. "And the three of them getting together on the Forty Steps." She shook her head in amazement. "They had it down to a science, didn't they?"

"Anybody who is dealing with that much money would be adept at hiding any possible criminal actions."

"How much money are we talking about, Hank?" Louise asked. "How much has been stolen?"

"This early in the investigation? It's impossible to tell. The books have to be gone over. The clients' statements are useless. And the only person left at the Tanner firm who could tell us anything is the office assistant Maya Vereen, and she doesn't appear to have any information beyond who's on the annual Christmas card list."

"But the investors?" Louise persisted. "Have they lost all their money?"

"It's not likely all of it is gone. As Althea said to Forsythe on that fateful night - she expected that the geese would keep laying eggs for them."

"When will they know?" Caroline asked, thinking of the fate of Teddy Ainsley's music center and Melody Granger's marriage.

"It will be a while before these forensic accountants can understand the financial holdings of Tanner. We know the money is not in the stocks the investors thought were being held in their accounts. That was Jason Cava's job, by the way. To falsify the quarterly statements for the clients."

"So that young man was smart to run," Louise said.

"Yes, the fellow in Bernie Madoff's office who was responsible for concocting the false statements for the clients in his Ponzi scheme got ten years in jail."

"I hope the authorities go after Mr. Cava," Louise said angrily. "He's caused a lot of hurt to a lot of people."

"I should tell you, Louise, that if Jason Cava returns to this country, he will probably be given a chance to enter a guilty plea in return for his cooperation against the other two. He'd get a very reduced sentence if his testimony would help to get the convictions of Epsberg and Forsythe. That happened with a few of the players in the Madoff case."

"That hardly seems fair, Hank."

"I know, Louise, and you're not the only one who thinks so."

*****

Once dinner was finished and Louise had gone to bed, Hank and Caroline went out on the veranda. The night air was pleasant, and the couple stood side by side enjoying the quiet of their surroundings. Hank's arm found its place around Caroline's shoulders, and she leaned easily into his embrace.

"This is how life should be," he said. "Me and my girl."

Caroline laughed. "You sound like the hero in a dime novel."

"Maybe I am," Hank said. "There have been times lately when I feel like I've wandered into a movie plot. Any day now I expect to see Matt Damon coming into my office."

"I wish this case was ending as neatly as the others we've solved together."

"We did get Althea's killer." He kissed the top of her head. "Mostly thanks to you, ma'am."

"I've been thinking back to the first time I met Althea Tanner in Val Ainsley's office. I was very impressed by her."

"I'm sure she was an impressive woman. Think about how she got her start. Someone like John Ainsley wouldn't have been easily impressed by an amateur. Althea had to be extremely talented."

"Yes, but after John died and she was on her own, things changed. I wonder why. She wouldn't have lost her abilities so quickly."

"After the 2008 crash it must have been hard to make a profit in the stock market."

"But every investor was having the same problem, Hank. Her clients should have realized that conditions in the markets were bad. They needed to be patient for everything to turn around... which it eventually did."

"Be patient where a lot of your money's concerned? I wonder, Caroline. Althea promised her clients big returns, and they expected them no matter what was going everywhere else."

"They must have been selfish fools."

"You really believe that all those wealthy investors were so foolish?"

"They needed to open their eyes to the truth. If they had been able to do that, a lot of lives would be better off now."

"Yes," Hank agreed, "but people don't always do what's smart."

"No, they don't."

"And when people read about this case, do you think that they will learn anything from what happened to these investors, Caroline? Or will they believe anyone who promises them high financial returns, no matter how unrealistic they might sound?"

"You know, Hank, I'm really not sure."

AUTHOR'S NOTES

Writing a book is a solitary occupation, but never do you do it alone.

Mastering the details of high finance and investment required a lot of research on my part. Thanks to all the reporters whose stories and reports educated me. Regretfully, the many articles in the media on insider trading, financial fraud, and Ponzi schemes gave me more than enough information with which to work.

I couldn't have written so knowledgeably about boats and sailing without generous input from my husband Dexter who kept me from looking like the landlubber that I really am. My son Tony, always there to encourage my work, answered my questions about the law. My son Jack turned my computer files into both the printed version of Invest In Death and the e-book. I am very grateful for his calm hand during this project.

Thanks also to the friends and family who always want to know how the book is coming. They are appreciated more than they know.

I'd also like to thank the Preservation Society of Newport County for their ongoing support of my work. They feature my books and regularly invite me for events where I can introduce my mysteries to visitors to Newport from all over the world. A special thank you to Laura Murphy and Maria Goldberg and especially the staff at The Breakers who always have the welcome mat out for me.

When I first had the idea to set a mystery on a sailboat I was fortunate to meet Julie Lassy of America's Cup Charters in Newport who gave me a tour of their 12-meter yachts. With Julie's help I was able to visualize how my story could work.

I love being a writer and ask only that my stories entertain.

— *Anne-Marie Sutton*

233

Made in the USA
Middletown, DE
15 February 2019